WORLD ENOUGH

WORLD ENOUGH

Clea Simon

This first world edition published 2017
in Great Britain and the USA by
SEVERN HOUSE PUBLISHERS LTD of
19 Cedar Road, Sutton, Surrey, England, SM2 5DA.
Trade paperback edition first published
in Great Britain and the USA 2017 by
SEVERN HOUSE PUBLISHERS LTD

British Library Cataloguing in Publication Data
A CIP catalogue record for this title is available from the British Library.

ISBN-13: 978-0-7278-8733-7 (cased)
ISBN-13: 978-1-84751-849-1 (trade paper)
ISBN-13: 978-1-78010-909-1 (e-book)

All Severn House titles are printed on acid-free paper.

Severn House Publishers support the Forest Stewardship Council™ [FSC™],
the leading international forest certification organisation.
All our titles that are printed on FSC certified paper carry the FSC logo.

MIX
Paper from
responsible sources
FSC
www.fsc.org   FSC® C013056

Typeset by Palimpsest Bo[
Falkirk, Stirlingshire, Scot
Printed and bound in Grea
TJ International, Padstow,

For Jon

ONE

September, 2007

T en o'clock, and the opener will be on soon. Opener! She laughs at herself. It's only the Craters and the Whirled Shakers tonight, and the bill was probably decided by a coin toss between them backstage. It's the Shakers she came to see, their psychedelic pop still gets her going, with its tambourines and the beat. But maybe she'll stay for the Craters. Depends on how tired she is. Depends on the crowd.

There are only about thirty people in the room. Twenty-something if you don't count the bartender, but after a long day at work, Tara is glad enough for the company and for the empty chair by the table up front. Beer in hand, she settles in, waiting for the music. Twenty-seven, she counts. Twenty-four if you subtract the two wives and a girlfriend. A good house, really, for two bands that have been around the club scene for twenty years. Then again, most everyone here has been, too. She knows most of them by sight, if not by name, and when she closes her eyes she can place them in the Rat, the Channel, Oakie's, Jumpin' Jack Flash. All the great old places, closed now, torn down to make way for condos and parking garages. Those cavernous rooms and black-painted basements are what she thinks of when she thinks of the '80s, back when she, the bands, and everyone here were in their heyday.

She opens her eyes to a bit of a shock. The women are all thirty pounds heavier than in her mind's eye. Or they've gone thin, like she has, a little drawn, a little leathery. The men have fared better. Gray, if they have hair, and some of them have gone from biker tough to resembling the butchers, delivery men, and press operators they are during the day. But mostly they're in good shape, if a little rough. Besides, it's her crowd and nothing new sounds as good.

Twenty years ago, the Shakers wouldn't have been playing a

pub like this, as much a burger joint as a music room. But twenty years ago, they'd been the hot new rising stars. The best of Boston, they'd pull in quite a crowd, a Friday like this, and there'd have been half again as many label scouts among the fans.

'Hey.' Tom from the Exiles pulls up the chair next to hers, settling his shot glass on the scarred wood table.

'Hey.' Tara has never known Tom well. She's seen his band a thousand times, can picture him in his Motorhead T-shirt banging out the bass riffs. But she only ever talked to him when he'd been behind the bar upstairs at Oakie's, those thick hands grabbing Buds four at a time from the reach-in. The upstairs – that had started for the overflow but it had become their hangout. The bar for the music crowd. Tom wasn't much of a bartender. Couldn't mix more than a screwdriver, but he knew everyone. His band wasn't much either, the kind of group you'd go see just because of who would be there – an extension of the bar. Social. Fun. Still, they'd kept at it. She knew he was still playing out, and he felt like family after all this time.

'Good crowd, huh?' They smile and nod, both happy enough to be there. Tara's about to ask him about the Exiles, just to be friendly, but right then the Shakers take the stage. Two guitars and a bass bash out the first chord. It's loud and lively, and the drummer jumps in with a fill, kicking everyone up to speed. More guitar and Phil, the singer, has grabbed the mike. He's smiling. Happy to be on stage. But that wide-eyed grin soon gives way to a rock-star grimace, eyes squeezed shut. Then he's prancing, the guitar taking over the song and Phil's body with it, as he swings the mike stand high, twirls around. Stadium moves. The guitars crash again over the driving beat of the bass. Joey, the drummer, solos, fast and neat, and the guitars are back. Phil is singing his heart out, and just like that, the song is done.

'Awesome.' Tom could be speaking for both of them. Twenty years ago, ten even, Tara knows she'd be up on her feet, dancing, in front of the stage. Maybe up on the table. Maybe next song. Joey counts off the next tune. 'One, two, three, four!' and the guitar-bass unison cranks up the pace before Phil joins in. Tara drains her beer. Maybe she will get up, dance right in front of the band like she used to.

She looks around for Min, knowing that she's not likely to

have shown up in the five minutes since she last surveyed the crowd. Min would've liked this. The band sounds good; everyone seems mellow. Not that Min's been out much recently. Unlike some of their old friends, the ones who've moved on to have families and buy houses out in Watertown or Medford, Min hasn't really replaced the rock scene in her life. But she's grown tired of it. When they meet for lunch – Min works at the hospital a couple of blocks from her office – she goes on about how sad it all is.

'How's it sad? Nobody's pretending we're twenty.' Tara is used to the usual complaints. 'We're having fun, and we still like the music.'

'It's just kind of pitiful. The dwindling crowd and all.' Min always shakes her head at this point, which makes Tara a little angry.

'It's the same as any other pastime. We're a group of old friends.' Even as she says it, Tara knows it's not entirely true. She and Min are friends. They've spent time together outside the clubs. Gotten to know each other. Helped each other through breakups and miscarriages (Min's) and divorce (Tara). But for the rest, it's clubland only. And Min has never had quite the feeling about the music world that Tara has, that it's her family. Her only real home. Looking around the room tonight, Tara pities her friend. This is something real. Maybe they are all outcasts, but they found each other, didn't they?

'Hey, kiddo!' As if on cue, Gina is there, collapsing into the one chair left. 'Don't they sound great tonight?'

'Killer.' Tara knows Gina drinks too much, knows that she's never gotten over Phil, even though the singer has moved on to a wife and two babies. She sees Gina glaring at Katie, Phil's long-ago ex, still a fan. Still a knockout, too, in her wan blonde fashion, her hair still silky smooth down past the shoulders of her black leather jacket. She looks like a star, even after a sunless work week, and Gina will never forgive her for that.

'What's the news?' It cheers Tara to see how Gina's doughy face brightens at the question, her one claim to fame being her connection with the band.

'They're talking about going into the studio again. You'll hear, they're going to do some of the new songs. They're really great.' Gina leans in, and Tara smells alcohol and sweat. 'I think this may be it!'

OK, so maybe Min has a point. They're all a little lost. But isn't it something that they found each other? That they have the scene?

'I'll listen for them.' The next tune has started and Gina is up again, shaking it in front of the tiny stage, standing between Katie and the band. Looking at her, her too-tight stretch miniskirt making indents in her waist and thighs, Tara thinks twice about getting up to dance. But just as she's reconsidering another song kicks in, a repeated guitar riff she knows in her sleep. It's 'World Enough', their hit. The song that almost got them onto a major label, out of Boston, out of all this. The bass joins in, four fast bars of building beat. Then the drums. Screw the years, it's time to dance.

If we had world enough, world enough and time . . .

Time's played them all for fools, but they're still here, and Tara loves it. In a minute, it's 1986 again. She's bouncing around, shaking it with Gina. For a moment, the years, the dinky pub, don't matter. She remembers descending into a steaming basement, working her way through a packed house, and hearing this riff, this command to dance.

I love you baby, and you know that ain't no crime.

The lyrics are inane. Tara knows that, and sings along anyway, shouting into the PA's roar.

World enough and time!

With a crash, the song ends, and the present-day world returns. Tara heads for the bar.

'You hear about Frank?' Gina is leaning over toward her. Gina always knows what's going on. Tara holds up her empty bottle – and two fingers – for the bartender, a tall, grizzled man whose name she can't recall. Gina's got an empty in front of her, and Tara's feeling generous.

'No, what?' The beers arrive, and she slides one over to Gina.

'He's dead.' Gina takes a swig, downing half the bottle. 'Some kind of accident.' Band and beer forgotten for a moment, Tara stares. Dead? 'I heard he fell down a flight of stairs. They're saying it could be some fucked-up form of suicide.'

'Shit.'

'Yeah, really. But this way, they get the insurance. You know about the baby, right?' Tara nods. She'd heard that Frank's only child, Mika, had been having problems. That her son – Frank's grandson – hadn't been right since he was born.

She takes a pull from her beer, tries to think of something to say. But Gina is gone, back on the floor for the next number. One of the new tunes, it sounds good enough but Tara has lost the urge to dance. Frank. Shit. Maybe Min is right. Tara used to think of this crowd as the lucky ones. The runts who'd survived. They were rejects and outcasts, and she included herself in that crowd, but they'd bucked the curse. They'd all been lucky enough to find each other, to find their own place, here in the clubs.

She'd never been able to explain it to Peter, her ex, but she'd always felt blessed to be included. He'd insisted that her outsider status was a choice, that she could join in the real world whenever she'd wanted. He hadn't understood, and had gone on without her. Now, she wonders if the luck has run out. We are the runts, she realizes, but we haven't escaped. Gina, Min, Tom and the other bands. And now Frank. We're sickly. We have fewer successful marriages and happy families. Too many of us have died.

'Why the long face?' Robbie from the Craters has pushed in beside her, an amber shot of whiskey in his heavily tattooed hand. 'It's Friday!' It's too loud to explain about Frank, about everything. So she nods and clinks her bottle to his shot glass. Turning to the stage, they watch the Shakers doing their thing, same as twenty years before.

It was the night she'd first worn her leather jacket. Tara remembers her pride in it, and the immediate, reflexive fear that maybe the black leather, with all its silver biker hardware, was the wrong look. Not that she could pull off pink. Not like Min.

'It's ironic,' her new friend had explained, yelling over the music the night they'd met, two weeks before. Sure enough, the way the bubblegum leather set off Min's hennaed hair was more tough than prissy, like a girl gangster from the '50s. Black was more conventional, and Tara had taken comfort in that. Besides, it was just so perfect. The way it zipped up, trim, as if made for her. The pockets, big enough for a reporter's notepad or even a CD, now that she had a player, and the way she'd found it at the back of the yard sale, buried in a box of T-shirts and old belts. She'd been glad of the cold that late September night, the early frost that made the dirt crumble beneath her feet. Only the day before it would've been too warm to wear her new find. Instead, she shivered as she dashed across the sad little median of a park, making her way toward Oakie's, her new home.

'Five bucks.' She handed over the money, nodding hello to Brian, the bouncer, and silent Thomas, the dignified older doorman who guarded the stairs to the basement club.

'Have fun.' Brian smiled at her. She was beginning to be recognized as a regular.

'Thanks.' She'd clomped down the stairs with the thrill of eagerness for everything new. Who would be there tonight? Would she know anyone? Meet anyone? The cold of the entranceway gave way to a humid warmth. Ten thirty and the room was getting crowded. She'd timed it right. Time to get a beer, look around, and not be the first person in the room.

'Hi, Tara, isn't it?' Gina was still girlish then, bordering on chubby but cute with it. Rounded. Outgoing, too: she was one of the first scene people Tara had come to know. 'Gonna be a good night.'

'The Sierras are supposed to be great.' She'd never heard the headliner, but she'd read about them in *Boston Rock*.

'Overrated.' Gina took Tara's wrist and pulled her forward, past the bar. 'You got here just in time.'

Tara recalls smiling and thinking she'd like a drink. But Gina didn't give her time to order. Pulled her instead past the half-bar where everyone piled their empties. They were right in front of the stage.

'Isn't it a little early?' Tara looked around. The club was filling. She recognized Katie; her hair a silky wave down her back. Rich from the *Free Press*, a few others. When she turned back to the stage, she saw four long-haired men, their hair cut in modified Beatle bobs. 'What's this?' They were plugging into their amps, an on-stage stack of Marshalls that belied their '60s look.

'The Whirled Shakers,' Gina yelled in her face as the drummer started a loud, rumbling roll. 'Whirled, like . . .' She twirled her forefinger in a blender motion. But by then the two guitars had joined in as well and a fifth had leaped onstage. The guitarists pounded out power chords, and for a moment she couldn't tell if they'd noticed the interloper. But then he grabbed the mike, swung the weighted stand above all their heads and yowled. One of the guitarists, the one with lighter hair, looked up and grinned. The singer howled again, then hunkered over the mike, and the band was off.

Forty minutes later, she was as sticky as the floor, her wet hair clinging to her face in tendrils. What a band! Sweating and bruised, from when the crowd had surged forward, pushing her hip-height into the stage overhang. She'd be sore tomorrow, black and blue. Just then she felt great, though. She'd looked up at the singer then, able to peek under his long, dark bangs. He'd been smiling. Why not? The crowd, the night was his, but before she could even close her mouth, the bodies holding her up had fallen back and she'd stumbled with them, only catching herself on the arm of a fat bearded guy who'd held her a little too tight as he helped her up.

'Thanks.'

'My pleasure.' He'd nodded and released her, acknowledging the liberty. She was glad of the leather then, a shield of sorts against the odd grope. The guy who'd grabbed her had been fat, but not soft. Biker big. She shook off the shiver of fear; this was her world, her home, she'd not be intimidated. But she'd been aware of him watching her after, as another song got everyone moving, and later still, when they'd all collapsed, sodden, on the bar.

'Buy you a beer?' He'd gotten there first. By the looks of him, he usually did.

'No, thanks.' Tara hadn't yet sussed out the etiquette of the clubs, but she knew she didn't want to owe this guy. She was saved by the bartender, who brought over a Rolling Rock without asking.

'I've seen you around.' She drank, nodded, willing the conversation to a close. 'You follow these bands?'

'Some of them.' She wiped the hair from her face. Squinted through the cigarette smoke. She must know someone else here.

'Do you write?'

That turned her around. 'What?'

'Do you write? I'm putting together a 'zine. A fanzine on the

Boston scene. Something like *Rat Turds* or the *FreeP*, but I want it to have real substance. Maybe interviews, maybe reviews. But something with some thought to it.'

Tara took another drink and held the cool beer in her mouth for a minute. Time to think. 'Yeah, why not?' She'd been looking for an in, a way to become a member of this community. She'd spent some time at the college newspaper during her years at BU, too. 'I can write. Do paste-up, too.'

'You can do production?' The fat guy smiled suddenly, changing his face from menace to beaming full moon. 'Excellent! You can be one of my editors.' He pulled a bulging wallet out of his back pocket and fingered through the papers, very little of it currency. 'Here's my card.' It was damp and dog-eared. 'Scott, Scott Hasseldeck. Good to meet you.'

'Tara Winton.' They shook hands and Tara realized she was smiling back. 'I'm very pleased to meet you.' Thus it had all begun.

'Who's the fat guy?' Gina had surfaced next to her, gesturing for the bartender's attention.

'His name's Scott. We're going to do a 'zine.'

Gina beamed at her. 'Cool. You'll write about me?'

And that was it. After a few months on the edges, wondering how to get in, to be a part of this frantic set, she'd done it. She and Scott and after a few months two or three others, as well, would gather in his Allston triple-decker and talk about the bands they'd seen. Who was coming up, who was coming to town. Everyone had their pets, and what was covered was decided often enough by Flicka, the photographer. If she wanted to shoot it, they had a cover.

Scott had already found a printer, back in Maine, who'd do a press run of a few hundred copies. They'd been to school together, and Scott put him up whenever he came to town – to party, meet girls, hear some music. That must have paid for the first issue, Tara couldn't see how else it came together. After a while, Scott sold some ads, too, though God knows how he convinced the used record stores and T-shirt places to part with that twenty-five or fifty bucks. And then, once a month or so – the first year, especially, the schedule was loose – she and Scott would make the long drive up to the printers, sneaking in on a Sunday, most times, and Tara would lay out the type like she'd done for her college paper, though her college paper never had a drunken printer or a leather-clad editor looking over her shoulder, egging her on to some of the worst headlines.

She'd sleep all day Monday, when they got back. But in the back of the van, they'd have those bundles and for the rest of the week, they'd be bringing them around. A tied bundle was as good as cover on a Tuesday or a Wednesday, the doormen waving them in when they came around. The bartenders, often enough, pulling a draft for her as she cut the twine binding on a fresh stack.

That was how she met everyone. *Underground Sound* never became a must-read, nothing like *Boston Rock* and with everything that happened, it didn't last long. But while it did, it got her name around. And Tara was glad to have her own way in, something besides her friendship with Gina. The paper got her into bigger shows, too, once it became established. Once people could count on it coming out on time. She remembers the first time she went backstage, into the cramped closet they called a dressing room at the Rat. She'd come to bring in an issue, but had forgotten about it from the moment she walked through the door. The room was tiny, and covered in graffiti. Sharpies, paint, ballpoint. The band names alone mesmerized her. She could've spent hours reading the walls, and she watched as the Painkillers, the band on the cover, added their names, dripping and sloppy with red nail polish.

That was where she first met Frank, too. The band name must have sparked the memory, but she could picture him, remember how startled she'd been, at first, to see his hulking form in the corner. The Painkillers were a post-punk girl group in the mode of Salem 66 or Oh OK. Despite their raucous laughs and tour-toughened looks, their sound was dreamy, all jangly guitar and vocal harmonies. Perfect for college radio, but Frank didn't seem like the romantic sort.

He'd been scary in those days. Heavier and always scowling back before he got married and found Jesus. She remembers stepping back, her quick intake of breath as she saw him, leaning up against the wall ('Circle Jerks! 1982').

'Hey.' He'd nodded, recognizing her from around. She managed a grin, a little lopsided, and nodded back. He was waiting, she realized. He'd slipped in to see the band before their sound check. That's when she figured out that he was in a band, too. Into the music, like she was, and once again remembered the paper. She ripped open the bundle and handed him a copy. He said 'Thanks,' and almost smiled. She was part of the scene, too. Legit. And nothing scared her.

TWO

In the end, it's Peter who comes with her. Peter with his old-school manners, insisting that nobody should have to go to a funeral alone. Tara had asked Min. Pressured her really, stressing the common friends who would be there, the fact that they had both spent time with the deceased and his widow. That Min had done more than that, all those years ago.

'It's been ten years since I saw her,' Min had responded. 'Maybe twenty. I don't even know that I'd recognize Neela. Or that she'd want to see me.'

'Come on, Min.' Tara tried. 'That was ages ago. Bygones and all that.'

Min had laughed at that. 'My point exactly. Another lifetime ago.'

Tara knew she'd lost her then. She doubted that the widow would remember Min as anything other than another scenester. Doubted Neela even knew about Min's fling with Frank all those years ago. They hadn't been married then, and Frank had still been drinking. They all had. But Min remembered. She'd gotten pregnant as the result of their on-again, off-again affair. Tara'd gone with her to the clinic. Years later, when she'd miscarried, she'd blamed that clinic – the abortion – for messing her up. She was working toward her master's by then and full of theories: septic conditions, micro tears, infection. She'd stopped talking about it, once Tara – by then a proper journalist – had presented her with facts and figures about the procedure's safety, about the clinic's reputation. She hadn't stopped thinking about it, though, Tara realized later.

Not that she'd told Peter about this, when he called to check in. He was as dismissive of Min as he was of all her old crowd.

'She can't make it,' Tara had said. 'She wishes she could, though.'

'Huh.' Peter's response – a noncommittal grunt – had said it all. Right after that was when he'd told her he'd pick her up at nine. 'Someone's got to be there with you.' She'd been too grateful to turn him down, no matter the cost to her pride.

He looks smart in a suit. She has to give him that. Certainly better than most of the small crowd assembled in the church. While the women pull off mourning pretty well – every onetime rocker having at least one black dress – the men all look like they're in costume, their jackets ill-fitting, their ties stained or ten years out of date.

'That's Gina.' Tara keeps her voice low. 'You remember her.'

'Kind of.' He follows Tara's gaze. Nods as she smiles at the latecomer, who has turned and waves as she squeezes into a pew two rows up. 'She's still kind of a mess, isn't she?'

Tara bristles. Gina's face is blotchy and swollen, her eyes delineated only by the smudged, dark liner. 'She and Frank were friends,' she responds. She can hear the edge to her voice and takes a deep breath to let it out. Peter has done her a solid, accompanying her. They are no longer married, after all, and this crowd has never been his. 'I think everyone is just in shock,' she says. She works to keep her voice neutral.

Peter nods, his silence his own peace offering. He is trying, she knows that. He hasn't commented on her car, for once. Hasn't pointed out that she could upgrade now to something newer and more reliable. Instead, he brought her a flier from a local open house – a condo development near his. 'It's a good deal,' he'd said, as he pressed it into her hand. 'If you buy in before they finish, you can get them to customize the furnishings too.'

'I can't think about that now,' she'd said. He'd held his tongue then too. It was a discussion they'd had before. How she was unwilling to move ahead – to make a life for herself. In her defense, she always pointed out how she had taken his advice. She'd left the newspaper where they'd met not long after he had. She'd met with the headhunter he had steered her way and landed her current job, handling corporate communications at three times the pay. Besides, she had wanted to point out, owning a home wasn't any sign of success. Not anymore. Frank and Neela owned their house, a ramshackle two-family in Somerville, and she knew they'd been struggling to get by. And now Frank was dead, having fallen down the basement stairs to the concrete floor below.

'Oh my God.' Even two rows away, Gina is audible, and Tara feels rather than sees Peter's eyebrows go up in a wordless rebuke. Still, she understands Gina's outburst. The pale, sagging woman who is being helped up the aisle is a far cry from the rambunctious rocker Tara remembers. Neela Turcotte looks twenty years older than her forty-odd years, her strawberry blonde hair faded to a washed-out grey.

'Poor woman.' Tara keeps her voice low, and Peter reaches for her hand. His touch is a comfort, still, if just because they know each other so well.

The service isn't long, and Tara is grateful for that. The minister gives an anodyne eulogy about Frank's steadiness as a husband and a father. He mentions the grandson and makes the usual vague reference to 'trials of faith'. Only when the assembly sits for yet another psalm that Tara doesn't know does she lean over to her ex and voice the question that had been echoing through her head.

'I wonder what happened?' she asks. 'I mean, it's so sad. Falling down your own stairs?'

Peter's face is unreadable. 'He was probably drunk,' he says.

'No.' She shakes him off. 'Frank was a twelve-stepper. Had been for years.'

'People lie about drinking all the time.' The censure is clear in Peter's voice. 'They fall off the wagon, and they're too embarrassed to admit it.'

'I don't think so.' Tara thinks back to the last time she'd seen Frank. He'd changed since those wild days with his band – with Min. He'd seemed to contract and condense, as if he were hunkering down to the real business of living. 'Being a parent changed him, and then the whole deal with their grandson.'

She can feel Peter watching her. The singing has ended; the minister is reciting some final prayer. Bestowing a blessing.

'I wonder if there was something else going on?' she asks again. Her neighbors turn toward each other. The kiss of peace ending the service.

'You still think like a writer.' Peter leans toward her. She feels his lips, warm and dry, on her cheek. 'But this isn't some story, Tara. This is real life.'

THREE

'What do you mean, there's no booze?' Gina's voice cuts through the hushed conversation like jagged glass. 'It's a funeral, isn't it? That's not right.'

Tara winces, grateful that Peter has left. He'd gotten that pinched look once the service ended, when Tara said she'd wanted to go to the gravesite and to the house after. At one point, that would have gotten Tara's back up. But the time for arguments has passed. 'Go home,' she'd said instead. 'I'll get a ride.'

'It's the Cooper deadline.' He'd been embarrassed.

'You did enough.' She absolved him. 'Really, I'm grateful.'

Now she's glad she insisted, that she waved him off with a smile when he pulled up to the curb. He doesn't fit in with this crowd. Never had, though he had tried when they were first dating, pursing his mouth in that same pinched fashion when he came back from the bathroom at the Rat. When he heard her friends – Min, Gina – laughing, drunk and happy.

She remembers all of that, including how she began to see their world – to see clubland – as he did. Sad and small. Funny how he stays in her head that way, even now. But she can feel those memories slough off her like dead skin, and she relaxes into her old self even as she makes her way up the cement walk. The door looks freshly painted. Peter had tried, Tara knows that, but she's glad she doesn't have to explain. That the toilet is broken and the pitcher on the back is for flushing, for example. Or whatever minor obstacle had been one too many this week. It doesn't bother her, not anymore. Even before Gina's outburst, Tara had been aware of a shift in herself. Peter would call it a regression, she knows. Funny how she still hears him. Funny now to think that they were ever married.

'Neela, I'm so sorry.' She'd gone straight to the widow. Her mother would be proud, even as she'd disparage this crew. This – Tara can visualize the way her mouth would tighten on the word – 'lifestyle'. That's when she hears it – when everyone hears it: Gina's cry of deprivation and of grief.

'Gina!' A hiss of warning. Someone's taking Gina out back, and once Tara has patted Neela's hand, hugged her daughter Mika, she follows, more concerned for her old friend than she wants to admit. She finds her on the tiny patio, sitting where a matronly type in a black cardigan has seated her. 'This is a sober house,' says the matron, standing over her. That hiss, surely Tara knows it. Carla, Tom's wife, her face grown hard with the years.

'But it's a funeral.' Gina is on the edge of tears, and Carla isn't helping. 'And there wasn't even a wake.'

'Come on, Gina.' Tara sidles up to her, pulling over another of the white plastic lawn chairs, and nods to Carla. She's taking over. 'You know that Frank didn't drink anymore.'

Gina sags forward and Tara pulls her close. Over Gina's head, Tara sees Carla shake her head. Exasperated. 'Go.' Tara mouths the word.

'We've got to respect what Frank would have wanted.' Tara talks softly, as if to a child. Carla rolls her eyes, casting a glance full of meaning at Tara before retreating back inside. 'And Frank would have wanted all his friends here, but he wouldn't have wanted anyone getting drunk.'

'He might have.' Gina, rallying the dead to her side. 'I heard they were fighting a lot. That's why people are saying he . . . you know.' Gina stops, as if to pronounce the word 'suicide' was to make it real.

'That's not how people kill themselves.' Tara nips that in the bud.

'It's that Neela.' Gina sniffs. 'She's become such a tight ass.'

Tara chuckles, covers her mouth with her hand. If she can lash out, then Gina's going to be OK. She won't melt down here, today anyway. And she's right. They've all gotten older, but it's taken them all differently. Gina's gotten sloppier. Carla, apparently, has grown harder, though Tara reminds herself that, despite the bulldog jaw, the other woman did take the time to escort Gina from the room. Did try to reason with her. Neela and Frank, though – they'd changed tons. Frank for the better. Despite his sobriety, he never became one of those holier-than-thou types. He'd turned in on himself, from what Tara hears. She remembers him as a somber man, the few times their paths had crossed over the last couple of years. Quiet and serious. But never sanctimonious. Whereas Neela? Tara closes her eyes, leans on Gina's head as if she were a baby, as if they were children still. It's warm out here, the early autumn heat captured by the close-set houses. As Gina complains, getting it out of her system, she remembers. Twenty years like it was yesterday.

'Hurry up!' Min had been rushing her. Actually taking her hand and pulling her through Kenmore Square.

'What's the rush?' Tara had been laughing, a little high. They'd smoked a bowl, back at Min's, while Min had gotten dressed. The liner, the mascara, painted on with a brush. Tara had shown up ready, hair slightly teased. It was Min who had held them up, changing her shirt three times and fussing more about her make-up than Tara had ever seen. Now she was grabbing Tara's hand, pulling her down the sidewalk.

'Just hurry.' The hardware on Min's jacket sparkling in the streetlight.

Tara had let herself be dragged. Min always kept things close, but it was clear this mattered to her. When they'd gotten to Oakie's, smiled their way past Brian at the door and down the stairs, she'd understood.

'Hey, Oaksters.' A scrawny man, his hair as black as his leather jacket, hunched over the mike. 'We're Last Call.'

A windmill and he sounded the first chord. Fast and loud, the band joined in, the beat coming strong from all three. The guitarist sang, too, his voice a rough bark. Only when he soloed did she get a look at him, the rooster hair almost reaching Oakie's improvised lights. A face like a hawk, eyes deep set even then. Something about his size, the way he stood looked familiar.

'They're good.' Tara turned toward her friend. Min nodded, her body bobbing with the music, and suddenly she was moving forward, making her way through the crowd.

'Min!' Tara reached for her. Oakie's didn't have a mosh pit, not really, but the crowd up front could get intense, especially with a band this high energy. 'Wait!'

She managed to grab her friend's arm, the leather cool to the touch, but when Min turned, she dropped it. The look in Min's face – there was no disguising it. She was ready to turn on anyone who stopped her. She'd have torn her own arm off if Tara hadn't let go, and suddenly Tara understood. Min had been distant for weeks. Had become vague about where she was going. Had even disappeared a few times, leaving Tara to find her own way home. Nothing major – clubland was home territory for them both – but curious, in its way. It was this guitarist. He drew Min like a magnet.

Tara caught up to her by the edge of the stage. 'What's his name?' She had to shout, even between songs. The crowd was sparked up. 'Guitar man?'

'Frank.' Min turned to her with eyes wide, and Tara felt like she'd earned something. Earned her trust. 'His name's Frank.'

Tara nodded, finally connecting the musician on stage to the hulking presence she'd seen around. There was more to know, clearly. But then the next song started and Min started to dance, arms above her head and head down, all hennaed hair and pale hands. As she turned, the light bounced off the pink of her jacket and softened her face. Warmed it, and Tara had danced too, happy to be in her friend's confidence. Happy to see her cool buddy shed some of her perpetual reserve for a guy.

With Min preoccupied with her own moves, Tara had snuck a glance up at the stage, checking out the man who had broken through to her friend. He wasn't looking down at them. That wasn't unusual. He was on stage. A star for the next forty minutes. But then Tara saw that he was focused on something – on some point off to her right. She turned, and that's when she first saw her. A skinny redhead in a cut-off T-shirt, black rubber bangles bouncing on her arm as she shimmied on the bar. And Tara's heart fell.

She didn't say anything. She couldn't, but she knew. All Min's preening would be for naught that night, not that she and Frank wouldn't hook up again. Whenever Neela pissed him off. When she went off, as she did periodically through their long and tumultuous courtship. But it was never the same after that. Not after Neela Johnson, wild woman, and the love of Frank Turcotte's life.

*　　*　　*

Maybe it was just as well Min hadn't come. Neela looks like she's at the breaking point. Tara watches her from across the room, a plate of pasta salad in her hand.

'Let's get something to eat,' she'd said to Gina, once the other woman had settled down. 'I don't know about you, but I didn't have breakfast.'

Gina had sniffed and nodded. The short crying jag that had followed her outburst had left her calmer and only marginally more disheveled than before, and Tara led her back inside with only the slightest shiver of trepidation. This was a funeral, she reminded herself. People were supposed to be sad, and the pudgy little rocker wouldn't be the only one whose mascara had been smudged by tears.

She needn't have worried. Despite the setting – the overcrowded living room done up like somebody's maiden aunt's – this was also still clubland.

'Hey, Gina, girl.' Richie had appeared out of nowhere, putting an arm around Tara's charge. 'How're we doing here?'

He didn't even look up at Tara as he led Gina away, so it was a shock when she heard her own thoughts voiced aloud.

'Gina being Gina.' The male voice startled her into turning. A voice she knew, although for a moment she didn't recognize the speaker. 'Some things never change.'

'Scott?' She had laughed in relief. The shared sentiment, the appearance of her old friend – all serving to lighten the day.

'In the flesh.' He smiled and leaned closer, and she was sure. 'A bit less of it these days.'

'You look great.' He did. The fat that had once seemed an integral part of his outsized personality had melted away. 'God, it's been – ages.'

'Seventeen years since I had a drink, so close to that long since I've been in the clubs.' He looked past her. 'Some people never change, I should've said.'

Tara turned. Gina was whimpering again, even as she shoveled pasta into her mouth.

'No, they don't,' she agreed. 'But I wouldn't mind grabbing a bite. Want something?'

'I'm good.' He hoisted his red plastic cup. 'Diet coke and

lime. My cocktail of choice. Get something and come back, though. I want to talk to you.'

'Aye, aye, boss.' They both grinned. That had always been her response, whatever Scott had asked of her – driving up to New Hampshire to cover some all-ages hardcore show. Tracking down the one English speaker of that Brazilian funk band. Distributing an extra three hundred papers the morning Tom quit in disgust after the 'zine had panned the Exiles single.

'Some turnout, huh?' Tom is there now, reaching past her for the rye bread.

'Frank had a lot of friends.' Tara had been considering the cold cuts but opts for the pasta salad. 'A lot of the old faces are here today.'

The bassist – former bassist? Tara doesn't know – nods, his mouth full. 'Kind of surprised,' he manages at last. 'Frank hadn't been around much.'

'Because of the program?' Tara takes a bite of her salad. She remembers Tom tending bar. Drinking, too. She can see Scott over by the corner, waiting, but she's curious.

'No, I don't think so.' Tom reaches for a pickle. 'You want one?'

'Sure.' She's missed this, the camaraderie. 'Thanks.'

She takes the pickle. Looks around. Scott has crossed over to Neela. The widow looks like she'll disappear into the flocked recliner. Was that Frank's chair, Tara wonders, as he kneels beside her. It looks too big for the pale wreck of a woman, the burnt orange all wrong for the faded pink of her hair. Grief has leached out whatever color she had left.

'You think he was drinking again?' Despite what Tara told Peter, she's not sure.

Tom sounds like he is. 'Frank? No, no way.' He shakes his shaggy head. The furrows around his mouth grow deeper. 'He was all caught up with the kid. He wouldn't.'

'Then what do you think happened?' Scott has stood up. 'Hang on,' she says, but Tom has moved over to where the chips are.

'There you are.' Scott turns down the fork Tara offers. 'No thanks, but I've got an offer for you.'

She raises her eyebrows, aware suddenly of her own full

mouth. Of her old friend's newly muscular body. She swallows, hard. 'Oh?'

'You know I'm at *City* now.' He looks at her, waiting for recognition.

She nods as she takes another, smaller bite. She doesn't read the glossy monthly, but she's certainly aware of it. Ad driven and silly as hell. Somewhere in the back of her mind, she recalls someone saying that her old boss had joined its staff. Was he in charge of features now? Was he the editor? She remembers an inane cover – a model in a parka eating ice cream – and hopes he wasn't involved.

'I've been given a mandate to make the mag more edgy,' he says, as if he can read her mind. He's keeping his voice low, and she realizes that he's not as comfortable here as she is. He hasn't slipped back into the old ways like she has. 'More street.' He laughs, embarrassed by the term. 'Anyway, management says I can bring in some more writers, and I was wondering if you'd be interested.'

'Me?' Her voice squeaks. It's the macaroni. She looks around for a napkin.

'You were always my best writer,' he says.

'Most reliable.' She can remember, even if he doesn't. 'The only one you could count on not to black out or go off with the band.'

'More than that.' His smile. Tara wonders if he's had his teeth capped. No, she remembers, he always had a nice smile.

'Scott? Scott Hasseldeck.' A manicured hand on his arm turns him around. Lily Clark. Tara closes her eyes. Lily always was a beauty. Unlike Neela, she's kept her looks. 'You're a sight for sore eyes.'

'Lily.' Clearly Scott remembers her too. But he turns back. 'Let's talk,' he says. Tara nods and goes back for more of the pasta.

'I'm looking to see who doesn't show up.' Two women, over by the food, are surveying the room. Tara listens, even as she refills her plate. 'It's not lovely Lily. She wouldn't dare show her face if it was her.'

Tara stands. 'Connie?' It's the voice that brings her back. The short black helmet of hair is cut into a softer shape, the color lightened with some auburn highlights.

'Tara Winton.' The speaker turns to take her in. 'You remember Robin. I'm afraid we're getting all gossipy. But if you can't gossip at a funeral . . .'

'Yeah, really.' Tara forces a chuckle. Nods at the third woman, who makes her own wan smile back. 'So . . .' Her voice drops in what she hopes is a conspiratorial whisper. 'You think Frank had someone on the side?'

A shrug. 'Don't know. But I do know he was preoccupied. Neela was complaining to me about how he had gotten all secretive. Making calls and not telling her who he was talking to.'

'Poor Neela.' Robin's voice as weak as her smile.

'Anyway, we're trying to figure out who isn't here.' Robin gives Tara a sidelong look. 'Guilty conscience and all.'

'Gotcha,' says Tara. She takes a bite of the pasta. Thinks of Min and hopes they're wrong.

'Hey, Joey.' She finds the drummer in the mudroom off the kitchen poking through a cooler filled with ice. 'Great set the other night.'

'Thanks.' Two-liter bottles of store-brand cola protrude from the ice, and someone has rested a six of Kaliber on top.

Tara reaches for the soda. 'May I ask you something?'

'Sure.' He breaks one of the non-beers from its plastic ring. ''Bout the gig?'

'No.'

He pops the can's top and takes a long pull, waiting.

'About Frank.' She's not sure how to ask. Not sure if the drummer – always taciturn, always the hardest to get a quote from back in the day – was the right person to approach. But he's here. She's here. 'Do you think Frank might have been stepping out? You know, on Neela?'

He turns with a muttered expletive and pushes past her, into the kitchen and beyond. She turns to watch him go and sees Tom, his face grown pale.

'I can't believe you asked him that. You asked anybody.' Tom is more adamant about this than he was about the drinking. 'Frank lived for Neela, for his family. He always said that anything else – you know, back in the day – was because of the drinking. It's always been Neela since day one. Ask anyone. Hey—'

He starts to call, to gesture, but she stops him. 'No, please,' she says, embarrassed. 'I'm sorry I even asked. It's just . . . well, it's such an odd way to go, you know? And if he wasn't drinking, then you have to wonder if there was a fight or some other problem.'

'You always were a snoop, weren't you?' Tom looks at her without blinking. His eyes are hard. 'Asking questions. Writing your stories. You probably started the rumors about Chris, too. Look, the man died. It was an accident, OK? It wasn't like he was a part of your life, but some of us here? We'll miss him until our own dying days.'

FOUR

Wine isn't the answer, but it helps. Tara has just topped off her glass when she gets Min on the phone.

'You wouldn't want to come over, would you?' She takes care to enunciate her words.

Min laughs. 'You need a drinking buddy? Was it that bad?' A thud and a sigh. Tara can picture her taking her shoes off. Collapsing onto the couch.

'Yeah.' Tara admits. There's no hiding anything from Min, not after all these years. 'I'll get pizza?'

'Sorry, I'm wiped. But hang on.' Silence as Min gets her own beverage. It's a routine they've developed, over the years: Tara, feet up on her sofa. Min with hers on the coffee table. Even when Peter lived with her, they kept it up, those nights when he was on a story, filing for third. Tara knows Min can visualize her as easily as she can her friend. It's comforting.

'So, what happened?' Min slurps at something. Tara wants to ask, to make sure her friend is also having something with a kick, but after the conversations at the reception, she feels shy.

'Well, Gina was there. Late, of course, and she had a bit of a meltdown at the house after.' Better to start with the known. Gina was safe.

'You went to the house?' A sigh and a grunt. Tara visualizes the pillows being rearranged. 'Did Peter go with?'

'Just to the funeral.' She kind of wishes she hadn't told Min about Peter. About how he offered to drive her. 'He didn't want to take the whole day off.'

'Uh huh.' She can sense Min nodding. 'He didn't want to deal with that freak show, that's what,' she says. 'Let me guess. Gina began bawling and Neela played the ice queen, accepting condolences from that throne of hers.'

'Kind of.' Tara wonders how Min knows about the chair. 'You've been over there?'

'Once or twice.' Tara is processing, but the wine has slowed her down, and Min erupts in laughter. 'Jeez, Tara. I mean, just to talk. Say hi. It's been years, you know?'

'Yeah, but.' Tara thinks back to the women at the wake. What they were saying. 'You were close once.'

'And I said goodbye to that, long ago.' Min's tone is definitive. Clear. Then again, Tara has heard that before. Which Min knows, too. 'Besides, I didn't like the man he was.' She talks as if she owes Tara an explanation. 'You know, toward the end.'

'So you spoke to him recently?' Tara sits up. Puts her glass on the floor.

'A few times.' Min always downplayed their contact. 'On the phone, basically. He was, I don't know, preoccupied. Wanting to go over the old days.'

'Oh?' That could mean a lot of things.

'The scene.' Min answers the unspoken question. 'Not us. But he was being weird about it. Just – not himself. Made me wonder if he was drinking again.'

'Tom says he wasn't. Swears it.' Tara thinks back to their last exchange. The anger in his eyes. The comment about Chris. It's been a long time since she heard that name.

'Well, yeah, Tommy would say that.' For someone who doesn't hang out anymore, Min stays current. 'He worshipped Frank.'

In the silence that follows, Tara reaches for her glass again.

'So, what's up with Peter?' Min is done with Frank, with that conversation. Tara can hear it.

'He's OK. On me to buy a condo near him.'

'I bet.' There's a lilt to Min's voice. 'I bet he'd like to show you some real estate.' Tara starts to object when Min gets serious. 'He's still into you, Tara. He's just been waiting for you to, you know, catch up.'

To grow up, Tara knows she means. 'Well, he should have come with me after then.' She means to deflect, but she also has more questions about the party. About Frank. 'Scott Hasseldeck was there,' she says. He didn't attack her. Didn't question her motives.

'Scott?' Another laugh. The wine is kicking in. Min is sounding loose. 'He's just looking for the gossip. For that rag of his, what's it called – *Shitty*?'

'Maybe.' Tara's feeling it too. 'But I'll tell you, he's looking good.'

'You're making me sorry I wasn't there,' says her friend.

'Me too,' says Tara, and they both drink some more.

Tara has a head the next morning, almost like in the old days. At least she has a private office, now, and once she closes the door she can sink into her seat. Downing two aspirin with her latte, she leans back, eyes closed. The good thing about the corporate world: she was dressed and on time. Nothing else seems to matter.

The clang of her office phone wakes her with a start. She jumps, eyes wide. No, the door remains closed. Nobody saw her napping.

'Communications.' She picks up the receiver. 'Tara Winton.' It's almost reflex, though the urge to say 'news desk' or even '*Underground Sound*' is never far away.

'Wow, you sound so official.' The laughing response is so close to her own thoughts that it stymies her.

'Scott?' she says at last.

'You sound surprised.' The laughter has left a lilt in his voice. 'I said I was going to be in touch.'

'So you did.' At the thought of her old colleague – of how he looked the day before – she starts to smile.

'I wanted to talk to you about a story,' he says, and she feels suddenly, unexpectedly let down.

'I'm not . . . I have a real job now, Scott.' Pride bucks her up. 'This isn't just a day job, you know.'

'No, of course not.' He ignores her protest. He always did, she remembers now. 'But I was hoping – well . . . I started to tell you. I've been given a mandate to bring *City* into this century. Make it edgier.' He pauses, and she can imagine him making air quotes. 'Urban.'

'Street?' She remembers, and she's chuckling now, too. It was always us against them with Scott.

'Exactly.' He knows he's got her. 'Anyway, I was thinking about Frank, about the whole scene, and I came up with the perfect cover story: "The Last Days of Punk Rock". It would be fun, sad. Our whole misspent youth.'

'I'd read it.' She can humor him. 'If you could get someone to do a halfway decent piece.'

'*You* could.' His conviction comes through the line. 'You always were my best writer. My best gal. Always.' Tara pictures him standing. Waiting for her to respond. Remembers what he looks like now. The pause threatens to become awkward. 'So what do you say?'

'I do have responsibilities here.' She's evading the question. He knows it. 'We'll give you a pseudonym,' he says.

'Like hell you will.' She falls for it. Like she always did. 'I want the byline.'

'That's my gal.' He's laughing again. 'And seriously, you have all the contacts, and all the research will be after hours anyway. It'll be fine.'

'Easy for you to say.' She's not sure if she's been played – or how she feels about it. She did have questions. About the scene. About Frank. 'OK, I'm interested, at least.'

'Why don't we get together to talk tactics,' he says. 'I've got some ideas. What do you say to dinner?'

By the time they hang up, Tara is more confused than before. But her headache has gone, and she's wide awake.

She heads back to the pub that evening, back to where it all began. There's no music tonight, and the place looks different. The tables are set for dinner service, the curtains behind the stage open to the street. The late sun slants in, burnishing the wooden tabletops, the wide, polished bar.

Only the bartender looks the same, and Tara starts with him, pulling up a stool as he makes his way over.

'Menu?' He puts down a coaster without asking.

'Thanks, but no.' She searches her memory. 'Nick, right?'

He nods. 'Good memory. Allagash?'

'Thanks. You, too.' She watches as he pulls the draft, a slight smile bringing a dimple to his grizzled cheek.

'Here you go.' He places the glass on the counter and waits while she takes a sip. 'Tara, right?'

'Tara Winton.' She nods and after a moment, holds out her hand.

They shake. 'I remember you,' he says. 'Not just from the

other night, but back in the day. Didn't you used to hang out at Oakie's?'

'Yeah, I did.' She looks around. The bar is empty, the bored-looking waitress has already seen to the one table. 'Hey, can I buy you a drink?'

'What the hell.' He grabs a lowball glass. Pours himself a shot. 'To old times, right?'

She touches her glass to his. Meets his eyes. They're blue and clear, and suddenly she remembers.

'You worked at Oakie's, didn't you? You were a bar back?'

He nods with a grin. The dimple – those eyes – erasing the grey and the lines. 'Brian ran me ragged, lugging cases up those stairs. It was Rolling Rock back then, not PBR. God, I hated those green bottles.'

'The green wall. I remember it.' She can picture it – the cases stacked in the basement. He's looking at her puzzled. 'Brian used to let me use the basement for interviews,' she explained. She doesn't mention that he would try to kiss her. Reach for her as she passed. 'Because the dressing room . . .'

'Was a shithole closet, I know.' His smile grows broader even as he shakes his head. 'I remember. You wrote for that 'zine, right?'

'Yeah.' It's satisfying to be remembered. It's also the opening she's been hoping for. She's not seriously considering the assignment. Not really. But it couldn't hurt to feel it out. See who might be available. Only just then an older couple – him with a white beard, her unnaturally dark bob – come in and walk up to the bar.

'May I help you?' Nick's shot glass disappears and then he's talking microbrews. Hops and witbiers. Like he'd never humped kegs from a cellar that reeked of piss and mold.

It was the smell that got to Tara, the first night she went down there. She had expected dirt and disarray, but not utter filth.

She'd never intended to go down there. Never had any interest. Oakie's was her club, her 'third place' between her walk-up apartment and the crap job she had doing paste-up at the weekly. But even the waitresses avoided those back stairs. 'Ankle breakers,' she'd heard one woman – the brunette with the retro beehive – call them. 'Ankle grabbers,' muttered her colleague, before she sent the young bar back down to fetch whatever it was she'd needed.

She could've joined them, Brian had made that clear. But Tara had never wanted a job at Oakie's, not in her wildest. 'Going deaf for tips,' the brunette used to say. No thanks. Tara would rather chronicle the scene than serve it. Still, Brian had been doing her a kindness in his role as gatekeeper, stray hands notwithstanding.

It was the summer of the Brit pop bands, when scrawny boys were climbing the charts turning out impossibly catchy records, raw hooks over even rougher guitar.

'They all think they're Mick Jagger,' she had said to Scott when another tour was announced.

'No,' he had disagreed, 'Keith.' But this one was different, he'd said. Better, and he wanted more than a review. 'Go talk to them. Get some dirt.'

She understood once she heard the record. It was good, with an edge most of the local bands lacked. Not the Whirled Shakers, of course. They could blow these boys away, but up against bands like the Exiles or even the Pugs, well, yeah, she could hear the difference. And so she'd called the label and set it up. No, she didn't need a backstage pass. It was obvious this band had never played Oakie's. She just wanted to give them a head's up. She'd catch them before their set. Fifteen minutes, just for some quotes.

'I'll put you on the list,' the publicist had said. Tara didn't argue. It would be pointless to explain that everyone knew her by this point. That Brian always waved her in. Besides, it made the publicist feel like she was doing her job.

Nobody had told the band though. Or maybe they had. When Tara had knocked on the door – 'backstage' at Oakie's being a former supply closet to the right of the stage – the singer was high as a kite, his pupils tiny pinpricks in his big grey eyes.

'Come on in, darling.' He'd stumbled backward. Waved her in. 'You're here for the party?'

'I'm here for the interview,' she'd said. 'I'm Tara Winton, with *Underground Sound*. Your publicist should have told you.'

'Oh, yeah, yeah, yeah.' He wiped his mouth and looked around. That's when Tara had, too. And seen the stocky one – the drummer? – shooting up on the sofa, his head already lolling to one side as the hit kicked in. The guitarist – Lesley? Lester? – stood just past him, leaning back against the wall as Gina sucked him off. Gina, who was in love with Phil. Another man, hand on his fly, stood waiting.

'Not here,' Tara had barked and grabbed the singer's wrist.

'OK then.' He'd followed laughing, as she pulled him back into the club. Only the room was growing crowded. The first band was about to play.

'Brian.' Her voice had become rough. Commanding. 'You have anyplace I can do an interview? Someplace quiet?'

He must have seen something in her face. Or maybe he simply knew – the bands, Gina. 'The basement,' he said. 'It's kind of a mess, but . . .' She'd been thinking of his office, when she'd asked about someplace quiet. Not the dank room down those back stairs. She waited, but he didn't offer. Only shrugged and so she'd nodded and pulled the singer after her. He still thought she was going to service him, she realized. But when she started peppering him with questions, he caught on quickly enough.

'Sheffield, yeah.' He'd even gotten into it, reminiscing. 'No, that story in the *NME* got it wrong. It was Dave's mum who got us the gig.'

They talked through that whole first set. Tara took more notes than she could ever use. Three times the lanky bar back had come down those stairs. She remembered his legs, feet sideways, as he made his way down. His eyes, as he looked over at them, curious. She'd felt better, knowing he was there. Safe.

The singer didn't care.

'So what do you say?' When she'd finally run out of questions. Pocketed her notepad. He'd reached for her.

'Hey, Nick.' She'd pulled away without comment and turned, instead, to the bar back. 'Are the Lowdowns still on?'

'Just finishing up, Tara,' he'd said, and then that smile. He knew what was happening.

So did the singer. 'I guess I should get back up to the boys then.' He'd pushed himself off the filthy wall, up to his feet. Began to follow her toward the stairs. 'Only one thing. You know that redhead? The one who dances on the bar?'

'Neela?' She'd turned back in surprise.

'Yeah, yeah, Neela,' he'd said. 'You know if she's here tonight?'

'Penny for your thoughts?'

Tara looks up into the impossibly blue eyes once again.

'Or another Allagash perhaps?'

A large hand wraps around Tara's empty pint, the scars of a hundred small cuts, of decades of work, marking it. Aging it back to the present.

'Oh, yeah.' She chuckles. How shocked she had been. How naïve. 'Yeah, thanks, Nick.'

While he refills her glass, she thinks back on the rest of that night. The set had been great, despite the turmoil backstage. Because of it? This was rock and roll, after all – the Brit boys working the crowd into a frenzy. Had the drummer been erratic? Off the tempo at all? She remembers watching him. Waiting to hear him falter or slow, but as far as she could recall, he'd been rock solid. It was that singer who had been sloppy, lounging all over the tempo like some louche suitor playing at love. Teasing, with the lyric, with the melody. Leaning back on a beat that caught him every time.

The dichotomy – the discipline, for lack of a better word – had been a revelation, ultimately informing the piece, though she'd been careful to leave out anything that could have cost the band its visa. Scott had been impressed. She pictures his face, round then, eyebrows raised at her grudging, even skeptical tone. 'You're getting some distance,' he had said. 'Good.'

In addition, she'd learned not to take Gina's claims of undying love too seriously. She also learned to recognize a smack high, a skill that would prove useful in the years to come.

'Here you go.' The fresh pint brings her back to the present, and she looks up at Nick. The same blue eyes, only older now. 'So what brings you around here?'

'I can't stop in after work for a beer?' She hears the flirt in her voice as she says it. 'Actually, I was hoping to talk to you.'

Those eyebrows again. 'Really?' A rag appears and he wipes the bar to her left, before turning once more to face her. 'What about?'

He's seen something. Heard something in her voice – in the switch she made mid-reply. He looks serious, and he's waiting. 'I was wondering about Frank Turcotte,' she says. That wasn't what she intended, but it is true. 'About what happened to him.'

'He died.' Nick sighs as he looks down at the bar. 'What else is there to know?'

'Doesn't it seem odd to you?' She leans in, keeping her voice low. The couple at the end of the bar aren't part of this. Neither, at this moment, is her once and future editor, Scott. 'I mean, a freak accident?'

'You think he was drinking again?' Nick faces her, all humor gone.

'I don't know.' She shakes her head. 'I know he was in the program. And I heard that he'd been secretive. So maybe that's all it was, that he was sneaking out to drink or something else . . .'

'No.' Nick cuts her off. 'He wasn't doing anything else. He hated all that – that other shit.' He searches her face. 'Don't you remember?'

Tara nods. She does. The piety of the convert. 'I wonder, though.' A thought. 'They probably did an autopsy, right? With an accidental death?'

'Search me.' Nick looks down at the other couple. Tara is losing him. 'You're the journalist.'

'I was.' She reaches out, her fingertips brushing the back of Nick's hand. 'Look, Nick, I'm not just looking for gossip. I'm – well, Scott has asked me to do a story on Frank, on what became of the scene.'

It's a gamble, and she half expects him to walk off. To her surprise, he laughs, and she wonders if he's been holding his breath.

'What became of the scene? You're asking about that now?' Something like a lilt has crept back into his voice. A tease, which just as quickly leaves. 'We got old, Tara. That's what happened.'

'Yeah, that's part of it,' she says. It's easier to be honest. To just talk. 'But we didn't all grow out of it. Get real jobs.' She catches herself before she confesses – to leaving journalism. To her own conflicts. One thing she learned – focus on the story. Not yourself.

'I mean you were there when everything was happening. When

Neela would get up and dance.' It works, the combination of flattery and nostalgia, or something like. His grin softens, his expression wistful.

'Yeah,' he says, his voice soft. He leans back, nodding, his eyes focusing on the space above Tara's head. 'I remember those days. That girl was trouble. She turned into a good mom though. Really turned herself around.'

Tara nods, but she's back there too. How sudden it had all seemed. The scene at its wildest, then a wedding. A baby. But Nick clearly knows more, and Tara gets that old feeling – there's a story here, and it's hers. 'Maybe she got it out of her system?'

'Neela?' He shrugs, focusing those blue eyes on her. 'Maybe.' Smiles like he has a secret.

'Wait.' Tara picks up on that. Lets a laugh sneak into her voice, jollying him along. Ventures a gambit. 'Is there some bartender code of ethics or something? Something that says you shouldn't talk to me?'

'Nah, we're good.' He shakes off the memory, but not the smile. 'Statute of limitations and all that.'

She hasn't lost it. He wants to talk. And it has been a while. More than twenty years. That wild girl is a grandmother now. A grandmother and a widow.

'Would you have time?' Tara asks, quickly, before the sadness kicks in. Before the window closes. 'I don't know, maybe this weekend. Or some night after work. Unless . . .?'

'No, it's fine.' He turns away. 'It's just me now.'

She looks up, confused.

'Patti got the house, the garage on the Cape, in the divorce.' That smile has tightened, turned wry. 'It's just as well. It was her father's place, and I didn't like running it. Dealing with the rest of the family. Here, I'm on my own again.'

'I know the feeling.' She raises her left hand. Wiggles her ringless fingers. 'I mean, I'm busy tonight, but . . .' She leaves it open. The story. Those eyes.

'Is that why you want to go back over all of this?' Instead of following up, he's gotten serious. 'Revisit old times?'

'I'm not sure.' Now it's her turn for a rueful grin. To look down at the bar. 'Maybe I'm simply curious.' She looks up. His eyes are still so blue. 'Curious and bored.'

She emphasizes the last word. Means it for a laugh, but Nick is serious now. He leans in, hands on the bar, and looks into her face.

'You know, writing about Frank, about the scene, isn't going to bring him – isn't going to bring any of it back.' His voice is low. There's sadness in it. 'Nothing will.'

FIVE

'So how the hell are you?' Scott ushers her into his place with a one-handed hug. The other holds a bottle of wine, the cork half out. 'Come into the kitchen,' he beckons. 'I need to get a splash of this in the sauce.'

Even without the invitation, Tara would have followed him, lured by the aroma of garlic and herbs. 'Wow,' she says, as he leads her through a living room dominated by a huge picture window. 'What a view.'

'That view is why I bought the place,' Scott calls from the kitchen, his voice accompanied by the clattering of pans. 'OK,' he says, wiping his hands on a dish towel as he emerges. 'What are you drinking? I've got most of that bottle left.'

'These are cold.' She lifts the six she's brought. Recalls, too late, what he'd said about not drinking.

'Excellent.' He takes it, turns back to the kitchen without missing a beat. 'Let me get us some glasses.'

She hears the clinking of glassware, her host humming a tune off-key, and she turns back to that window. Skyscrapers and the harbor beyond. Her office is somewhere in the other direction, one of the new faceless buildings that make up the new waterfront. The view from her office is nothing like this, though.

'Doesn't look like Boston.' She's talking half to herself, but Scott has come up behind her, frosted glass in hand.

'Not from here, does it?' He hands her a beer, sips at his own beverage – cranberry red, slice of lime – as if he'd never shotgunned a Rolling Rock fresh from the Store 24 cooler. 'But the town's changed.'

'I gather.' She looks around. 'You've done OK.'

She means it. The cream sofa matches the chairs. The bookshelves of light blond wood. Still, she can hear the note of reproach in her voice.

He must, too. 'Yeah, I know. *City.* Who'da thunk it?' He takes a seat on the sofa, motions for her to do the same. 'But I paid my dues, Tara. The start-up I left town for? It went belly up. So did the next two. I was toiling away at *Portland Business* when Jonah called me.'

'He called you?' Tara remembers Jonah Wells. A little man – always in a suit – he ran the Casbah, a onetime warehouse down by the same docks she's now looking over. That lot – the one with the cranes, she thinks. That was it. 'And how'd he get into publishing anyway?'

Scott shrugs as he takes another sip, and Tara finds herself wondering if he's stalling. 'Well, he wanted someone with local experience. Someone who knew the city "from the ground up", he said. And, I confess, I'd been putting out feelers. I mean, there's only so many profiles you can do on tech start-ups you know are going to fail.'

Another sip. 'As for the magazine, well, he was always a businessman first.' He laughs softly. 'He was never in it for the music.'

'I believe that.' Tara drinks, looks out the window. The sky is darkening, green and orange slipping into a deeper blue. The silhouette of the cranes has started to disappear. 'Though I heard he was in it for the musicians.'

Scott snorts. 'Hey, he's my boss now.' His tone is light, but Tara stops. She doesn't need to elaborate. They both remember the Casbah's reputation, as rough as the waterfront then was. Bands had to fight for their money, sometimes literally, as the bouncers seemed to enjoy beating on anyone who got in their way. Some bands, anyway.

Even before the end, when it became a pay-to-play joint with bad suburban cover bands 'selling' tickets to their friends, it had a rep for the way it treated musicians – and their fans. The Cash Bar, everyone called it, a nickname that even made it into the *Underground* after a well-known funk star had nearly walked out when he found the Crown Royal specified in his rider had been opened and, presumably, watered down. Everyone had said Jonah had pitched a fit when he heard that the bar manager had given in. Everyone said it was his call that the funk star hadn't been booked back.

'So what have you been doing?' He stretches one arm along the sofa's back, and Tara blinks. He looks so comfortable. As if he belongs in this tony, high-end space. 'I mean, I knew you left the paper when I stopped seeing your byline.'

'You read me?' She's tickled. She forgot how it feels. 'God, Scott, I miss it. I really do.' She looks down into her beer, as if the past were all that golden hue. 'I don't know. It seemed like a good job. A natural move what with the writing I'd been doing for you. What we did with the *Underground*. I mean, I'd always wanted to write. But then the *Dot* started cutting back, and Peter – well, he'd already moved on. He's doing consulting now, with one of the big firms, and we were married by then. And the scene, well . . .'

'Yeah.' He nods. 'The fun ran out.'

'Exactly.' It's as good a description as any. They drink in silence, and Tara finds her mind wandering. 'Hey, what were you humming?'

'What?' He shakes his head. 'I don't know. I don't remember.'

'I thought . . .' She stops. Smiles at the memory. 'I saw the Whirled Shakers the other day,' she says. 'They were still good.'

'Phil and the gang? They're still at it?' A ping from the other room. 'Hey, keep talking,' he says, rising from the sofa. 'Tell me all about it while I finish the glaze.'

She does, leaning on the door frame as he whisks butter into a small saucepan. 'I even ended up dancing,' she says. Scott has been fussing over the food while she talks, and she feels self-conscious, like she wants to see his face. See his reaction. 'Min thinks it's all kind of pitiful,' she admits.

'Min Kahler? You're still in touch?' He looks up from where he's crouched by a low cabinet, before extracting a tray. 'What's she up to?'

'Still at County.' This is safer ground. The jobs – no, the careers – of their friends. 'She could move into management, I think, but she likes just working her shifts.'

'Hmm.' He stands and looks at the tray. 'Sounds like someone I know.'

'What?' They're back on familiar turf. 'I moved on. Went from *Underground Sound* to the *Dot* and Zeron. I'm the manager of corporate communications, I'll have you know.'

He raises an eyebrow, the corner of his mouth drawn back as if to smirk. 'Yeah, that was real risky for you, Tara.'

She shakes her head, confused. 'What do you mean?'

'You said it yourself. You're a writer.' He reaches for an oven mitt. 'That's why I want to get you writing again, Tara. *City* could use you – but I think it would be good for you, too.'

He opens the oven. The aroma is intoxicating. Tara doesn't cook, never did, and certainly never like this. She feels almost lightheaded, it smells so good.

'Not that I don't have my own selfish reasons.' He stands. Placing the pan on the cooktop, he glances over his shoulder. That old smile, the real one she remembers so well. 'Shall we?'

'I didn't expect to hear from you tonight.' Min's voice is low, her words innocuous. But Tara's known her long enough to catch the insinuation.

'It's Scott, Min,' she says. The exasperation, at least, is real. 'I mean, I've known him forever.'

'You knew him, how long ago?' In the pause following Min's question, Tara hears the flick of a lighter. The inhale. The satisfied exhalation that follows. 'I mean, hey, I never had a sense of him, other than as a fat guy who made you do all his dirty work. But now . . .'

'Yeah, he looks good now.' Tara thinks back on the dinner, on how it felt to see her old friend again. 'But who knows? I never saw him with anyone back in the day, either.'

'As previously stated: fat guy.' There's an audible purr of pleasure in Min's voice, though from the smoke or the conversation, Tara can't tell.

'And he didn't make me do all the dirty work.' Tara doesn't like this. Doesn't like Min when she gets all catty and cool. But she has questions for her friend, and Min has been hard to pin down lately. 'He gave me a chance to write. As you may remember, I was stuck doing paste-up at the *Dot*. Maybe I got a record to review, like once a month. And Scott and I – we made something.'

'Exactly.'

Tara closes her eyes. Lets Min have her point. Besides, she's not sure where she and Scott stand. It was so easy to fall into old patterns. The meal had been great – green olives and lemon spicing up a game bird. Potatoes crisped and tender. Somewhere along the way, Scott had learned how to cook. But even before they had tucked in, they'd been talking business. Scott was full of ideas – opening with the funeral, jump back to clubland's heyday, when A&R men would saunter into Oakie's like they belonged there.

'Are you going to want me to get the Casbah in there?' Tara had been only partly teasing. She still couldn't get her mind around the idea of Jonah as Scott's boss. Jonah in her world.

'I don't know about that.' Scott had sounded reticent, and for that Tara was grateful. And he'd changed the subject, then. Pushed forward. 'Let's not set anything in stone yet,' he'd said. 'I want you to do some research. I know you know what happened, but why don't you see what's out there now? See if anyone has an interesting story. You know, hellion transformed into church lady. Someone who made it coming back to get the band together.'

'That would be something.' Tara had sat back, then, remembering the previous night. The Whirled Shakers at the pub. That wasn't what Scott meant, though, and she knew it. 'You're looking for someone big, though. Right? Someone like the Aught Nines?'

'Exactly.' He'd paused. They had locked eyes over the table, remembering. 'Only, you know, someone who survived.'

'You were right, you know.' She blinks back the memory. Throws a bone to Min, who has grown quiet on the line.

'Of course I was.' She chuckles. 'In what way?'

'About us – about the scene. So many people didn't make it. The drugs and all, and now Frank.'

'Wait a minute.' Tara can hear her friend adjusting. Maybe even putting her cigarette out. 'I didn't say "us". Not us. You and me, we were never self-destructive like that. The drink and the drugs. We kept our heads.'

Tara nods. She's not sure how true that was. Yes, they'd come through OK, but as she recalls, much of that was luck and fear.

'And Frank, well.' A sigh. Or Min has picked up her ciggie again? 'I don't know what was up with him, but the man was sober for – what? – twenty years? Not that he didn't have reason to drink again.'

'He was having problems?' Tara thinks back to the women at the reception. To the gossip. 'He called you to talk?'

A chuff of laughter – or maybe a cough. 'Tara, the man was

an old friend. When he called me for advice, what was I going to do?'

'Advice?' She does her best to keep her tone level. Nonjudgmental.

'Mm-hmm.' Min takes a drag. Exhales. Tara can picture her, lying on that old sofa. 'A few weeks ago. When they got the news about Mika's baby. He wanted to know everything.'

'And he didn't trust the doctors?' Something was off. Tara was fishing, but she didn't know for what.

'Tara, I'm a nurse. He'd known me for more than twenty years. His grandson was sick. It was serious.' Min was not one to be probed. 'He wanted the straight dope, OK? He's – he was – an old friend. Kind of like Scott is for you. Sound familiar?'

'That's . . .' Tara stops. Maybe it isn't different. Maybe Min is right. 'I'm writing a piece for him, Min. A piece for *City*.'

'Let me guess: ice cream?' Min is almost laughing.

'No.' Tara cuts her off. 'It's not all . . . I'm writing about the music world. About the community we had.'

'Oh, that's rich.' Min has her back up now. Tara can hear it. 'Just what you need – more time in the clubs. Talk about addicts, Tara, you're one. You've got to let it go. Move on. I was thinking when you told me your old playmate was in town, that he was looking good, that he'd be good for you. You could jump his bones finally. Get laid. Consummate that strange relationship you two always had and get Peter out of your system along the way. But now I'm thinking your ex sounds better and better. Your old buddy – Scott? – he's enabling you. Using you just like he used to, only you're in so deep you don't see it.'

'Min, stop it!' Tara takes a breath, or tries to. Peter. Scott. Her interest in the scene. Min has thrown so much at her she doesn't know where to start. 'It's an article. Freelance. A feature for the magazine. I've missed it, you know? I mean, I'm not going to quit my job, but Scott's given me an assignment, and he's letting me run with it.'

'Uh huh.' Min's voice dripped with sarcasm.

'It's a possible cover.' But that's the least of it for Tara, and Min knows it.

A pause as Min takes another deep drag. 'Writing about how

it used to be,' she exhales the words. Tara can almost see the
smoke.

'Maybe.' Tara has to give her that. 'But also about what
happened and why. You know? How things fell apart. Who's left,
who's still doing it. I mean, it's for *City*, so I'll be focusing on
the big names. The Cars. Til Tuesday. The Aught Nines.'

'Oh, that's rich.' Min is readjusting. Sitting up – or lighting
another cigarette. 'The Aught Nines.'

'You've got to admit, they had a great story.' Scott remembered.
He'd loved it.

Min, however, sputters. 'They'd have been one-hit wonders.
Their album wouldn't have gone anywhere.'

'Well, that's just it.' Tara's back on solid ground. The music,
the history. She could do something with this. 'We'll never know.'

When Tara first became aware of them, the Aught Nines were like
so many other bands she knew. Nice guys with nothing much
going on beyond the usual garage punk thrash. A repertoire that
was half covers of Stooges songs and half originals that didn't
sound as good. The kind of band you saw if you got there early
enough, when they were third on a bill on a Wednesday. Jim, the
guitarist, and Jerry, the bassist, were brothers and they were pretty
honest about their motivation: girls. They'd started the band back
in high school and had never really moved on. Of course once
they were of age, the free beer kept them going. And when their
singer, another childhood pal, left – something to do with his
father's painting business and a freelance tax bill that had never
been paid – it seemed likely the band would break up. But that
month the *Dot* was offering a deal on musicians' classifieds. The
first 10 words for free. It was supposed to drum up business and,
besides, who could say everything they wanted in only 10 words?

Jim – or maybe it was Jerry – saw it as a challenge. Kind of
like when the bartender at Riddles told them they could only
drink free while they were on stage, and Jerry managed to chug
five pints while playing open strings. He'd approached the *Dot*
ad the same way, getting the word count down to seven: *Gigging
band needs singer Iggy Ramones Dolls.* The box number was
free. That was all they really needed, but it was Greg who insisted
on fleshing it out: *No preppies allowed!*

'We talked about that,' Greg had told Tara, when they'd sat down for a profile. His moon face had been serious, the bulk of him lending weight to his words. 'I mean, Jim and I wanted someone we could hang with. Jerry was pushing for something else. Something like "Chick magnet wanted". But Jim and I had girlfriends, so we overruled him.'

'Funny what you ended up with.' Tara tried to stay out of her own stories, but this one was obvious. She can still remember Greg nodding slowly, the peculiarity of life obvious to all.

They hadn't had many responses. That week, much to the ad manager's delight, the paper had been stuffed with classifieds – Tara had heard the yelling as pages were requisitioned to handle the overflow. And most, according to the plan, had offered a bit more detail – either about the repertoire the aspiring band mates would be expected to learn or the perks of private practice spaces or regular residencies that paid. Two singers, Greg had told her, had hung up as soon as they'd heard what band they were hoping to audition for.

'We were bummed,' the big drummer admitted. 'We figured that was it.' Still, there were some plusses. They'd each been kicking in fifty bucks a month for the practice space, he'd recalled, money none of them could easily spare. Besides, they figured they'd get some wild 'last show ever' gigs out of it, too.

And then Chris had called. Chris Crack, he called himself. 'Crack,' he'd said. 'Like the drug.' It wasn't his real name, obviously. But this was rock and roll, and the brothers were amused. 'Sure,' Jerry had said. 'Come on down.' It wasn't like they were doing anything else on Monday nights, and they had the space till the end of the month.

It wasn't until a few weeks later that they learned the truth. Chris 'Crack' Kantrowitz wasn't just a preppie, he had no experience being in a band or even on the scene. By then, it didn't matter. The kid from the suburbs with the bleached blond hair was a natural, a rising star who would catapult the Aught Nines to weekend bills – and then headline slots – in record time. When the suits from New York began to show up – town cars idling outside Oakie's, outside the Rat – nobody was surprised. The only question, by then, was what had taken them so long.

Tara was one of the first onto the reconfigured band, tipped off by something Nick had told her. 'No, really,' he'd been laughing as he stacked cases by the bar. 'Patti's brother's band has the space next to theirs.'

'The Aught Nines?' She'd not believed it. 'They've probably let their space. Or they just had their boom box cranked.'

Still, she'd shown up. Nine on a Tuesday – the promise of those farewell gigs had faded once the band had spread it around that they were not going anywhere. Brian had raised his eyebrows to see her so early – making his usual protest as she fended off his outstretched arms. 'Darling, you're breaking my heart!' Still, he had stamped her hand, no doubt expecting her to surface after the first song finished, if not before.

As soon as Greg counted off the opening number, it was clear that something had changed. Tara was used to the brothers' full-throttle attack, guitar and bass together as if volume alone could make up a song. But that night, Jim seemed to be sitting out, standing to the back of the stage as Jerry began to build a bottom line. When Jim came in – one simple, fast riff more metal than punk – she waited for the vocals. Even when Paulie had been on the mic, the brothers had always sung along. Going for the volume again. Gang harmony, they'd called it. Only what she heard was not something the Aught Nines had ever done before.

Chris Crack – the name stuck, despite its affectation – didn't enter so much as pounce. A glam rock throwback in a woman's eyelet blouse two sizes too small, he leapt onstage, grabbed the mic stand and swung it – narrowly missing Jerry – before opening his mouth for a caterwaul that had Nieve at the bar looking up, open-mouthed. Dropping from the falsetto scream into a rough baritone, he delivered the lyrics of the Aught Nine oldie – 'Beer for Fools' – as if it were the gospel. And when he tore into a new song – Tara, at least, had never heard it – he pushed back into that falsetto, letting it fade away into something as soft as a lover's sigh.

By the end of the set, he had lost the shirt, and under its sheen of sweat, his pale torso glistened. He looked like what he was fated to become: a rock star. And all five people who heard him that night knew it.

SIX

'So, what do you want to ask me?'

Saturday afternoon, and Tara is at Nick's spartan Back Bay apartment. He's sitting in a repurposed kitchen chair. She's on the nubbly beige couch. 'I'm not sure I know any more about Chris Crack than you do,' he says. 'And it's been, what, fifteen years? Twenty?'

That's the story she's given him – the rise and fall of Boston's golden boy – but for a moment it throws her.

'Chris, yeah,' she says, remembering. 'Chris Crack and the Aught Nines.'

She called Nick after an email exchange with Scott, following up to make sure the offer was real. Half hoping the dinner was something else. And now here she was, not sure exactly where to start. In the old days, she'd had a Rolodex with the direct line of every publicist at every label in the country. These days, most of those labels no longer exist, and those contacts – always good for a story and at least a drink when they came through town – had moved on long ago, their industry jobs made redundant by streaming services and a new definition of fame.

'Actually, it's more of a general story – the end of the scene,' she says, reaching for a small figure on the blond wood coffee table before her. A horse, she sees, carved from some darker wood.

The story will be about death, she'd told Scott. The death of a subculture. Only now, with someone who knew the deceased, she feels a little funny about the word. It's easier to talk to the carving.

'Did it end?' She glances up at his question, but he's not looking at her. Instead, he's tipping his can back. Diet Coke – it's two in the afternoon and they're no longer kids. 'I mean, the Aught Nines, sure. And Chris . . . But Oakie's hung around for a few years after I left. Bun's is still around, only with a different name.'

'Yeah, and a DJ on weekends. Dance nights.' Tara doesn't have to explain the scorn in her voice. Not to Nick. 'And by the end Oakie's was booking cover bands.'

She catches herself. This isn't about her, she wants to say. Not about what she had once hoped for. What she misses. Or not entirely.

'I know there are bands playing out now.' She puts the horse back down. She wants to focus. 'I know some of it is age. But for a few years there, something was happening. We made something, all of us. Something we shared.' She pauses. This is the part she can't quite explain – not to Peter or Min, not to herself. 'And then it all fell apart.'

That's all she's got thus far. For two days, she ignored the piece. Ignored Scott's emails, the ones asking for more, and tried to focus on Zeron. On the boss who relied on her, and the staff whose work she would ultimately present to the shareholders. The quarterly report might not be thrilling, but it did demand careful attention. Or so she claimed, not that her protest fooled anyone. Certainly not Scott: *Don't tell me you couldn't do that gig with your eyes closed*, he had written, after she had pled deadline. *Don't tell me you're not bored to tears.*

When she hadn't responded by Friday, he'd followed up with a threat. *I've got a freelancer, all of twenty-five, who's eager for an assignment. How badly do you think he'll mess this up?* That had done it. She'd emailed back that she would begin over the weekend – that she'd have some notes for him by Monday. Tara knew the damage a reckless twenty-five-year-old could do. After all, wasn't that part of her story?

She is aware, suddenly, of the silence.

'It all fell apart?' His voice is quiet, and Tara can't read it.

'Well, yeah,' she says. She feels coarse, suddenly. Clumsy. 'I mean, I know lots of people went on to do different things. And a lot of bands stayed together. We both heard the Whirled Shakers the other night. They still sound great.'

'But they're not the Aught Nines.' He's nodding slowly. He gets it.

'Yeah.' She feels a bit braver and builds on her theme. 'It was like, everyone was having fun and getting nibbles on their lines. Then they – *he* – had a chance to break through. I mean, for real. And it all got more serious.'

'That's one word for it.'

Tara knows what Nick means. The big unspoken – the drugs. What had been recreational, an accompaniment to all the drinking and the fooling around, had gotten bad, right around the time when the Aught Nines were drawing major label attention. That night with the Brit boys had been the first time Tara had seen anyone shoot up. It wouldn't be the last.

'So, you think it was the smack?' She keeps her voice low. Nick never used, not as far as she knew. But he'd been the one to find Brian, slumped up against the wall out behind the Casbah, she'd heard, the needle still in his arm. He'd lost other friends, too. They all had.

'I don't know.' He looks down at his soda, at the coffee table between them. 'Maybe it was all just a crazy dream. Prolonged adolescence – no, fuck that. Prolonged childhood.'

Tara follows his eyes. Sees the apartment as he must. He had a home, she's learned. A house, a marriage. Now – this. A pull-out couch for when his boys visit. A coffee table from Ikea or, more likely, Goodwill. A bachelor pad without the sense of fun. Featureless, except for that carving. She picks it up again.

'You like that?' Nick's question interrupts her thoughts. His smile is unexpected.

'Yeah.' She turns it over. The surface is smooth and polished to highlight the grain, the piece balanced to show the horse in motion. 'It's nice.'

'I did it.' He sounds proud but also a little wistful. 'For Jack, my youngest. He's too old to play with horses now.'

She looks up, seeing him anew. 'I didn't know you carved.'

'Whittled,' he corrects her. 'Yeah, it gives me something to do with my hands. Keeps me sane.' He chuckles softly. 'Maybe that's why I didn't get involved in any of that shit. You know, back in the day.'

'Could be.' She hands him the figurine. He turns it over, rubs a finger along its body, as if it testing the polish, the finish.

'But it was special, for a while. Wasn't it?' She speaks quietly. This is a side of the man she doesn't know. He replaces the little horse on the table between them and sits back.

'Yeah, it was.' This time he meets her eyes.

'That's what I want to write about,' she says, gathering steam. 'Not what happened with any one club or even one band. Just – how it came together and how it all came crashing down.'

'You talked to Neela?' He raises an eyebrow.

'No, not yet.' Tara thinks back. 'I'm going to have to, even if I don't bring the story up to Frank, poor guy. I mean, she was at the center of it.'

'That she was.' Nick's comment has a note in it – wistful? Amused? – that makes Tara wonder. 'Now, she's a story.'

'She was,' Tara says, not realizing how she's changed the tense until the words are out of her mouth. Timing. It hits her. 'Actually, she might be. I mean, she and Frank got married just as everything was falling apart.'

'Yeah, they got out just in time.' Another silence, more thoughtful this time. 'Frank started going to meetings. Neela had Mika. They built a life.'

'Poor Neela.' Tara thinks back to the pale and faded woman she saw only a few days before. Remembers the sexy redhead in the torn jeans, gyrating at Oakie's. Remembers when she tried to climb up on the bar at the Casbah. It took two bouncers to carry her out, and some jokester laughing that if her tits were only a little bigger they'd have let her be. It was a wonder any of them ever went back there. That the place made any money at all, not the least enough to set up Jonah Wells.

'Did you ever work at the Casbah?' She looks at Nick, at the half smile that still lingers on his face.

It disappears, his reverie broken. 'What made you think about that place?'

'No reason.' He's watching her, and she feels bad about lying. 'It's the magazine,' she confesses. At least to a partial truth. 'Did you know Jonah Wells owns it now?'

'Jonah Wells.' He repeats the name slowly, thoughtfully. 'And he knows you're doing this story?'

'I don't know.' Tara ponders. 'I know he told Scott – my editor – that he wanted the magazine to be more urban. Edgier.'

'Edgy.' Nick has his hands on his knees. He faces the table as he pushes himself to his feet. 'That's a hoot. No, I never worked at the Cash Bar. Thank God.'

* * *

Nick is used to this role. Support. The constant bar back. Tara feels a little guilty about plumbing his memories, but after that little outburst – after a break for a refill, which she doesn't really need – he gives her what he can freely and without reserve. The phone numbers for the rest of the Exiles. A place on the Cape where he thinks Brian's old girlfriend lives. Katie's married name, which she's kept.

It's enough for Tara to get started, and she thanks him. She'll work him into the story somehow, she promises herself. A credit, if not a quote. He was there.

Besides, she wants to see him again. After an hour or so of reminiscences, the two catch up on their current lives. He's into cycling, he tells her. Takes his boys out on the weekends, when he has them – twenty, thirty miles at a pop. But he does shorter rides, too, he says. Does she know the Minuteman Trail? It's the best way to see the foliage, and it's easy enough to pack a picnic.

By the time she leaves, she's no longer thinking about the apartment. About its pre-fab uniformity, the sad beige couch. Instead, she's buzzing from the conversation – from the possibilities that have begun to present themselves. About the little carving and the care it showed, about his deep blue eyes.

She spends most of Sunday making phone calls. The nuts and bolts of reporting that she remembers well. Only this time, instead of looking for a quote about a trend – stories about a new band or, God help her, a new paint color all falling within her beat – she's asking about a dead man. A friend, and the circumstances of his last few months. It's not the story she outlined to Scott, not exactly. It's what she's thinking about, though. Her way in.

'So your hook is the dead guy?' Peter's voice is gentle, his question less so. At least that's better than the last few months of their marriage, Tara thinks, even as she shrugs a noncommittal affirmative.

'Yeah, in a way,' she says. He's called to check in. See how she's doing, he says. Tara wonders. These last few months, he's been calling more often. Some of that is about the condo, the 'logical next step', as he puts it, now that she has the good job. He's always pressured her to think ahead. To be smart. Some of that is, well, something else.

Tara knows what Min would say. Will say, when Tara admits

that she's told Peter that she could use his help. That she's told her ex-husband, 'Sure, come on over.' But it's not romance or even regret that prompts her former spouse. He worries about her, she knows. Worries that she hasn't made some crucial step. That she's getting lost.

For instance, there's his critique of her story, what there is of it thus far: a few notes and a list of people to call back. They're sitting on her sofa – once their sofa – each in their old, accustomed places. He's holding a beer. She's got her laptop open.

'You're not that kind of a journalist, Tara.' He's heard her out, but that hasn't changed his conclusion. 'You're great on features. Always were. You have a style. Why don't you just do this as a feature? A look back on a particular subculture.'

He's trying. She knows that. The compliments are his way of patting her on the head. Sending her on her way. But she's no longer the star-struck newcomer. The former paste-up girl who's had her first big story and seen the star news guy reading it.

'Because I don't want to write a retrospective.' She remembers how he looked up and caught her staring. How he'd smiled and introduced himself. 'Some kind of rose-colored rock and roll history.'

He'd helped her at first. She won't deny that. She'd just been put on staff and didn't know what to write – how to find a story beyond the newest band, the latest record – and he'd given her tips. Told her to start stockpiling numbers. People to call. Sources.

'Journalism 101,' he'd said. It sounded like a joke, but she knew he meant it. That he'd gotten a degree in it, even after years on small community newspapers. He'd taught her about fact checking, about sourcing quotes, about talking to everyone and everybody. Basic research. 'Do your homework,' he'd say. When he offered to help, at first, she had been so grateful, she hadn't seen beyond her own need. Hadn't even questioned when the tutorials turned into more.

'I don't know what I want to do with this story exactly. Not yet.' All these years later, she's learned to stand up to him at least. Learned not to be cajoled into a compromise. 'I don't want it to be stale.' She emphasizes the last word. Remembers that they're no longer married, for better as well as for worse. 'But thanks,' she says, knowing how lame this sounds.

'It just seems . . .' He breaks off with a heavy sigh. She looks up at him and waits. Unlike her, Peter always finishes his sentences. 'I don't understand why you're doing this,' he says.

She nods. 'I know,' she says, gathering her thoughts. 'Some of it is Scott. I'm excited by the opportunity. I mean, *City* is a big deal. A glossy.'

He eyes her as he drinks. He brought the good stuff, not that over-hoppy brew he usually orders.

'Peter, you know I've missed it,' she answers the question he hasn't had the chance to form. 'And it's not like I'm quitting my job.'

'There's something about that guy I don't get.' He shakes his head. 'Always was.'

'What's there to get?' Tara turns back to her laptop, eager suddenly to hide her face. Her defense of Scott is as old as her relationship with Peter. The two men never developed any kind of rapport. Only her stock dismissal of her ex's concerns reminds her of her new awareness of her old editor. Of her new interest, and she can feel the heat rising to her cheeks. 'He's just Scott.'

'Hmm.' She resists the urge to glance up and thus can't judge his intent. 'So, what can I help you with?'

'That's just it.' She focuses on the screen, willing her few notes to make sense. 'I guess I'm looking for a structure. Some way of making sense of why everything fell apart.'

'Why?' He huffs out something like a laugh. 'Tara, are you serious?'

She keeps her face still and doesn't comment. It took her years to learn to do this. To not rush into an argument. Better to let Peter wear himself out.

'Tara, you always romanticized the rock world, the people who hung out in those clubs. You were a bright-eyed college grad, and they were – I don't know – local toughs.'

'Min wasn't.' She breaks her own rule. Stops there.

'OK, but most of them. I'm not saying they were bad guys, but they weren't what you wanted them to be. And, yeah, OK, maybe there were a few other exceptions – it sounds like Scott has done something with himself. But basically, you had a bunch of townie kids amusing themselves before the inevitable.'

The last word makes Tara gasp. She looks up to see that he's put his bottle down. His face, at least, looks pained.

'I mean, before their girlfriends got knocked up or their dads made them start paying rent.' There's a note of exasperation in Peter's voice, high and tight. 'But, yeah, there was always substance abuse. So, yeah, the rest of it followed.'

'The rest of it.' Tara turns away from her former husband. Her eyes are hot. 'I can't believe you're such a snob, Peter. I thought . . .' She shakes her head. But they're not married. Not anymore. She's going to finish her thought. 'All those shows you came to with me. All those songs I played for you. I thought you heard what I did. I thought you understood.

'Maybe most of us weren't going anywhere.' She focuses on her computer, the wisp of a thought hovering. 'Most of us weren't stars. And I'm including myself in that.' She starts to type, to capture it. 'But there was a community. There was some kind of camaraderie and support that made something possible. That made something special happen.'

She's typing quickly now, and to his credit, Peter has the sense to shut up. He sits as she works. Drinks the rest of his beer and does his best to peer over her shoulder at the words forming on the screen. The sun has set before she's done, the light from the computer illuminating her face. When she looks up, his face is in shadow, and she realizes how the time has passed.

'Sorry,' she says, slightly abashed as she comes back to the dark room – to her ex.

'No problem.' His voice is soft again. Tender. 'It looks like you've found your story.'

She smiles, her flush flooding her with warmth. 'Well, I think I have a direction, at least. A line of questioning. But as you always told me, now I've got to go do the work.'

They order pizza from their old place, and she has a beer and then another to celebrate. He spends the night. It's something they do now and then. It's not like either of them is seeing anyone else. Or not exclusively. Tara knows Peter has lovers. That he plays the field. There's something comfortable about this, though. Maybe it's as simple as the familiarity. He knows her body, as she knows his. Maybe it's the lack of expectations.

It is considerate sex. Courtly, even. Though the one time she told Min that, her friend had rolled her eyes. 'Sounds thrilling,' she had said. 'I'd rather have a doughnut.'

Some things Min will never understand, Tara thinks to herself, as Peter pulls on his clothes the next morning. As he leans over to give her a chaste kiss on the cheek.

Her friend thinks she is spinning her wheels. Sating her hunger with her ex as a way of avoiding getting out there. Meeting someone new.

Like Min should talk, Tara chuckles softly as the front door closes with a click. Like Min has moved on. Like any of them really have.

SEVEN

The arrival of Chris Crack changed everything, and not just for the band. Suddenly, the clubs were crowded – even Oakie's. Even on a Tuesday. And although Scott tried to pass off the newly packed venues, the lines at the doors, as the return of the students – 'September,' he'd said. 'Lemmings. They'll have moved on in a month.' – he'd been infected, too. Up till this point, he'd left Tara to her own devices. Now he began pressing her on when she was going to write up this new wonder kid. This bright, bratty, golden boy who was bringing them in. By the time her piece came out – *Underground Sound* being a monthly – the band was already headlining weeknights. The story was tagged to their biggest upcoming gig to date: a Saturday night at the Casbah.

A backlash was inevitable. This being Boston, the focus was on Chris's suburban roots, his penchant for thrift-store finery, rather than his talent.

'It's an affectation,' said Scott, as they opened the reader mail – real letters in those days. 'It goes to credibility.'

'What are you?' Tara had sniped back. 'A lawyer or something?'

He'd paused and blinked up at her, hurt showing on his round face.

'Sorry,' she'd mumbled and pulled another from the stack of letters. She'd been surprised, as well, by the snark in her own voice.

'He's not yours anymore.' Scott might as well have been reading her mind. 'I remember when that happened with the Cars.'

'It's just too many people.' She'd not wanted to be that way, to resent someone else's success. 'I mean, last night at the Rat, I could barely get from the stairs over to the bar. It's got to be a fire hazard.'

'Hmm.' Scott had nodded, as if he hadn't heard, and it hit her.

A man – a large man, like Scott, anyway – had no problem pushing his way through a crowd.

'Maybe I should climb up on the bar,' she'd said, the snark returning to her voice. 'Do like Neela.' When he still didn't say anything, she pushed further. 'It certainly works for her.'

Her editor hadn't responded. Hadn't had to. Neela's trademark move had made her a local celebrity. More than local, if you figured her for the inspiration to 'Dancing Girl' by the UK stars GlitterBot, as almost everybody in their crowd did. And along with the attention came the access – Neela was always on the list. Always backstage, and often enough on the arm, if not the lap, of whatever touring rock star wannabe was headlining that night. Not that it mattered to Frank much – or not that anyone could see. When whichever big-name band left town, the two of them would show up together again, same as always. If her wild ways bothered him, he didn't let on.

'Tour rules,' he'd say, and laugh, the implication being that he, too, took advantage of local talent when Last Call were on the road.

The Aught Nines, though, they were local. And although Neela had begun showing up at their gigs fairly early on – Tara had seen her at the Chet's show, three weeks after that first crazy gig – at first she had kept to dancing. Her usual routine, more about her moves than any one band.

Tara could still remember the night that changed. More crowded than that first gig, by far, but not so bad that you couldn't make your way up front. Not so packed that you couldn't see if you chose, as Tara did, to lean back on the bar, bottle in hand, and take in the room.

Neela was part of that scene, by then. She could still picture the slender redhead, jeans riding low on her hips as she lost herself in the Twist and the Frug, a go-go-girl for the garage-punk age.

'Something else, huh?' The voice, right by her ear, had startled her, and she'd turned. Phil, from the Whirled Shakers, his dark eyes wide, reflecting the light from the stage.

It had taken Tara a moment to realize what he meant. That he was talking about the band blasting out the throbbing tune, not the sexy woman gyrating to the beat above them. They were playing 'Hot Shot', the song that would be their biggest hit. Tara didn't know it then. Nobody did.

'Here's a new one,' Chris had called out, the satin ribbon around his neck already dark with sweat. Ever the flirt, he had eyed the crowd, with a smile that caught the light. 'Hope you like it.'

Behind him, the drummer – all chained intensity – barked out the count, and the band was off. He'd grown into a powerhouse, Greg had, all that bulk proving to be muscle, laying down a foundation for Jim's bass tattoo. Even Jerry had changed, his solos reined in somewhat but harder, faster. What they'd be calling speed-metal, in a different context. But not here, not now. All because of Chris.

'*And then you kick in,*' he sang, half caterwaul, dragging against the furious beat. '*Kick in like the lightning tightening up my veins. You're a hot shot, baby. A hot shot.*'

By the second chorus, Tara realized she was singing along. Everyone was, those who weren't dancing, anyway, heads bobbing to that unrelenting beat.

'*Hot shot, baby. You're a hot shot.*' Tara caught herself. Took a swig of her beer. Phil had moved up. She could see the back of his head, nodding in time. Face turned up to the stage. Still, it wouldn't do for her to start dancing. Not at this show. She would be talking to the band tomorrow. Meeting them in the old practice space, the one they'd almost given up. Jim and Jerry she knew well enough. Greg too, if it came to it, but the new guy – the singer – he was a wild card, a young Adonis slick with sweat. She'd learned by then how bands viewed writers. Female writers anyway. If they looked into the crowd, they would see her back here, at the bar. Keeping her perspective on the whole thing.

Still, it was catchy. '*Like lightning, lightning in my veins.*' She put her bottle down and made a note to ask them about it. To find out about any plans to record. Just then, the band broke for a drum fill, Greg as relentless as an avalanche, and Tara's beer went over. She saw it, just out of the corner of her eye and jumped up, grabbing for the neck to right it. Above her, Neela was spinning, eyes closed. Chris's voice – a wordless howl – was pouring out over Greg's drums, carrying Neela along with it.

Tara grabbed a napkin, but Brian was on it, wiping up the spill before she could reach it. A moment later, he was handing her a new bottle. She was a regular, and Neela – well, the gyrating redhead was in her own world. Only something was different. Something had changed. Instead of her usual go-go moves, Neela was writhing, patterning her rhythms along with the vocals. Dancing for Chris, making his music flesh. Tara needn't have worried about the band – about what the singer would think of her, a lone journalist in the crowd. She saw him now, that ribbon hanging off him. He was staring at Neela. She might as well have been the only person in the room.

She was mesmerizing. Only after Tara had handed Brian the foaming empty did she notice that Phil had rejoined her at the bar. His eyes, however, remained fixed on the stage. Not only was he not watching Neela, he hadn't noticed the accident either.

'They're the real thing,' he'd said, once the song ended. His voice had grown quiet, in the brief lull, and Tara recognized the expression on his face as wistful. Not even jealous, she realized. Simply struck by the band on stage. 'He is, anyway.'

'Oh, you're as good.' Tara had coughed up the compliment, a little in awe of the man beside her. A little envious of his unadulterated concentration. He didn't even reply, just stared up at the stage as if the sound could save him.

Katie had been there that night. Up front, by the band, her waterfall of hair shimmering in the stage lights. Enjoying the thrust and the volume, even as her boyfriend retreated to take in the bigger picture. Tara remembers her. Remembers how she and Phil both had been spellbound.

Tara calls her later that morning, once the 10 o'clock meeting is over and she's back in her office, door politely ajar. She keeps her voice low, when she gets voicemail, aware all the while how her colleagues like to drop in on the way back to their own sterile workspaces.

'Katie?' She eyes the door. To close it would be too much. *The Zeron climate is a cordial one.* She'd written that line herself. 'It's Tara, Tara Winton.' She gives her cell and then, on a whim, the office number. 'I'm working on a story, and I'd love your input.'

That's the line she'd perfected, back in the day. Enough information to intrigue, but not enough to scare anyone off. Who didn't want to have input? As she hung up she made a mental note – that was something she could use in the quarterly report, too.

Not that Katie was ever talkative. Tara had considered the willowy blonde a bit standoffish during her first few months in the clubs. She'd seemed aloof, drifting through the sea of black leather so ethereal and pale. Tara figured that to Katie, she just didn't matter. Figured the blonde to be one of those women to whom only men counted. She tried not to let it bother her. After all, she had her own place in the scene. By then, she was a writer, a rock crit, not just some fan. Still, she figured some acknowledgment was necessary. She'd nod at Katie, but she didn't expect anything more, despite the fact that they inevitably saw each other several nights a week.

It was only after the debacle with the Hinies – the drummer so drunk he vomited and fell off his stool, passing out before the band could play a note – that she'd found out how wrong she was. As the stench had emptied the room, the bassist shouting, the band in disarray, she'd taken refuge in the back alley, slipping out through the stage door where everyone loaded in. Most of the room was crowding around the front, trying to get their five-dollar cover back, but she found Katie back there, doubled over against the wall by the dumpster and laughing like a hyena.

'What a buffoon.' Katie wiped her eyes as she straightened up. She'd had a couple of tall boys cradled against her body and held one out to Tara. 'Want one?'

As they drank, they'd bonded over the mishap – and over the poor souls who would have to clean up the mess. And although they'd never become close, Tara had learned that night that despite the attention she appeared to attract, the pretty blonde was simply shy.

'I'm not even that much of a music fan,' she'd said, licking the foam from her upper lip. 'I mean, not loud music anyway.'

The unstated exception had been for the Whirled Shakers or, more accurately, for Phil. He had seen her at her waitressing gig, she told Tara that night in the alley. She had no use for 'some punk rocker', but he had not let up until she'd gone out with him. Over time, of course, she'd grown to appreciate the music, or at least the culture that had grown up around it. 'It's like a family, you know?'

Even after they broke up, Katie had kept her allegiance to the band, her shining fall of hair a constant at Whirled Shaker shows as she and Phil worked out some kind of enduring friendship. She and Tara had never grown close; that conversation behind the Rat remained the longest one-on-one the two ever shared. But Tara had a new appreciation for the pretty blonde after that, no matter how Min rolled her eyes whenever she was mentioned.

'That girl needs to move on,' Min would say, when they saw her out, dancing to the Whirled Shakers. 'Get a life,' even as Katie would turn to flash a smile.

Tara knew better than to point out the obvious comparison to her friend by then. Knew how Min could close right up. And so when she wants to talk about Frank, Tara calls Katie.

'Tara.' Katie rises to greet her as she walks in. They work within blocks of each other, they'd realized, when Katie returned her call. Lunch at the Bagel Bar had been an obvious choice. 'So good to see you.'

'You too.' Tara takes a seat. Katie has chosen a table by the big front windows, and the sun streaming in highlights the fine lines around her eyes, the slight sag around her jaw. 'By daylight, I mean.'

'That's right.' Katie nods, a smile brightening her face. 'You were there the other night. The boys still sound good, don't they?'

'They got me dancing,' Tara acknowledges. The other woman chuckles, and then it becomes easy, Tara explaining about the article – about venturing back into music journalism, just a bit, thanks to some odd combination of nostalgia and boredom.

The conversation pauses when the waitress comes by, her full sleeve of tattoos making Tara aware of the generational differ-ence, of how the young woman must see them: middle-aged. Staid. But Katie seems unconcerned, and is quite happy to pick up the conversation again once they've ordered.

'So, what can I help you with?' She sips her sparkling water as she waits, and Tara finds herself looking at the glass, at the rising bubbles. It is lunchtime on a working day. 'I mean, you probably remember as much as I do.'

'To be honest, I've been thinking about where everyone is today. I mean, those of us who survived.' When Katie starts, almost imperceptibly, she realizes how that sounds. 'I'm sorry.' She shakes her head, as if she could shed her thoughts. 'It's just – losing Frank made me think of everyone else who's gone. Drugs, booze . . .'

'But Frank's death was an accident.' Katie breaks off. Turns to thank the server. The Bagel Bin does a credible niçoise, Tara sees, already regretting her own lox and a shmear. 'I mean, he'd cleaned up,' Katie says.

'Well, that's just it.' Tara picks off the red onion. She loves it, the way its sharpness brightens the oily fish, but she's going back to the office. 'Did he?' She takes a bite. 'I mean, falling down the stairs . . .'

'No.' Katie holds up a hand as she reaches for her glass, sipping to clear her throat. 'No way. I've spent a fair amount of time with Frank and Neela, and he was definitely sober. Neither of them drank, in fact.'

'Neela too?' Tara isn't sure why she's even asking. Maybe it's the memories.

Katie is nodding. 'Neela, too,' she says. 'She gave everything up when she was pregnant. In fact . . .' She stops and sighs.

Tara waits. This is gossip. It won't relate to her story, but you never know. When a source wants to talk, you let them. Unless they don't. 'Katie?' She prompts, after the moment has grown heavy.

Another sigh. 'I don't think there's anything to this. I mean, Mika's baby being sick kind of proves it.'

Tara shakes her head, confused.

'Henry – that's Mika's son – always had trouble, from Day One. He couldn't keep milk down – or not enough. He's been below weight. Anyway, it turns out that he's got some kind of enzyme disorder. He doesn't digest . . .' She gestures to her own midriff. 'Anyway, Neela was super worried during her own pregnancy. Worried that she'd harmed her baby in some way. You know, before she knew. Frank put the fear in her. Dragged her to some clinic up in New Hampshire even before – well, even when she was still kind of with Chris. Right at the end, there. But that really must have scared her, because she cleaned right up.'

Tara thinks back – the drinking. The smoking. 'She did?'

'Yeah.' A nod, a faraway look. 'Chris's death, well, you know.'
Tara does. 'You've got kids now, right?'

Katie smiles, a private smile. 'Max and Moira, yeah.' She
nods. 'But I was never that wild.'

A beer behind the Rat. She and Peter never discussed kids,
not really. Things always seemed too tentative. To her, anyway.

'We had some fun, though. Didn't we?' Katie's voice interrupts her thoughts, and Tara looks up. Katie seems lost in her
own reverie. She's staring out the window, but Tara doesn't think
she's seeing the men in suits. The women in their heels moving
just as fast, jostling for position on the sidewalk. Here, where
the Seaport meets the Financial District, everything is busy,
bustling in the daylight – so far from the city they knew and
shared. No, Katie is looking beyond them. Above the crowd. The
sun shows every line, but she's pretty still. Delicate, with that
half smile. 'Do you remember the Whirled Shakers record
release?' Her voice is soft with memory.

'Like it was yesterday.' Tara's with her now. Back at Oakie's,
back before the Aught Nines had eclipsed everyone. It had
been summer – supposedly the dead time – but you wouldn't
have known that from the crowd. 'Weren't the Aught Nines on
that bill?'

A nod. 'Yeah.' Katie chuckles. 'Poor Phil. And they sounded
so good.'

'They did.' Tara remembers. It was the Whirled Shakers' night.
The band was tight – as good as they'd ever been – stoked by
all the regulars and the handful of fat men in suits who had
crowded into Oakie's. Fire safety be damned, the room was alive,
a hot battery, shooting sparks. Tara remembers how eyes glittered,
how sweaty everyone was even before anyone began to play.
Frank's band had opened – Last Call making their brash punk
cri de cœur sound as good as it ever would. Tara remembers
drinking beer after beer – you had to, in that heat – and feeling
nothing. The buzz came from the volume, the rhythm. The way
the crowd was moving even as Frank's last solo wound the set
up to its close.

By the time the set finished, Tara was on her third beer –
maybe her fourth. She remembers Nick, stripped to the waist

and dripping, yelling to Brian. Something about the taps. The lines. She remembers him heaving a case of empties onto his shoulder as if it were made of air. The stage light caught him as he humped past, the spot picking out the muscle on his back. The sheen of his skin. She'd looked away. She and Peter were serious by then, and besides, the Whirled Shakers were taking the stage.

The excitement could have been too much. When Joey had called out an insane tempo, Tara had gasped – waiting for Phil to call him off. For the false start. But it wasn't and in two beats the band joined in, winding the impromptu mosh pit into a frenzy of guitar and pounding bass. Against the rush, Phil took his time, stalking like a panther. Bigger than Chris Crack. More muscled, and darker, he prowled the stage, dominating it, and when he grabbed the mike, swinging the weighted stand out over the crowd, the response was deafening.

If we had world enough. World enough and time . . .

Tara catches herself. She's singing. She's at lunch, daytime, and Katie is nodding. 'That song,' she says. 'That summer it was all over the radio.'

'Yeah.' Tara can hear it still. 'Bad luck, I guess.'

'Bad timing.' Katie corrects her.

'You mean, that night?' Tara hadn't thought about it at the time. Sometimes people left before the last set, what with the T closing soon after midnight and all. The Whirled Shakers wanted to party – they'd earned it, all the work they put into that single. Eleven o'clock set, and then they'd be free. Time enough to meet with the suits. To retire to their loft for the inevitable after party. For the inevitable triumph.

Getting the Aught Nines to close had made sense. Not only were the band members old friends, mostly, the new lineup was getting buzz. It was smart, offering something new after the old-school garage throb of Last Call and the Shakers. It was generous, too.

Only they hadn't counted on Chris Crack. On how a skinny, pale suburbanite could draw the eye and hold it. As sleek as an eel, the singer made Phil appear hulking by comparison.

'Like lightning. Like the lightning in my veins . . .' She can hear it still.

'Maybe if they hadn't opened with "Hot Shot",' Tara says.

'Maybe.' Katie looks down at her plate, sighs. The bright shining moment has passed. 'I always preferred "Boy in a Bubble". There was something tender about it. Something vulnerable.'

Coddled, fondled, packaged, bundled. I barely survived, barely got out alive.

'You weren't the only one.'

Katie looks up, and Tara catches herself. 'I meant, the suits,' she says. Because that was the song. 'Hot Shot' was the opening salvo, the one that made them turn back – from the bar. From Phil and Joey. The song that had them sidling through the crowd again, to see this other band. The one they didn't know. But when 'Hot Shot' lead into 'Bubble', the Aught Nines' fate was sealed. The Whirled Shakers', too, if they'd known it.

'Yeah,' says Katie. Her smile has twisted into something wry. 'That was the tune that emptied the bar,' she says.

She and Tara lock eyes, and Tara remembers. Neela had been dancing, of course. Brian had worked around her, handing over the bottles – the shots – rather than leaving them on the polished surface. All through the Whirled Shakers' set she'd been up there, her retro sequined top reflecting and amplifying every chord change, every move. She'd paused during the set break but stayed in place, accepting the drinks handed up to her as her due. But maybe there were one too many, the room too hot, the tempo too wild. Once again, her moves changed when the Aught Nines started. Slower and more sinuous, working against the breathless beat that served as Greg's starting point. Weaving something more sensuous around the vocal snarl. And Chris had responded, singing more slowly still, leaning back on the beat. Almost pulling the band apart as 'Hot Shot' thundered to its close.

Maybe she'd sensed something, though how she could have heard anything – gasp, or cry, or whisper – in that room was beyond her. For some reason, Tara had looked up, just as the next song started. But for once, Neela wasn't dancing. And as 'Boy in a Bubble' built toward the bridge – *'Coddled, fondled, packaged, bundled'* – she'd jumped down to make her way into the crowd. Toward the stage. Toward the beautiful boy who had stolen the night.

'Poor Phil,' says Tara, remembering the aftermath. The Whirled Shakers had had their shot. A month earlier. A different bill, maybe they'd have made it – a contract with Elektra or CBS. Money to record and to tour. As it was, the single they'd made here, the one getting all the radio play, ended up being it. Instead of the first of many, 'World Enough' became their only hit.

'Poor Frank,' says Katie. And Tara looks up. Everyone knew Neela left with Chris that night. Their absence at the loft later a glaring breach of clubland decorum. Frank had been there and gotten royally drunk. Tara left before the fights began, but she heard about how he'd threatened Greg, tackled Jim and been pulled off by Jerry. And then he'd started on his own band.

'That was the beginning of the end in a way,' says Katie. Her thoughts clearly on the same track. 'I think that's when Frank's drinking really started. I mean, when it became bad. But who can blame him?'

Tara looks at the woman sitting opposite her. Knows she's since married – and remarried. Moved on. Still, she understands about heartbreak. About carrying a torch.

'Phil got over it,' says Tara, as gently as she can.

Another smile, this one sad. 'Did he?' The smile grows. 'Yeah, he has, I think. He's got a good life, with Sue and the boys. And the band still plays out, sometimes.'

'And it worked out with Frank and Neela,' says Tara. She feels like she's asking. Like she wants Katie to confirm the happy ending.

'Yeah, really.' Katie stares out the window again. What she sees, Tara can't tell. 'Neela got lucky, didn't she?'

EIGHT

Her office phone is blinking when she returns, and Tara feels her stomach clench. She stayed out too long. The quarterly report is on everyone's mind.

'Hey, Tara.' Peter's message begins. She feels the tension slide away. 'Call me?'

'What's up?' Tara gets him right away. Like her, he's got an office job now, which makes him easy to reach. Still, she grabs her pad. Peter's instincts have always been good. If he has an idea for her story, she'll listen. It's easier these days, now that they're apart.

'I was thinking.' He laughs, which gives her pause. 'Would you want to go out for dinner this weekend?'

It's her turn to chuckle. 'I thought the point of dinner was to get the girl into bed,' she says. 'Let me guess, you want the Santarpio's special only you need someone to justify the extra cheese?'

The moment of silence that follows throws her. She puts her pencil down. 'Peter?'

'No,' he says at last. 'I meant, someplace nice – like Chez Louis. I was thinking, maybe Saturday?' He can't see that her mouth is open. That she's speechless. She's saved by a soft knock, as the bald head of Rudy from Development peeks around her door.

'One second.' She mouths the words, holding up a finger. 'Peter, I've got someone in my office. May I call you back?'

'You could just say yes.' He doesn't sound happy.

'Yeah, sure.' Rudy is waiting. 'Yes,' she says. 'That sounds fine.'

When her phone rings again, she ignores it. Rudy shouldn't have had to come to her, she knows that. And even though he says he's glad to get away from his desk, she understands that his time is more valuable than hers in the Zeron scheme of things. Besides, she really doesn't want to think about Peter. About whether she wants to go out with him – a date, it sounds like. Yes, pretty unmistakably a date. Or whether she should duck out.

She could avoid the issue. Come up with an excuse. She hadn't checked her calendar. She had other plans. But Peter knows her, and to do that would be to make a statement, a decision of another sort. Would end the easy camaraderie that has grown over the last few months. The uncomplicated sex.

No, she doesn't like being pressured like this, and so she lets the phone ring. Lets Rudy drone on about goals and incentives for the coming quarter. Her own goals are vague enough, and she needs time to digest. To think about what she really wants.

'So you can do your magic?' He's standing, and so she stands too. 'You have enough?'

'I believe so.' She nods and smiles in what she hopes is a confident manner. She's been at the job long enough to fake it. The language never really changes. 'If I need anything, I'll leave word with Sally.' Sally being the secretary for the executive wing. 'But I really appreciate you coming in,' she says. A little oil on the waters. 'I should have a draft for you by Thursday.'

'Great, great.' He's nodding. Order restored. 'Back to the salt mines.'

She laughs softly as he makes his exit, waiting until he's disappeared before hitting voicemail once more.

'Tara, it's Nick.' She stares at the phone in astonishment. 'I'm sorry to call you at work, but I thought I might have a better chance of reaching you there.'

She grabs her cell. Sure enough, it's off. She powers it back on as Nick's message continues. 'Anyway, I was wondering if you'd want to have dinner this weekend. I mean, I'm working on Saturday, but the boys are with their mom this weekend, so I'm at loose ends otherwise. Would you want to do something on Friday?'

To Min, there's no question.

'Have you lost it?' Her friend's tone conveys her urgency, despite its on-duty hush. 'Have you gone completely mad?'

'Min, I wouldn't have called you at work if this was simple.' Tara is standing, facing the corner, her voice low but urgent. She doesn't dare close the door, but this is personal. 'I mean, I don't really know Nick and—'

'That's the point.' Min's voice rises almost to her natural speaking volume. Behind her, something beeps. 'He's new blood. He's a nice guy, right?'

'I guess, but Peter . . .' She glances over her shoulder.

'Is your ex.' Min bites down on the word. 'Your comfort fuck, right?'

'Yeah, but . . .' Tara pauses. She feels missish about what she's about to say. 'I mean, if I end up sleeping with both of them—'

'Then you'll be getting more action than I am.' Her friend breaks in. 'Go for it, girl.'

Still, she avoids calling Nick back for the rest of the afternoon. Tells herself she needs to get some work done – the work she's being paid to do – and ignores the phone when it rings two more times. Anyone in the building can just drop in. Anyone in the building knows she's on deadline for the quarterly report.

Only Peter knows how little of her brain this corporate crap actually requires. And so when she drafts the thing – so much of it boilerplate she thinks of it as typing rather than writing – she's tempted to call him. To laugh with him over the ease of it: three hours for what was supposed to take all week. Only she can't call him. Not now. Tara stares at the phone, its message light blinking. This is almost as bad as those first few months after he moved out. When it finally became real that they were splitting up. Her first response for so long had been to talk to Peter. Not being able to do that, she felt like a stranger to herself.

'Welcome to adulthood, kid.' Min had gotten her through the bad days. Not only the divorce, but the move. Neither had wanted to stay in their old apartment, the walkup they'd found right near the paper's old offices. Peter had been checking out condos for months before the end.

'I feel so rootless.' Tara had tried to explain. She was in her new place – her current place – by then. Boxes unpacked and lying on the sofa that Peter hadn't wanted. It must have been her third or fourth night there, and she was trying to stay. Trying not to spend another night on Min's sofa. 'Homeless, almost.'

'Not with your salary.' Min had grown a bit terse by that point.

Tara had been leaning on her a lot, and really, Min had been a doll. 'Hell, maybe you should have checked out some of those places, like the one Peter's buying.'

It was an old argument. Min pushing her to keep after Peter, to spend more time with him. Tara trying to explain that, no, she was glad when he went out alone. She knew what Min thought, that Peter was having an affair. But they weren't like that, not like Min's on-again, off-again with Frank. Peter really did just get more pleasure from high-end furnishings, from thoughts of equity, at least at first.

'No, it's not about the apartment . . .' Tara got tangled up, trying to explain. She'd started the Zeron job by then, largely as a result of Peter's pushing. The *Dot* was going under anyway. 'It's just . . .'

'Rock and roll never forgives?'

'That's not how it goes.' Tara had laughed. Min's singing. The misquote. 'But, yeah, I miss . . . I don't know. The scene.'

'Start going to meetings.' Min was joking, happier now that she'd jollied Tara into a chuckle. 'You'll see all the old, familiar faces.' When Tara hadn't responded, Min softened her tone.

'You're not missing anything, kiddo,' she'd said. 'You know that. It's not the same as it was. It hasn't been since Chris died.'

She needed to speak to Jim. To Jim or Jerry, or even Greg. Someone who had been close to Chris Crack. Someone who'd been there. She'd been a journalist long enough to know where the story was headed: Frank might be the news hook, but Chris Crack – the rise and fall of the Aught Nines – was the meat of it. The body. Yes, she could use Frank's story – Last Call had pretty much collapsed after that night. The Whirled Shakers limped on – hell, they were playing out still – but between Frank's drinking and his general belligerence, his band had burned out pretty quickly. Nobody wanted to book a group whose guitarist might or might not show up, and pretty soon his band mates grew sick of covering for him.

Still, Tara realizes, Last Call have a place in the article. Sitting back down at her desk, she starts a search. Tony K – she can't remember his last name – was the drummer. Ralph on

rhythm . . . no, she can't recall his last name either. But Onie
Dee, she finds him quickly enough. Onie Dee, Plumbing and
HVAC, with a smart website and an in-town phone number.
She thinks of the bassist, a muscular man with hands like
catcher's mitts. One of the few African Americans in the rock
world in those days, he'd been the calm, sane counterpoint to
Frank's self-destructive storm.

He'd have had to be, Tara realizes. Clubland was more open
than much of the city – hell, everyone knew the two women in
Let's Kiss were a couple – but Boston was still Boston, and
alcohol brought out the racism of the chowderheads who
would pack the clubs after a Sox game on a Saturday night. Well,
good for him, she thinks, picking up the phone. Onie Dee made
out all right.

'Tara? Tara Winton?' He picks up, and laughs when she begins
to explain. 'Sure, I remember you. How could I forget? My
mother loved that story you did on us. Kept it on her fridge until
she went to assisted living.'

Tara smiles, unsure how to respond. She'd never thought of
the families of the people she wrote about. That the black bassist
might have a proud mom.

'So, how are you doing? You've got your own firm now?' She
could kick herself. Of course he is, but he's happy enough to
explain. To tell her about his business and his family, about the
crews he employs.

'Once I hit forty, I realized I didn't want to be fumbling around
in basements for much longer,' he says, sounding proud. The
years have been good to him. 'But if you need any work done,
let me know. Melanie's gone home for the day – that's why I
picked up – but I'll tell her you're a priority. That you made the
boss a star!'

'Hardly.' She shakes her head, as if she could clear it. She'd
forgotten that piece. That Last Call had had some good days,
at least by Boston standards. 'But actually, that's kind of why
I called.'

He's quiet while she explains about the assignment. About the
points that interest her. Only when she gets up to Frank, to his
funeral, does he begin to speak again.

'I heard about Frank,' he says, the levity gone from his voice.

'About the troubles he was having. His grandson.' His sigh carries over the line. 'I thought about going to the funeral, but work's been so busy and it's been so long since I even talked to him. I don't know, maybe I should have.'

'Would you want to talk about him? About the band?' Tara winces, glad he can't see her face. This is the part of journalism she always hated: the ask.

'Maybe,' he says, as if the question holds no offense. 'I don't know how much I remember really. We were all drinking too much back then, and it's been a lifetime ago.'

He pauses, as his words hit home. 'You know, Frank called me a few weeks before he died.' Onie sounds wistful, or maybe simply sad. 'He wanted to talk about the old days, too, but I was busy. I never called him back.'

Silence on the line, and Tara waits.

'Yeah, sure,' the onetime bassist says at last. The voice from the past, sparked once again. 'Why not?'

He agrees to meet her at a Starbucks in Cambridge. 'Unless you want to trek out to the 'burbs.'

'No, that will be great,' Tara responds. 'My ex lives right near there. I can probably park in his guest space.'

'Sounds like you've figured things out.' He's laughing, and Tara realizes how odd that probably sounds. 'Anyway, I'm about out of here.'

Tara closes down her computer for the night, and takes one last look at the phone. She ought to call Nick back, she knows that. She ought to listen to those two new messages, too. Telling herself that maybe she'll be off the hook, that maybe one of her suitors has dropped out, she hits the play button.

The first message is from Scott: 'Hey, Tara,' he says, 'I'm wondering if you've had any more thoughts on the story? I'd love to hear how it's going, maybe talk deadline. Art. Whatever. Call me?'

Whatever, she thinks, and catches herself. Maybe Min has a point. Maybe she's been out of circulation for too long. She lets the other message play. Nick.

'Hi, Tara?' He sounds tense, she thinks and catches herself. She doesn't know him that well. She doesn't know him at all. 'Something's come up, and I'm going to have the boys this weekend. I don't know if you got my last message or anything, but if you did – could I have a rain check?'

Somewhat to her surprise, she realizes she's disappointed.

'Hey, girl, don't you ever answer your phone?' Scott's in transit. She can hear crowd noise. A truck. 'I didn't want to bother you at your job, but you weren't picking up.'

'Sorry.' She brightens. 'I turned it off because I had lunch with a source.'

'Excellent!' An ambulance in the distance. 'So this story is happening?'

'It's happening.' She tries to sound confident.

'Good, good. We should talk. Not now.' A voice – male – calls Scott's name. 'Let's touch base tomorrow?'

'Sounds like a plan.' She's not faking the cheer now. By tomorrow, she'll have one more interview done. A few more hours to think this through. And, yeah, Scott's out with another man. 'Go Sox!'

He's still laughing as he hangs up, and Tara heads out to her car.

Despite what she'd said, Tara doesn't take Peter's guest space. Bad enough that they're sleeping together, that he's taking her out on Saturday. Instead, she circles until she finds a quasi-legal spot and notes the time. Cambridge roulette, although she's too close to a corner rather than taking one of the coveted resident spaces, and she'll play the odds that the meter maids won't be quite so stringent on a Monday.

She doesn't recognize Onie, not right away. Not until she realizes that the only person looking up toward the door is also one of the only people of color in the coffeehouse does she put two and two together.

'Onie.' She holds her hand out as he rises to greet her. 'It's Tara.'

'Good to see you.' His grip is firm. Up close, she sees that he's grown big – solid, but not fat. His close-cropped hair is grey, receding a bit at the temples. He looks like what he is, the realization hits her: a prosperous middle-aged man. And since he already has a beverage, steaming on the low table in front of him, she nods toward the counter. When she returns, a decaf latté in hand, he's the one to get things started.

'Now, tell me about this article of yours.' He drinks. Chai, she thinks, as the aroma reaches her. Something spicy and warm.

She does, playing up the nostalgia a bit as he sips his tea. A pensive smile creases his face.

'Yeah, they were good,' he says, when she's done speaking of the Aught Nines. '"Hot Shot" got the airplay, but it was just a teaser, something to lure the labels. If they'd had access to a real studio, not some basement in Roxbury . . .'

'You helped them record, didn't you?' The memory tickles the back of her mind.

Onie's smile broadens. 'Yeah, that was my real dream. Well, besides being a rock star. I thought I could be a producer.'

'"Hot Shot" got a lot of airplay.' She can hear it still.

He chuckles, shaking his head. 'On the college stations. We had four tracks and a decent board, but what I didn't know about mixing . . .' He waves away the past and all its possibilities with one large hand.

'What were they like?' She's taking notes, but it's more than that. She really wants to know.

'The Aughts? Well, they weren't like any other band on the scene. Not like Last Call, anyway.' He sees her puzzlement and continues. 'Most of us were groups of friends. I mean, I knew Frank from high school. That's how the Aught Nines started, but by the time we all went into the studio, they were a different animal.'

'More professional?'

He tilts his head. 'You could say that. I mean, Jim and Jerry were never much for discipline. Greg, neither, though he had a good sense of time. No, it was Chris. He was running that band like a drill sergeant. He made sure they were on time, they were rehearsed. I mean, it was a cheap little studio – the owner made his nut recording commercials for the local AM station – but Chris was as serious as death in there. There was no fucking around for the Aught Nines when the band was on the clock.'

'Well, yeah, they were paying for it.' Tara's skepticism is shaken off with a close-mouthed grin.

'Nah, believe me,' says Onie. 'I worked with other bands. The Whirled Shakers? They would still be figuring out the arrangement, asking me to weigh in.'

'You worked with the Whirled Shakers?' Tara looks at the man across from her with new appreciation. 'On "World Enough"?'

He nods.

'I love that song!' She's beaming now, gone totally fan girl.

'Thanks.' He looks down, slightly embarrassed, as he begins to sing, his voice barely audible. '"*If we had world enough and time*". Talk about another lifetime!'

'But Chris . . .' Tara can't let that go. 'He was together then?'

She doesn't need to say any more. 'Yeah.' Onie sounds a million miles away. 'I mean, I guess he was using. I heard the same rumors as everyone else. You'd see him at parties . . .' Another bad memory to wave away. 'But in the studio, he had it all under control.'

'For a while.' She speaks softly, but he hears her.

'It seemed like a lot of people were getting into it then.' His smile is gone.

She remembers those parties, too. Someone nodding out on the sofa. Min telling her not to go into the back room, not that anyone was fucking in it – not anymore. 'You have any idea what happened?'

'No.' He's lost, staring off into some distant space. 'Just suddenly . . . that shit was everywhere. I can't tell you how many people thought I'd be able to hook them up.' He turns toward her, his eyes serious despite the wry grin that once again pulls at the corners of his mouth. 'I wasn't into reggae, either.'

She huffs out a half laugh and shakes her head. Sympathy, or despair. 'Was anybody in Last Call . . . was Frank into smack?'

'No.' A vehement shake of his head. 'He hated that shit with a passion. No, with Frank, it was the drink that did him in. I mean, the band . . . we were no great loss. But he was really hurting for a while. Couldn't hold a job. Last I remember, he was at the Casbah.'

'The Casbah?' Tara's voice spikes with disbelief. 'Jonah Wells gave him a job?'

'No, no way.' Onie laughs at the thought. 'He wasn't pretty enough. But Brian was managing by then. The bar, anyway. He got Frank a gig working the door. Only Frank was too angry – too angry and too drunk. He beat up some kid. Some poor junkie, stoned out of his head. Kid was screaming it was a shakedown, but it was just Frank being Frank, pissed at the world and wasted. Even Brian couldn't keep him on, after that. If anyone had asked me, I'd have thought he'd have been the one to go – not Chris.'

NINE

I t all comes back with the legwork. Phone work, really, although these days it really is only the phone – no more Rolodex of scrawled and crossed-out names. By the time she leaves work on Wednesday, she's played phone tag with Jim and Jerry, with Nieve, who still tends bar over at the Drift, and left messages for Phil and Robbie from the Whirled Shakers, as well. Even if one or two of them drop out, she's got the bones of the piece. Not the structure, exactly. Not yet, but a sense of the narrative. Of the flow. A story of creation and community, of struggle, and a tragic near miss. Of the survivors who still warm themselves at the embers.

Of course, she'll need to talk to Neela. Frank's widow ties together the two parts of the story, past and present. She was there with Chris, and, obviously, now, with Frank. Only his funeral was just last week, and it's too soon. Tara can still picture her. How pale she looked. How exhausted. She'll reach out to her – spend some time with her – sometime before her deadline. She tells herself it's only human to give the grieving woman a bit more time. Anybody would.

Still, she's hesitant to call Scott back. She remembers well enough how bullheaded he can be, and he clearly wants this piece. That there's a story there, she no longer has any doubt. But as it begins to take shape, she's starting to question if it's the one he'll want. The one she's half-promised her old buddy she could deliver.

It's nearly six. She's hoping for voicemail, but he's still at his office, and so, with her notes spread on the coffee table, she outlines what she has and what she hopes to get. It's all professional, smoother than she had feared, and they quickly come to loose terms. Four thousand words. Five, maybe, if she gets something really good. A dollar a word, with a bump if it makes the cover. She'll get him something in three weeks. A draft, at least, but even before, she'll keep in touch. So they can talk about art, he says. Photos or an illustration, maybe. But she knows Scott. He wants to be able to shape the piece as it happens. And then he begins to riff.

'Sex and drugs and rock and roll.' Scott is chuckling, a deep rumble bouncing his words along. 'We've got to find a way to work that into the lede.'

'Wait.' Tara jumps in before he can say more. This isn't what she meant, what they've been discussing. 'Are you serious?'

The pause that follows worries her. Makes her more aware than Scott's new look, new job – more than anything – of the time that has passed. How much has her old friend changed?

'Well, you are talking to the widow, aren't you?' Scott always did have a sense for Tara's weak spots – urging her on when she shied away from something hard. 'I mean, she's your story.' He's getting carried away. Taking what she's told him, only twisting it slightly. 'Neela Turcotte – the dancing girl turned grieving granny. From cranked-up Chris Crack to sober Frank Turcotte. That's your piece, Tara. Neela, Chris Crack, and the aftermath. Sex and drugs and rock and roll.' He says it again, the phrase rolling out of his mouth, like he's selling something. Like he's a suit, jollying her along. 'Yeah, that's it. I like it.'

'Scott.' She hears the peevishness in her voice. The slight whine, but really, she has cause to be annoyed. Or, no, disappointed. 'You can't be serious.' She pauses. He's the editor of *City* now. He *is* a suit. 'Are you?'

'Well, sort of.' He has the grace to sound abashed. In the silence that follows, Tara finds herself drifting back. The old Scott – the fat, sloppy Scott – would have scoffed at that tag line. It was cheap – no, 'easy', he'd say, as a precursor to urging her to dig deeper. To think harder about the people involved. The personalities. Not just a hook for the uninitiated. For the tourists.

'I'm sorry, Tara.' What he hears in her silence he doesn't say. Clearly, he's picked up some of her unhappiness. No – she corrects herself – her ambivalence. '*City* isn't a 'zine. It's a glossy monthly, with a circulation of more than three hundred thousand, ninety-nine percent of whom will never have been in the clubs. Will never have heard of any of these people. They hear "Boston rock", they think Aerosmith or maybe, *maybe* the Cars. And they're our readers, too.'

Tara swallows her response. He's right, though that final 'too' is a bit much. She didn't know Scott had this gig because she never reads the magazine. 'I guess I'm not the target demographic,' she says, her voice soft. An offering of peace.

'But you are!' He's excited again. 'College educated, gainfully employed. Soon to be a homeowner, maybe.' As he talks, she wonders – did she tell him about the condo? 'Well, you don't have kids, and most of our readers do. But you can write, Tara. You just have to' – the pause is telling – 'broaden your scope a bit. Just to bring them in. The story is still yours. Still what you were telling me.'

'I guess.' She thinks back to their dinner. His apartment – how he looked. For the first time since seeing him again, she misses the old Scott, stained hoodie and all. He would have understood her reservations.

But she's changed too. 'I'm just not sure anymore,' she says. She never used to balk at any of Scott's suggestions. Then again, she'd been a novice then – and he'd been a good editor. 'It seems like maybe you want something more sensational than I'm comfortable with.'

'Nonsense!' She hears the old Scott in his voice. The enthusiasm, the passion. 'I want the real story, Tara. I want to know what happened. What went so horribly wrong, and you're in a unique position to find out.'

'I am?' Something isn't right. He's selling it too hard.

'You're one of the best writers I know,' he says, and she tries to resist the glow his words conjure. 'I've been meaning to get you into the magazine. Been meaning to get in touch since I've been here. And you've got perspective, Tara. You were always in the scene but never really of it.'

'Oh.' One short syllable is all she can manage. She knows what he means, as much as she wishes she didn't. For years, she told herself it was her role. A critic needs some distance. Needs to maintain some kind of objectivity on the goings-on around her. But she knew that was only part of the truth. Everyone knew that redhead from *Boston Rock* fucked half the bands she wrote about. That Tom was doing lines with Brian – and probably with every other bouncer or barkeep who let him in early to drop off his copies of *Underground Sound*. And she didn't even want to think about Min. It wasn't just Frank, like it wasn't just coke, after a while. There was a reason her friend kept her away from the back rooms. Only now, Tara finds herself wondering.

'Were *you* part of the scene, then?' She visualizes the man on the other end of the line: trim and clean-shaven. Soon he'll have his feet up on that glass coffee table. The sun is setting, and the view over the docks, over the water, will be amazing.

'We were there, Tara.' She hears him sit up. The conversation is coming to an end. He wants to go home. 'Hey, I met you because of it. And I also met Jonah. I'd say we did OK for ourselves.' She pictures that window. The view. 'Maybe we were on the fringes. Outsiders looking in. But at least we survived.'

Scott's only being smart. Being what Peter would term 'adult'. She knows that. He's guiding her toward the piece he can use – something 'edgy' enough to titillate his corporate master, but still sufficiently mainstream for the majority of his readers. Still, she's disappointed. No, she realizes as she sits and stares at the silent phone, hurt. She had thought they were a team. She had thought, maybe . . . no. She shakes her head. This is a gig. A story. Nothing more.

While she's been sitting here, in her own living room, the sun has set. The soft September twilight faded, leaving her in darkness.

'God, I'm a sad case.' She talks out loud, to cheer herself up. For, as Scott would say, distance. But after switching on the reading lamp, she grabs her phone again.

'Nick!' She's so happy when he picks up that she forgets why she's called. He'd invited her to dinner – and then called to rescind the invitation. 'I'm – ah – returning your calls?'

It sounds lame, even to her.

'Tara.' His voice is warm. She likes the way he says her name. 'I'm glad you called. And, I'm sorry – that was all sort of half-assed.'

'No,' she responds. 'No problem. I mean, is everything all right?'

His sigh turns into something like a laugh. 'Just the usual drama,' he says. 'Patti – my ex – was having problems with the boys. I mean, they're teenagers. But, well . . .' He hesitates. 'She hasn't had an easy time of it. Would you hang on a minute?'

She waits as he talks to someone. He's at the bar, she realizes, saying something about the register. About a delivery that came in. When he gets back on, she apologizes.

'I guess I caught you in the middle of things,' she says.

'Not at all.' He sounds better, almost chipper. 'In fact, I was just leaving. Hey, I know it's last minute, but . . . would you want to get a pizza or something?'

'Yeah,' she says. 'I would.'

They agree on Bertucci's. It's closer to her place, but he's got his car anyway, he points out. After a day in the office, she's glad to walk. It's full dark by then, but even mid-week the city is humming and she feels the old lift, the surge of energy and hope that comes from going out. Maybe it's not the culture she misses, she thinks as she makes her way into Central. Maybe it's simply the night.

He's not there when she arrives, but there are no new messages on her phone. No last-minute cancellation, and so she gets a table. Orders a glass of wine and tries to quell her sudden nerves. It's Scott, she tells herself. He put her on edge, with his talk about the scene, about the piece. It's all silly, really. Her old friend is merely being pragmatic. 'Adult.' Peter's voice sounds in her head again. Still, Tara feels uneasy. Unsure what she has committed to. Unsure, if she is going to be honest, about why she wants to write this piece.

She looks up, but nobody has entered in the few minutes she's been sitting there. She thinks about calling Min, but she already knows what her friend would say. Min never really liked Scott. And besides, Nick has just walked in.

'Just in time,' she says, as he sits down. Before she has a chance to stop herself.

'Bad day?' He seems to get it, and she nods, grateful.

'This helped.' She raises her glass, and then catches herself. 'I mean, I'm not . . .'

'No, I know.' He raises his hand to stop her protestations and, then, to flag over the waitress. 'Would you want more? Let's have a carafe.'

By the time she brings it, Tara has finished her glass. By the time they order, she only feels a slight pang of guilt – the sausage and banana peppers is Peter's favorite, though Nick doesn't go for the extra cheese. She sips her second glass slowly, aware of the pleasant buzz, but when he asks how the story is going, she ends up telling him about Scott. About her reservations with his editorial direction. And with his flip description of her detachment.

'Maybe I'm being silly,' she says. She dips her finger in a drop of wine, circles the rim of her glass. She's not hungry, not anymore. 'But, well, I always felt like the scene was my family. Maybe because my real family wasn't particularly emotive or expressive. And now, I guess, I wasn't either. I guess I held myself aloof, too.'

She hears herself talking, and it's as if she's hearing Scott all over again. 'I mean, was he right, do you think?'

'Aloof? No.' He speaks softly, his blue eyes sad, and she realizes that she was worried that he wouldn't take her seriously. 'An outsider? Maybe. But we all were. I mean, wasn't that the point, sort of? We could all be misfits together.'

'Maybe.' She thinks of her friends. Of Min and Frank. Of Scott, who she thought she knew so well. 'Maybe I did keep my distance.'

'Maybe you had good instincts.' He reaches over, puts his hand on hers, just as the pizza arrives. 'Fantastic,' he says, sitting back as the waitress places the pan between them. 'I don't know about you, but I'm famished.'

Tara separates slices and plates them. Biting into her own, she finds her appetite, the knot in her belly gone. When Nick picks up the carafe, hovering over her glass, she nods. Why not? She's not driving. Besides, she hasn't felt so good in ages.

'I insist,' he says, when she laughs off his offer to walk her home. 'Central Square hasn't changed that much. Besides,' he lowers his voice to a conspiratorial hush, 'I could use some air before I get behind the wheel.'

She doesn't protest. The street has grown quiet, and, besides, she's enjoying his company. They've moved off talk of work and their respective families. It turns out, he's a reader. 'History, mostly, but anything I can get my hands on.'

'My ex was into history,' she says. By this point, that's not a conversation stopper, though he does make a face, which in turn sets her laughing. 'No, really. That's not a bad thing,' she clarifies.

They've reached her building by then, and when she turns to tell him, she finds herself hesitating. It's not his eyes, or even the lean, muscular bulk of him, so much more fit – more physical – than Peter ever was. When he leans down to kiss her, she kisses him back, wrapping her arms around him to draw him close. To bring him in to her body. To her world.

TEN

'So what did you decide?' Min's question startles her out of her reverie. She's on her way to work, singing one of the old songs to herself. 'Are you lining them up for the weekend?'

'Oh, sorry.' She catches herself. Thinks back. 'I don't – things have changed.'

'Let me guess. Scott called, too?' She hears Min settle in. Thursday, her day off, and she always had an ear for when something was on Tara's mind. 'Tell.'

Tara takes a moment before she responds. She hasn't been thinking of Scott. She hasn't been thinking about much, actually, which is how she'd like to keep it. She feels good. Happy, even, and not yet ready to unpack her thoughts about the night before. And so she decides to answer the question that Min gives voice to, rather than the more salacious one implied.

'Yeah, we talked about the piece. He's pushing for something a bit more sensational than I had in mind,' she says, as she makes her way toward the office. At this moment, she can't quite remember why Scott's coaching bothered her so much, and she tries to conjure the discomfort she felt. Min will expect it. 'Something a little cheesy.'

'Well, it is *City*.' Min is enjoying this, Tara can tell. Almost as good as sex. 'Soccer mom central.'

'Yeah.' The problem with revisiting the conversation. It does begin to bother her again. What Scott said, how he said it. This was really not the time to dredge it all up again. She's got work, even if Min doesn't.

'Do you think the scene was made up of outsiders?' She posits the question as she walks up the stairs to Zeron's main entrance. That's not really what she's thinking, but it's close enough.

'Island of misfit toys? Maybe.' Min's lying down, Tara can hear it in her voice. Hears her stretch and reach for something. 'At least some of them. Why?'

'I was thinking about Chris Crack,' she says. And suddenly, she is. 'He seemed like a golden boy, didn't he?'

'Well, yeah, to us.' Min laughs. 'But, really? He was just a rich kid from the suburbs.'

'But, think about it.' Tara steps aside to let others pass. She's trying to articulate a thought, 'I mean, most of those guys just formed bands to meet girls. Chris was different. He was, like, a star.'

'You're such a romantic.' Min isn't laughing now, but there's a note in her voice. One part mockery, one part affection. 'He could've been a stockbroker or something. One of the doctors whose shit I have to deal with. Only he had a rough childhood and so he decided to strut around like he's David Johanssen. Big fish in a small pond, if you ask me. And look where it got him.'

'He had a rough childhood?' Tara sees the VP for Marketing come up the stairs. She smiles and nods.

'Rough's the wrong word.' Cellophane ripping. Paper. 'But didn't you ever listen to his lyrics? Something was wrong with him.'

Tara tries to remember. When Min's like this, she doesn't like to ask. As she stands there, she hears the unmistakable sound of a match being struck. Min is smoking again. First thing in the morning, too.

'What about you?' She softens her voice. Knows her friend too well. Knows the signs. 'How are you doing?'

'Right as rain.' Tara hears the heavy exhalation. She can almost see the smoke. 'Thank God I'm off oncology.' She laughs a graveyard laugh, not trying to hide anything.

'Why don't you come over tonight?' Tara tries to keep it light. 'We can watch *Lethal Weapon*.'

'Nah, Gibson's getting too old. I can't even get it up for him anymore.' Another deep huff. 'But, sure. Why not? Hey, I've got some errands to run later. Why don't I meet you at the factory?'

She means Zeron, of course. Tara looks up, as if someone could hear. 'Great,' she says. 'I'll be out front by five fifteen.' One of the perks of a corporate gig.

'If you're not, I'll come in and get you.'

*   *   *

It's just as well she's already drafted the report. Tara can't focus. It isn't just Min – or the night with Nick – it's the story that's distracting her. What was it Onie had said?

'Suddenly that shit was everywhere.' She remembers. October, it must have been. That cold, clear weather that makes you forget you're in a city. The sky so blue it looks fake. But cold at night. Frosty. That's why she was confused by the small crowd huddled outside Oakie's. The way they were all turned toward each other. Smoking hadn't been prohibited, not yet. And when she'd asked Min, her friend had merely laughed.

'They're all looking to score,' she'd said. 'But Brian's had enough. He's kicked them out. He can't risk the license.'

It took Tara a while to understand what was happening. Pot was a constant in the clubs, so much so that people smoked openly, almost. Backstage could give you a contact high. And everyone did lines in the bathroom, at least if they could afford them. She'd done her share herself – the cheap coke cut with enough speed to have her bouncing off the walls.

But something was changing – some factor she didn't quite grasp at first. She remembers. That huddle was the first time. Or was it when Min pulled her back, her hand on Tara's shoulder, just as she was about to snort a line.

'You don't want that,' her friend had said. 'Come on. I need a beer.'

There's nothing for it. She needs to talk to more people. To someone who was closer, who knew more about what was going on. She steels herself and dials Neela's number. There's no answer, and when the voicemail beeps she hangs up. An hour later, she tries again. This time, she leaves a message.

'Please call me,' she says, so the widow won't think this just another condolence call. She leaves both her numbers. All through the daily meeting, she keeps checking, her phone hidden in her hand. Even as she's neatening up her desk to leave – old habit, never lost – she's waiting.

'Hey, stranger.' Min is leaning against the building, cigarette in hand, when Tara descends the steps. Thirty pounds heavier, she's let her hair revert to its natural brown. Let the grey begin to show too. The pink leather is long gone, replaced by an Army surplus jacket. Generic. Warm. 'Long time, no see!'

She pauses to grind out the butt, leaving it on the sidewalk before reaching up to embrace her friend. Tara looks around, hoping none of her colleagues have seen this, have seen Min, with her cat's-eye shades and black high-tops.

'What?' Min holds her at arm's length, examining her face for the cause of her unease.

'It's the piece.' There's some truth in that, and Tara shrugs, shamefaced at it – and at her lie. 'I've been trying to work on it all day, despite this.' She lowers her voice. 'Despite the gig. Only I'm not getting anywhere.'

Min links her arm and the two start walking. Her friend smells of ash and the pack she's smoked today, even out here, but with each step Tara breathes more easily. 'I think I really have to talk to Neela before I go any further,' she says. 'Only now I can't reach her. I mean, she can't be back at work yet. Can she?'

'Neela? No.' They've reached the T, but Min hesitates. She wants another cigarette. Tara can see it in the way she rubs her fingers together. In her distraction.

'You want to walk?' Tara doesn't like her smoking. Not this much, anyway, but Min is clearly in a bad way. 'I can use the exercise.' She almost says 'air'.

'Me, too.' Min's response is a little too hearty, and before they've gone a block she has another cigarette lit. 'So, anyway, did you try Mika?'

'Her daughter? No.' Tara looks at Min. 'I don't really know her.'

'Hm.' Min pauses to pick a bit of tobacco from her lip. 'Nice gal. She was kind of wild when she was younger. No surprise, huh?' She glances toward Tara but doesn't wait for an answer. 'These days, though . . . ugh.'

'Her son?' Tara thinks about what Katie told her. Something digestive. 'It's serious, right?'

'Could've killed him.' Min's so matter of fact, it must be the nurse in her. 'He'll be OK now, though. Now that the doctors at Mercy have gotten their heads out of their asses long enough.'

'Oh?' At times, it's hard to remember Min's training. Her

expertise. She could've gone to medical school. Tara has thought this a million times.

'Fabry's disease.' Her friend nods to herself. 'Or some variant. I told Frank. Finally, they got him tested.'

'Fabry's?' Tara's never heard of it.

'The kid is missing an enzyme.' Min waves the cigarette. 'Without it, he can't digest most food. But with it . . .' Ash flies. 'Anyway, they caught it, though the kid has some catching up to do, and Mika's been through the mill. Anyway, Neela's at her place, most likely. Doing her mother hen thing. Frank always said she felt responsible for everything.'

Frank. Her friend says the name like it's nothing. But the smoking – the archness – they're worse than before.

'When was the last time you saw Frank?' That's not what Tara really wants to ask. Anything to get her friend talking, though.

'God, a week, maybe five days before he died?' Those shades hide her eyes. 'He'd called, you know, about the baby. He was at his wit's end.'

'So he called you for medical advice?' Tara keeps her voice low. She's not one to judge.

Min looks at her, over the glasses. 'We were friends, Tara. We weren't humping in the restroom anymore, if that's what you were thinking. Speaking of, you've got some weekend lined up. Tell me about this Nick. I'm not sure I remember him.'

Tara can't help it. She blushes, and then she's telling Min everything. Or almost. The talk about alienation – about the scene, their failed marriages – feels too intimate to share. And so it comes out more like a drunken hookup. Too much wine and no regrets in the morning.

By the time she's through – and answered all of Min's questions – they've reached her building. As usual, someone's propped the front door open with a brick, and as they go in, Tara kicks it out of the way. Peter would have a fit, talking about security and the crime in the city, and he's probably right. But as she reaches her landing, she sees a manila envelope on her mat, marked only with her first name. It is lumpy, misshapen, and as she opens it to see what has distended it so, she is suddenly filled with joy. A shake and onto her palm slides the little carving of a horse.

'What's that?' Min starts to reach for it, but Tara pulls back. Holds it close, admiring the grain of the wood. The curve of the legs captured in mid stride. The way the flag of a tail splays out to give the illusion of speed.

'It's one of Nick's carvings,' she says. 'He whittles,' she corrects herself. 'He did this one for one of his kids.'

'Creepy,' says Min. 'Come on. I need a beer.'

Min doesn't want to talk about Frank. That much is obvious as Tara ushers her friend inside. Still, his presence hangs over the room, thick as the smoke as Min lights another cigarette. In the silence, as Tara struggles for the right words to say. Instead, or maybe simply to stave off her friend's inquiries, Min presses Tara about Nick – about that carving.

'Think he's a stalker?' The way she asks it's more like a statement. 'Did he seem, I don't know, obsessive that way?'

Tara hesitates, already uncomfortable with how much she's told her friend about the encounter. She fetches an old mug for Min to use as an ashtray. On the way, she ducks into her bedroom to put the little horse away where Min can't casually handle it. Can't pick it up to examine.

'I think it's kind of sweet actually,' she says when she emerges. This feels like an act of defiance. 'His son liked horses when he was younger.'

Min looks at her, one eyebrow raised, and waits. But Tara has learned a few things over the years of their friendship, and instead moves on to safer topics. To work, to what they want to eat. Not that there's much discussion. They always order Chinese. Dumplings and moo shi. But an hour later, Min has barely touched her bowl. She's said something about her weight, gesturing with her latest cigarette as if that's a reason. But she's on her third beer, and Tara knows her friend too well.

'You must be missing him.' Tara's had a beer as well. It makes her brave. Besides, her friend is clearly hurting. 'I mean, you'd become friends.'

Min shrugs, but lets out a sigh that seems to release all her tension. 'Ah, shit,' she says, and, leaning forward, covers her face with one hand and starts to cry.

In a moment, Tara is beside her, arms around her as she sobs, her cheek against her friend's bowed back. 'Oh, Min,' she says. There are no words, but they've been through this before – or something similar, anyway. 'Min.'

'It's not like I lost him,' Min says, with a hiccup, as she surfaces. 'Not really.' Tara hands her a takeout napkin, and Min blows her nose. She is still, Tara sees, holding her lit smoke.

'Don't.' Min shakes her head, though if she's warning Tara off a lecture or more questions, Tara can't tell. 'I mean, we were barely even friends anymore.' Min stubs out the cigarette. The former, then.

'Well, you guys talked, right?' Tara tries to piece together what Min has told her, even as she reaches for another napkin. 'I mean, when his grandson was sick, he called you.'

'Yeah, I'm cheaper than a doctor.' Min wipes her face with two rough swipes, as if she were angry at her eyes. 'He changed, after they were married.'

Tara knows better than to comment. Knows that Min can hear herself.

'It wasn't just Neela.' Min glances over, a little sheepish. 'Or, you know, being married. I think it was the drinking. Something happened when Frank quit drinking.'

'Well, yeah.' It just comes out, but Min doesn't seem to mind.

'No, I mean, he closed down somehow.' Her friend appears to be struggling.

'Maybe that's how he needed to be.' Tara strokes her friend's back, like she would a baby's. 'Maybe that's how he managed.'

'No.' Min sputters and reaches for her cigarettes again. Lights another without looking. Without, Tara decides, even being fully aware. 'There was something else going on.'

'Well . . .' Tara stops herself from saying any more. There was a lot going on, and they both remember it well.

It had been early March, the tail end of a miserable winter that had dragged on for far too long. For Tara, it was all about the bands, but even there a deep freeze seemed reluctant to give way to spring. Scott had dubbed it 'the winter of our discontent', adding, 'cause everyone sucks just now'.

'Not everyone.' Tara had come over for an editorial meeting, which really meant having a few beers and some gossip. 'Maybe the Aught Nines will finally ink a deal.'

Scott snorted as he scribbled notes, pawing through a pile of fliers from fledgling bands. But Tara was hopeful. Every week, the rumors promised that a contract was near. Epic. Elektra. MCA. All the labels had come courting. Numerous professional management firms, as well. But like some airhead debutante, Chris Crack had kept them all at bay. Playing them against each other, as if for the sheer fun of it. They'd been flown out to LA – down to New York – so often that their gigs were becoming rare occurrences, and between the slush and the cold, the on-again, off-again of clubland's new favorites was straining everyone's nerves.

'Don't hold your breath,' Scott said finally, handing her a Xeroxed sheet. 'What do you think of these guys? Want to check them out?'

'Might as well.' Tara looked at the announcement. The Casbah, that night. Chris had blown off an interview, and not until she had called his mother in Hamilton as a last resort had she found out that Chris was down in New York, supposedly hammering out the last details of a contract. 'If we hear from the Aught Nines, I can always write it up as an "in review".'

'Yeah, sure.' Scott glanced at another flier. Crumpled it and took a shot at the wastebasket. 'That might still happen.'

'You think they're playing too hard to get?' To Tara, this seemed impossible. Despite – because of? – the rarity of their gigs, the band had never sounded better. Chris, meanwhile, had perfected his rock-star moves. Rarely still once he was on stage, his writhing body glowed like some phosphorescent sea creature.

'Things don't always work out,' Scott had said, with a shrug. 'The bloom doesn't stay on the rose forever.'

That night, at the Casbah, Tara decided her editor was crazy. There were three bands on the bill, and none of them could hold a candle to the Aught Nines. The first had been thrash metal, but too disorganized to get the mosh pit moving. And at the Casbah, there was always a mosh pit. The second had some boy band singer – cherub lips and golden curls. But his voice had been so bad, Tara had ducked out, despite a frigid wind that cut through the waterfront like a knife. That's when she'd seen Frank, collapsed against the wall.

'Hey, you OK?' Tara had never gotten close to the man. But really, it was too cold to let someone pass out out here. 'Frank?'

'Huh?' He'd turned to face her, and she recoiled. Frank Turcotte had always been a bit scary: rough-looking, with a permanent scowl under those heavy brows. The man who turned toward her now looked not so much a bully as a victim. His eyes seemed barely focused in his pale face, his wide mouth hanging slack.

'Frank!' Tara reached for him, pulling on one leather-clad arm.

'She's gone.' He shook his head, even as he let Tara pull him to his feet. 'I can't reach her.'

'Come on, Frank.' Tara draped his arm over her own shoulder, as if she could actually support his weight. She knew better than to argue with a drunk, especially this drunk. 'Let's go inside. It's not that bad.'

As they staggered back toward the door, Tara debated calling Min. Her friend loved this man, for reasons she couldn't decipher. But really, foisting a melancholy drunk on her was not an act of friendship. Especially when she – when everyone – knew the reason for Frank's state. Neela had moved in with Chris Crack. Was living with him openly, last anyone had heard. From the looks of Frank, Tara figured the redhead was in LA with him right now. Or was it New York? She couldn't keep the stories straight.

With the last of her strength, Tara managed to pull the door open.

'Oh, no.' Mick, the bouncer, stood in their way. 'Not in here.'

Tara closed her eyes, as Frank slumped against her. 'Please,' she said, at last. 'You can't leave him out here. He'll die.'

She never knew if it was her words or some fleeting sympathy for the man who, until recently, had been a colleague, but the burly bouncer relented, taking hold of Frank as if he were a ragdoll and dragging him over to the small room that served as a staff office and de facto lost and found.

'You might call your friend.' He dropped the man into one of three folding chairs. Let him slump against the cardboard box that overflowed with scarves, mittens, and, apparently, a forgotten coat, before closing the door behind him. 'Have her pick him up.'

Maybe it was his tone. His casual assumption that a woman would always come when called. Maybe it was concern for Min. Or maybe, Tara had wondered, sometimes, late at night, it was that she was jealous. The passion Min felt for Frank. The love. But she didn't make the call. Looking back, she asked herself once again, if she should have.

'He was in really bad shape, Min,' she says now, sitting in her living room. Watching her friend smoke. 'He needed a change.'

'He needed to get over Neela, that's what. He knew what she was like.' Min takes a long drag on the new smoke, then grinds the butt out anyway as if it were the mug that had broken her heart. 'He knew, but he didn't care.'

ELEVEN

Would things have turned out differently if Tara had called Min? She doesn't know. Can't know. Can't talk to Min about it, either, that night years ago still the great unacknowledged shadow between them. Even now, as she goes to the kitchen for more beer, to put the leftovers away, Tara feels its presence. Wishes she'd never stepped out the door. Never found Frank. Though, maybe, if she hadn't, he would have died, and everything would be different now.

She takes out two more cans. Leans her head against the fridge, a moment for herself. It was so long ago, but she remembers.

As it was, Frank soon came to, sobering up in the staff room of the Casbah, where the doorman had stored him. Where Jonah wouldn't see. Tara didn't know it then, but she heard after. Much of the club did, at least those by the door.

Neela hadn't been off with Chris, it turned out. Chris hadn't even been in New York. His mother had lied to Tara, covering for her son. Trying to protect him, most likely, from a world she must have considered toxic. Chris, they all heard later, was in a program – some kind of detox – and although he wouldn't stay, it would turn out later to have been prophetic that he was gone that day, that night. Because Neela had been left alone and at loose ends. And Frank, drunk and miserable, had found her. The resulting row sounded like the end, by all accounts. Bottles had been broken in tears and rage, until finally both the lovers had been tossed out of the club once more. And although the two had not left together – Tara remembered Onie talking to Frank, Onie reasoning with him, talking him down from hanging around – that night had proved a turning point. At the time, it sounded like Frank and Neela were really over. Maybe they'd just needed to air all the bad will out.

'You fall in?' Min's voice from the other room brings Tara back.

'Sorry.' She dismisses the past. Conjures a smile and returns with the fresh drinks. 'I guess I was thinking of how lucky we are.'

Min's expression says it all.

'No, really.' Tara's chuckling as she hands over the beer. As she takes her own seat on the couch. 'When you think how many of our friends ended up twelve-steppers – or worse.'

'You're thinking about Chris.' Min takes a long pull, dried out by the tears.

'Yeah, but not just Chris.' Tara bites her lip. She's remembering Min, during one of her bad periods – one of the times Frank was back with Neela. She'd walked into the ladies – was it the Rat? Or Oakie's? – and seen her friend and two other women, hunched over a CD case, white lines laid out on the smooth plastic.

'A little blow?' Tara dabbled, not that she wanted to butt in on anyone else's party.

'No, not this.' Min had sniffed and stood, blocking her from the case, from the woman – Rita from the Callers? – holding it steady. 'Come on, kiddo,' she'd said, reaching for Tara. 'Let's go get a beer.'

'But I have to pee.' Tara had ducked away from her friend and the other two women had laughed. One, Rita, had slumped back against the stall wall, eyes closed.

'Knock yourself out, honey,' she had said.

'There was a lot of shit.' Min looks at her now like she can read her mind. 'It was just everywhere, and so cheap.'

'Were you buying?'

A shrug. 'We were young. I mean, we were chipping. It wasn't like we were shooting or anything.'

Tara keeps her mouth shut. What matters is that her friend survived.

'I mean, Rita got in over her head.' Min turns from her. Reads the label on the beer. 'That could have happened a thousand different ways.'

'She didn't – it wasn't a bad shot, was it?'

'No.' Min shakes her head, her face grim. 'Rita OD'd plain and simple. She was blue when the paramedics brought her in.'

The room falls silent. Min doesn't talk about work, and this wasn't what Tara intended anyway.

'Hey,' she says at last, when the weight of memory has begun to disperse. 'Do you want to watch that movie or not?'

* * *

Tara's too tired for second thoughts the next day, and when Jim and Jerry call her back, she puts them off till next week. It's Neela she needs to speak to, and she doesn't have the heart to leave another message. Not yet, anyway.

'Have you thought about art yet?' Scott's call catches her off guard. She's picked up the phone without thinking, having just walked in from the budget meeting.

'Scott, it hasn't been forty-eight hours,' she says. 'And I'm at work.'

'No shit!' He laughs, and for a moment she sees him as he was, her brilliant unkempt pal. 'But I'm psyched about this one, Tara. I want some vintage photos. Something vérité. This is going to be good.'

'Maybe.' She circles her desk, settles into her chair. She could just do the job. That would be easy.

'And I have a little something to get you going.'

She closes her eyes. Memories from last night. A little something, indeed.

'The boss likes it. He's really interested in what you're writing.' Scott keeps talking. 'I think we can make this the cover.'

'You talked to Jonah about this?' The idea makes Tara squeamish. Like she's in too deep.

'Yeah.' Scott seems to take it all in stride. Jollying her. Teasing. 'We had a meeting. The publisher likes to know what big features are pending, Tara. It is his magazine, after all.'

When she doesn't answer, his tone changes.

'I thought you'd be happy about this.' He sounds more rational again. More adult. 'That you wanted a big story. Something to break you back in.'

'I do.' She closes her eyes. Rubs her forehead. Two nights in a row: too many drinks and too little sleep. 'And I'll get on it, Scott. I'm sorry.'

'Hey, why don't you come in.' He's immediately conciliatory. 'You haven't seen my office. And you probably haven't seen Jonah since back in the day. Am I right?'

'I've got this budget report, Scott.' It's not an answer. It's all she's got. 'My deadline is Friday.'

'Monday, then.' Scott always managed to bring her around. 'Lunch? You've got to eat lunch.'

'Monday lunch.' It's far enough away. In the meantime, Tara knows, she's got to steel herself. She's got a number somewhere for Mika. Frank's daughter will know where Neela is.

'Why?' It's not the question Tara expects, but it's the first word Neela says, when she gets her on the phone. 'Why do you want to dig all that up again?'

Tara sits there, unsure what to say. The hard part, she thought, would be making the call. But Mika had been quite receptive. Had been encouraging, in fact, when Tara reached her and explained what she was after.

'That sounds great,' she had said. 'I think it would do Mom good to get out of her own head for a while. Make her talk about when she and Dad were young.'

In the background, Tara could hear the crying of an infant, but Mika hadn't sounded panicked. Just busy, and happy to pass off care of her mother to an old friend. It was Neela who was resistant.

'I'm not dredging up anything,' Tara says, stumbling toward a response. 'I mean, I'm doing this article about the music scene, and I thought, since you knew so many of the players—'

'You want to talk about Chris, right?' Neela cuts her off, her grief making her sharp.

'Well, yeah.' Tara has to admit the truth, even if it does sound bad. 'But also Frank, of course. You know, everybody on the scene.'

'Of course.' The other woman starts to laugh. But just as Tara is beginning to worry – is Neela hysterical? Can she reach Mika somehow? – she stops. 'Look, come by on Sunday morning. My daughter will be at church, and I'll be babysitting. That'll be a good time.'

Tara hesitates. Not only does the widow sound unhinged but Tara will be seeing Peter the night before.

'You know where she lives, right?' Neela rattles off an address in Medford. 'See you then.'

That's enough for the week, and Tara puts her head down. Writes the stupid report. No matter what she told Scott, she gives it no more thought than she would to pumping gas. Only she gets paid for this, she reminds herself, as she makes herself skim the numbers – a proofread of the most desultory sort. Maybe that's why she feels so empty, once she turns it in. So bored.

Writing for *Underground Sound* had never left her enervated. Even the *Dot* gig had been invigorating, despite the hours. She sleeps badly and wakes late. Saturday, but she doesn't care.

'Do you think I should get a cat?' Afternoon, and Tara is still lazing in bed.

'Do you want to never get laid?' From the slight hush in Min's voice, Tara can tell her friend is on the ward. Weekends are the busy times at the hospital. 'Don't become even more of a stereotype.'

'I don't know.' Tara ignores her friend's question. Waking up alone is getting old. 'I mean, I loved Smiley.'

'Smiley was special.' Min has a soft spot for the tuxedo cat still. Partly, Tara recalls, because Smiley always kneaded Min's leg when she came over. 'My little masseuse,' she called him.

'Is this about your bartender?' She's not reminiscing now. 'The blue-eyed stalker?'

'He's not—' Tara catches herself. 'No. I don't know.' She kicks back the covers. Considers coffee. The day. 'I know he's busy this weekend. I guess I was hoping he'd call.'

Min surprises her. 'You know, you could call him.' Voices in the background. A machine starts beeping. 'He did leave you that little thingy. And don't you have another date tonight?'

'It's not a date . . .' Too late, Min is gone, leaving Tara to wonder what exactly her night will hold. It's too much to contemplate, not without coffee. And so she gets up to start her day.

'You look nice.' Peter rises to greet her. He speaks gently, like he used to.

'Thanks.' She takes her seat and looks around. Away. His gaze is too direct. Too needy, she can already tell. Besides, she hasn't been here, to the bistro, in months – no, years. The art on the wall is the same: watercolors of some village, somewhere. The knickknacks – the flowers, that ceramic pig – are familiar, too, but the color has changed. They've painted, or maybe it's her memory. Time flies, and when she picks up the menu, she remembers why. It doesn't matter that she's earning a corporate salary. Spending that much on a piece of halibut just seems wrong.

'May I offer you a cocktail?' The server appears by her side, deferential and way too young, and she hesitates. She could use a beer or – something. She tries to think of something French.

'I thought we'd have wine with dinner,' Peter interrupts, and she smiles and nods. Some things never change. But when the server retreats, Peter leans forward. 'Is that OK? I thought we'd get a nice bottle. That white Burgundy you always liked.'

'I don't know what I'm having yet.' The menu makes a handy shield. Against what, exactly, she doesn't really know.

Maybe that's why she orders the halibut as he rattles on about his week. About work, and about the condo again. Drinks the Chablis without really tasting it, throwing it down too fast to savor the limestone and the lime and grunting when he tries to draw her out. When Peter hesitates before refilling her glass, she feels like she's won a round, or at least survived one.

'Enough about me,' he says, once he has relented and poured. His voice isn't so soft anymore. Isn't so warm. 'But I've found out something that might interest you.' His voice suggests otherwise. 'Something about your friend.'

Is it her imagination or has his smile grown a bit tight?

'My friend?' She puts the glass down, uncertain.

'Frank Turcotte. I made some calls, you know. After the funeral.' He's watching her and she sees it. He's not aiming to hurt her. He's bragging. Peter has the connections. Peter always gets the scoop.

She waits, regretting suddenly that first, quickly downed glass.

'They did an autopsy, of course.' He glances up from his steak. 'His wife – widow – said he was alone when he fell, so that was par for the course.'

'Yeah.' Tara gives him this, to urge him on. They were married long enough. She knows the law. 'So?'

'They're investigating. It's open.' He takes a bite of his steak but his eyes stay on her. He's looking to see if she understands. She knows this, and it infuriates her.

'For Christ's sake.' She puts her own fork down. 'I understand toxicology, though everyone is swearing up and down that Frank was sober, but—'

Peter is shaking his head as he chews.

'You can't mean.' Tara is confused. The wine. 'Suicide?'

Peter shrugs as he saws off another piece of meat. 'Don't know yet.' He has eyes only for his dinner now. 'But if you're going to take a trip down memory lane, I thought you might want to know. Maybe things weren't so rosy, so happily ever after. Maybe he was drinking again and fell down the stairs. Maybe he did it intentionally, because he couldn't stand his life anymore. Or maybe—' he looks up, a hunk of flesh on his fork – 'maybe Frank Turcotte was murdered.'

'I never said anything was rosy.' Tara ignores the speculation. She knows what Peter's after now. 'Particularly not Frank and Neela's life.'

They're still in the bistro. The candle still casts its golden glow. But Tara has pushed her full wine glass aside, and her fish is getting cold. 'You think I'm sentimental. That I don't see things – people – as they really are.'

'You're nostalgic.' He states it as a fact, once more focused on his plate. 'You've never gotten over something that never was.'

'So that's what this is about.' She should have guessed. 'The story. The fact that I'm writing for Scott again.'

'Really, Tara?' His tight smile contorts as he forks another piece of meat into his mouth and starts to chew. 'You think I'm jealous of Scott Hasselback?'

'Hasseldeck,' she corrects him automatically and when his smile broadens gets madder still. 'I don't know what's wrong with you, Peter Corwin, I really don't. You seem to view me as some kind of outdated child, some naïve infant who you're going to educate.'

'I just hate to see you wasting energy.' He motions with his fork, his appetite unabated – no, spurred – by her growing fury.

'I'm not your problem anymore.' Her hands, on the table's edge, are clenched into fists. Her voice is an angry hiss. She makes herself breathe. Opens her hands. 'This,' she says, 'was a mistake.'

'It doesn't have to be.' Peter puts his silverware down. Reaches across the table to place his hand over hers. 'Tara, please.'

His face, she sees, is sad. Not smug, or not now. 'I'm sorry,

Peter.' She is. Not that it makes a difference. 'I shouldn't have come tonight.'

'Tara.' A note of warning, and that's what cinches it.

'Please.' She doesn't mean it this time, but she knows him. Knows her own smile, pasted on, will sting more than any invective. 'Thank you for the dinner. I'm sorry to embarrass you, but I really have to go.'

With that, she pushes her chair back and stands, the plastic grin still in place. And with a nod to the server, hovering just out of earshot, she walks to the door and is free.

TWELVE

'Holy shit!' Min laughs when Tara tells her what happened. 'So much for comfort sex with the yuppie ex!'

'Yeah, I guess I burned that bridge.' She chuckles, grateful for her friend's reaction. Realizing that she's more shaken than she knew. The anger may have burned off as she stalked off, but now that she's home, the implications of her abrupt departure loom large. 'I just – he gets so smug, you know?'

'Hey, you married him.' Min never did like Peter, Tara recalls. 'So, you going to see the blue-eyed bartender tonight?'

'No.' Her laugh catches in her throat. The idea of stacking men like that – as if she was ever that free. That in demand. 'I think I've had enough excitement for one night.'

'Different kind of excitement. Best remedy for one man is another.' Min has finished her shift. She's at home and at liberty, too, but Tara knows better than to bounce the bromide back to her.

'Yeah, I don't know about that.' Tara still hasn't heard from Nick. Still hasn't called him, either. Though she has been thinking about him. Was, perhaps, thinking about him during dinner. She looks at the carving, which she's taken back into her living room. Picks it up to admire the work. 'Besides, I've got an appointment tomorrow.'

'An appointment?' Min lingers on the word. 'On a Sunday?'

'Yeah, I'm going to talk to Neela,' Tara admits with some reluctance.

'And the grieving widow isn't going to be in church for her sins?' Min must have picked up on her tone. Still, Tara works to tone down her reaction.

'Hey, she's had a rough time.' Jealousy. It could be the theme of the evening. 'And I do think she'll be good for the story.'

'Maybe now she'll be able to give you the real dirt on Chris.' There's something in Min's voice that Tara can't place.

'The real dirt?' She's gotten over playing coy, at least about Chris Crack.

'You ever stop and think about where all that shit came from? How come all of a sudden everyone was snorting or shooting up?'

Tara catches herself before she interrupts. 'Not everyone,' she wants to say. But she's unsure what Min is driving at, and she wants to know.

'I always thought it followed the coke,' she says instead. 'That it was cheaper, you know?' Tara rarely bought, but she knew people were spending big bucks. Money they didn't have.

'"It followed", like what? A stray looking for a home?' Before Tara can respond, Min's backing down. 'Oh, never mind,' she says. 'I forgot who you were writing for there.'

'Min.' Tara's not hurt, exactly. But twice in one night . . . 'That's unfair. You know I want to do a good story.'

'Yeah, I'm just remembering.' Min is herself again. It's been a long day. A work day for her, and she's sad. 'Remembering and regretting, I guess. Poor old Frank.'

'Hey . . .' Tara catches herself. She'd been about to say something stupid. Something like, 'at least he got the girl'. She closes her eyes, musing on her own blindness. On her friend's unacknowledged loss. 'Are you OK?' she asks, at last.

'I'm good.' The voice on the other end of the line sounds tired. Sounds old. 'As good as I'm likely to be.'

Chris was hardly the only junkie on the scene, even if he was the best known. Not that Tara knew it at the time.

'What's with the thermals?' She had been poring over contact sheets in the *Underground* office. Trying to find a cover shot that would actually look good. For the January issue, probably, which meant it would have been December fifteenth, more or less. Not that you could tell from the weather. Before that deep freeze set in, the winter had been unusually warm. Even the zine's crappy office had been comfortable, despite the cracked window and the radiator that the landlord never fixed. But as she and Scott went over Flicka's contact sheets, all she saw were bands dressed for winter.

'Did Mass Surplus have a sale or something?' Grunge hadn't yet hit the East Coast. Not like these guys would ever be fashion plates. But they weren't lumberjacks or longshoremen, either, and Tara was at a loss to explain the preponderance of waffle weave before her.

'What do you mean?' Flicka grabbed the loupe and pulled the sheet over. 'Oh, yeah. You're right.' Picking up a red grease pencil, she crossed out a photo.

'What's wrong with that one?' Tara had thought it had personality.

'Too many closed eyes.' Flicka slid the magnifier again, her brow furrowed as she examined the next shot. 'I must have been high myself. All these guys are nodding out.'

'They are?' Tara nudged the photographer aside for another look. Leaning over the scarred Formica graphics table that served for layout and paste-up both, she examined the quartet. The Fitzhughs – more garage than punk, with a growly singer who almost made up for the rudimentary musicianship of his colleagues. Under the little magnifier, she saw them, leaning back against the brick wall outside their practice space. It was a nod to the Ramones, of course. But she'd thought it fit them. That it looked street. Rough. Only, she hadn't grasped the full extent.

She squints to see better. To see their faces. 'I thought . . .'

'You thought, what? They were all sleepy from the cold?' Flicka took the loupe back and made another cross. The third shot she circled. 'There. They look like proper thugs in this one.'

'Let me see.' Scott pushed between the women to take the lens. 'Yeah, that works. You think you can get a story out of them?'

That was to Tara. She peered at the photo Flicka had chosen. The tiny photographer had a good eye. Here was Dougie, leaning over to spit. Stu holding a cigarette to his lips. She was right: this shot made the band look more interesting than she had thought them.

'Sure, boss.' She stepped back, ceding the sheet to Flicka, who had moved on to another sheet. 'I'll find something in my notes.'

When Scott had first proposed she cover them, she had complained about how dull the band was. How derivative.

'Maybe,' he'd said. 'But everyone goes to their shows.'

He was right. In a way, they'd taken over the Aught Nines' slot as the band who nobody really liked, but everyone went to see. The guitarist tended bar around town, the drummer worked as a bouncer. That afternoon, in their practice space, they'd answered her questions in monosyllables. She'd wondered if they resented her for some reason. If they sensed her poor opinion of them. In retrospect, their unresponsiveness made sense.

'Mr Friendly,' she said, musing to herself. 'We could use that as a headline. "Everybody's Best Friend".'

'I don't know if you want to do that.' Flicka, still bent over a contact sheet, didn't usually get involved in story discussions.

'Oh?' Tara asked. Scott was being uncustomarily quiet.

'Everybody's connection would be more like it.' She still didn't look up, but at that Tara turned toward Scott, who only shrugged.

'Come on.' Tara had heard the rumors. 'It's not that bad.'

'Really?' Flicka reached up to adjust the lamp. Scott had retreated to his desk. 'Weren't you the one just asking about all the long sleeves?'

That's when it hit her. Min in the bathroom. The huddle outside. 'Where's it all coming from?'

Flicka had shrugged, still glued to her loupe. 'You're the reporter. You're in the clubs. Maybe you can figure it out.'

THIRTEEN

D rugs and who did what way back when are not what she's going to open with. Tara knows that as she makes the drive out to Medford the next morning. Min's comments have stuck in her head. Peter's too, if she's being honest about it. His implication that she's unrealistic and imma-ture. That she idealized the music world and all its various players. Romanticizes it still, twenty years on.

She tries to shake it off. It's not like she had been equipped to investigate anything back then. She'd been a music critic, writing for a 'zine in an era when cocaine was giving way to cheap brown heroin. When nationwide, smack was moving out of the inner city to ruin the lives of white kids, too, and the hard-partying rock community was fertile territory. No, she's not denying that substance abuse was a problem for too many musi-cians. Too many of the fans, as well. Heroin helped destroy it, her little world. She knows that, even if she doesn't know how it happened, the exact route it took. What Peter doesn't get – never got – was that what mattered to her was the music – well, that and the camaraderie. The family of choice she found, she'd thought she'd found . . .

What was it Nick said? That they were all misfits? Maybe that's why so many fell prey to the drugs or the drink. Why there were so few of them left. She's thinking of the other night, when the Whirled Shakers were playing. She'd been happy then, despite it all. And then she'd heard about Frank.

Was this a mistake? Trying to interview Frank's widow barely a week after his funeral? She shakes her head as she cruises through the unfamiliar suburb, the directions in her lap. It's too late to call and cancel, but part of her hopes she won't find the turnoff. Won't find the blue split level that Neela's daughter and son-in-law, and now her new grandson, call home.

Scott is pushing too hard, and she should have pushed back. In the old days, he'd urge her to try things. Jolly her into stories, like the one on the Fitzhughs, half the time simply because he needed eight hundred words to finish an issue. Though looking back now, she wonders about that story at that time. The guitarist had been working at the Casbah. Could Scott have been angling to get in with Jonah Wells even then? No, that was crazy. Her old friend has simply changed too much. It's not the weight loss or the new clothes. He's bought into the whole glossy lifestyle, and now he's pressuring her to deliver.

She catches a street sign and pulls a hard right, leaving behind the strip malls for a residential area. The subdivision Mika and her husband live in is one of the older neighborhoods. The houses are small, by current standards. But the trees on the street are mature, their shade making up for the peeling paint and cheap siding as she slows to look for a number.

The setting is peaceful, and Tara finds herself musing on how different life must be here. From the tense crowd at Neela and Frank's, after the funeral. From the upscale sleek of Scott's urban roost. From her own cluttered, makeshift home. She should get a cat.

If it weren't for the ambulance, she would have missed the house. As it is, she slows, waiting as two EMTs roll out a stretcher. She can't make out whether the figure being lifted into the back is male or female, but she sees the blanket folded down, an oxygen mask over the face, and feels an almost superstitious rush of relief. That's when she notes the house – blue, with shingles – is Mika's.

'Oh my God, What happened?' Tara pulls up to the curb. Rushes out the door. One tech turns toward her and then back to his partner. The figure on the stretcher is still. 'Neela?'

'Excuse me.' The tech blocks her with his body. Turns back to the house. 'Ma'am?'

A petite brunette is gesturing – her neat pageboy, no-nonsense slacks and blouse at odds with the panic on her face. Her face is white. 'I . . . my baby.' She makes a feeble wave back toward the house.

'Go,' says Tara to the EMT driver, the situation clear. 'I'll take her.'

The tech waits only for Mika to nod in confirmation before climbing in beside the stretcher. In a moment, they are gone.

'Mika, I'm so sorry.' Tara follows the younger woman into the house. Watches as she begins to pack up a bag. Diapers, wipes. 'Can I help?'

What she wants to ask is what happened. Why is Neela – for it must be Neela – in the ambulance? And did she – her questions, her arrival – have anything to do with it?

'Here.' Mika shoves the diaper bag at her as she collects bottles from the fridge. For a small woman, she seems able to hold a lot. She works systematically, checking labels and choosing from among five. In the other room, a baby starts to fuss. 'Oh, honey, I'm sorry.'

Tara follows the young mother into what is clearly a nursery. The yellow walls are bordered with trains and teddy bears. A glossy white crib takes pride of place, before a changing table and cabinet, flannel clothing – blankets, perhaps, or onesies – all looking as soft to the touch as their pastels are to the eye.

Only the industrial-looking scale and a shelf lined with prescription bottles seem out of place. Tara steps toward these as Mika bends over the crib with a coo.

'I know,' she says. 'That was loud. That was scary.' The bottles are for liquids – 'pediatric formulation', Tara reads. The labels all have long Latinate names.

'Thanks for this.' Tara turns. Mika has the baby dressed. Everything is covered except for the round face that stares at Tara with blatant curiosity. 'I didn't want to hold them up, but getting Henry ready to go takes time.'

'No problem.' Tara raises her car keys, the diaper bag over her shoulder. 'Anything else you need me to grab?'

'Oh, I don't need you to drive.' Mika breaks into a smile, as unexpected as a snowstorm. 'I just couldn't go with the ambulance, and you broke the spell, I guess.'

'You sure?' Of course. A suburban mother has a car. She's an adult, with a baby.

'Well, if you wouldn't mind driving my car.' Mika's smile softens her face, with its sharp angles. The short, sharp haircut. 'I'm a little shaken up, I'll confess.'

'Of course.' Tara swallows, wondering what she's gotten herself into. How long she'll be at the hospital. Reminds herself she can afford cab fare. Escorting Mika is the humane thing to do.

Besides, as she follows Mika out to the SUV, this will give her a chance to find out what happened. It's not like she had other plans for the day.

'Mercy,' says Mika, as she buckles herself into the passenger seat. Henry, strapped into his child seat behind her, chortles with apparent delight.

Tara waits, turning to the younger woman. Unsure how to respond.

'Sorry.' The hand to her face doesn't hide Mika's embarrassed giggle. 'Mercy Hospital. On Beacon?'

'Got it.' Now it's Tara's turn to be confused, but Mika gets her started and soon Tara is driving through the subdivision. The SUV is big. Tara feels like she's looking down on the parked cars as she drives by. On the houses and their shady lawns. But it handles smoothly, and soon she's acclimated.

'So, I'm sorry.' She begins with another apology. That seems to be the order of the day. 'But what happened? Did Neela – your mother – did she have an attack or fall?'

'Mom? No.' Out of the corner of her eye, Tara sees Mika look out the window. Sees the muscles in her neck work as she tenses and swallows. 'I shouldn't of . . .'

Another swallow. Mika's long neck would look graceful under other circumstances. Like a swan's. From this angle, all Tara sees is the tension, the sinews shifting through the delicate skin.

'Don's away this week.' Mika shifts to stare straight ahead. The better to talk, it seems. 'With all the time he took off with Henry, he really couldn't say no. He's in sales over at CepCo. And so after Dad – well, it just seemed like a good idea to have Mom come stay with me for a while. I don't know.' She turns toward the side window again. The houses have given way to the strip mall, where she told Tara to make the left. 'Maybe it was just selfish of me, wanting a little help. Wanting to have some normal mother–daughter time.'

Tara glances over. Mika is no longer smiling.

'I knew Mom was in a bad way,' she says. 'I shouldn't have put any pressure on her. I shouldn't have left her. I tried to get her to go to church with me. I thought it would be good for her. I was raised in the church. She and Dad took me every Sunday, not just holidays, and Father Ray – he's a good guy. He's been a rock.' She chuckles. 'Sounds biblical, huh? But really, he's been great, when we thought we were going to lose Henry and then, after I heard about Dad. Don wasn't raised Catholic.'

She turns to face Tara and even with her eyes on the road, Tara sees how she lights up when talking about her husband. 'He used to tell me how square my parents were. How strict.' She laughs again, but it sounds a little sad now, and she shakes her head. 'I told him about Dad being in a band. About how Mom used to dance on the bar.'

Tara glances over quickly. 'Yeah, I heard about that.' Mika is grinning. 'Mom's old friend Gina told me. You must know her, right?'

Without waiting for an answer, Mika continues. 'Right at the light, then you'll see it. Anyway, he knew about my dad being in the program. His father is too, so I guess that made sense. And I like that he doesn't drink either – not really. I mean, he'll have a beer sometimes, with his friends. But it's not something either of us grew up with, and I like not having to explain that. I thought that meant we were healthy. That we'd have healthy babies . . .'

Tara sees the hospital up ahead, but there's a light. She turns and looks at Mika. The young mother appears lost in thought.

'How is Henry?' Since they've pulled out of the drive, Tara hasn't heard a gurgle from the baby in the back seat.

'Oh, he's fine now.' Mika twists to look. 'He loves this car. Thinks his dad bought it for him. But, I'll tell you, it was rough for a while. And I think – I think Mom took it to heart. She blamed herself. She thought, I don't know, the drinking or maybe there were drugs . . .' Tara bites her lip. 'Anyway, you'd have thought that when we got the diagnosis, that would've helped.'

'He has – Fabry's?' Tara struggles to recall what Min has told her.

A vigorous nod. A hand goes up to smooth the hair. An automatic gesture. 'Genetic,' she says. 'Not because his grandpa might've drunk too much or his grandma got wild. Over here.' Mika points and Tara guides the big car into a small lot. 'I got to know this hospital very well, what with Henry and all.'

'I should check and see if they're admitting her.' Mika

is out of the car. She has the back passenger door open and is unbuckling the car seat. 'The EMTs said Mom will probably be kept overnight. I mean, considering her condition, and everything. But she was doing better even by the time they arrived. When I came home, I didn't – I just, you know. You see things on TV and in the movies.'

Tara stands beside the young mother, thoroughly confused.

'I told them, when they arrived.' Mika takes the diaper bag from Tara's hand and slides it over her shoulder. 'I'd gotten her to sick it all up.'

'Sick it up?' She should be carrying something, only Mika appears to have this down. To have everything under control.

'You know, vomit,' she says, over her shoulder. She is walking toward a glass door. The door slides open, welcoming them inside. 'While we were at church, Henry and me. I came home, put Henry down for his nap. I thought she was napping too. And, well, she was. But I'm used to watching people sleep. To hearing them, and something just seemed off. I went into her room – the guest room – and she was just too still.'

Mika pauses. Turns back toward Tara. She looks so young, suddenly. Baby and all. 'It was pills,' she says. 'My mom took an overdose of pills.'

FOURTEEN

The weather should have warned her: the winter thaw ending with a deep freeze that almost kept Tara at home. It wasn't the party itself she dreaded. The Whirled Shakers' loft would be crowded enough so that its draftiness, its general lack of heat, would be a good thing, and Tara knew she'd end up sweaty and red-faced, especially once the dancing started. It was the drive there. The sudden plunge in temperature had frozen the slush into something treacherous, and she knew her old Buick wasn't up to black ice. Even though she'd begun to freelance for the *Dot* – two record reviews and the editor had invited her to pitch a feature – she still couldn't afford new tires. By next winter, maybe. If the staff job that the editor had hinted at came through. If she could keep the Skylark on the road till then.

It was the thought of the *Dot* that forced her out into the cold. She'd already semi-promised Scott that she'd write up the party – the party and the local compilation it was celebrating – for the *Underground*. The Whirled Shakers, easily the best band on it, had recorded a track, and they'd be the natural hook. But the Crudz had a cut too, and she could pitch them as the focus instead, if she had to. She hadn't heard their song yet, but the power trio was reliably high-energy, with a grinding guitar and bass sound that mined deep metal for its gut punch, and this was their first outing on vinyl.

It was a feasible angle, but the truth was, as the new year began, she'd already begun to look ahead of the 'zine. To look to her own future. If the compilation took off and the Whirled Shakers were willing, well, she wanted something really prime to offer the *Dot*. The weekly actually paid. They were the big league.

Tara turned down Thayer and felt her rear tires skid out slightly. Winter sucked, especially in the city, where any fresh snow soon turned black with soot. At least, she reasoned as she fishtailed up the narrow street, it kept the tourists home. Up ahead, she recognized Phil's van and the little Fiat that Katie somehow kept running. The burned-out hulk that served as a street marker was there as well, and Tara slipped ahead of it and parked, close enough to step onto the broken curb and avoid the slushy muck below.

Min was already drunk by the time Tara mounted the stairs. Tara heard her before she saw her, that hyena bark of a laugh topping the noise of the crowd and the stereo both. She followed it across the open space, to find her friend over by the sink. The loft didn't have a real kitchen, although some previous resident had rigged up a small electric stove and a full-sized refrigerator that looked like it hailed from the Eisenhower administration. The fridge was probably on the fritz again, Tara noted, because the sink had been filled with ice, a motley assortment of beers and a jug of wine poking through. A knife lying on the sideboard had already mauled two limes. The tequila bottle lying next to them was nearly empty.

'Tara!' Min turned toward her, wild-eyed. She was slouched against a pimply blond boy, her move throwing her deeper under his arm. 'Have you met Billy? Billy's the best.'

'Hey.' The boy raised his beer, a broad grin on his spotted face. He looked eighteen, at the most. 'Marge was telling me about you.'

'It's Min.' Beer in hand, Min pushed at the boy's chest and left her hand there, steadying herself. 'And I have not. Silly.'

'Uh, hi.' Tara looked around. 'Is Frank here?'

'Frank who?' Min nearly shouting.

That was ominous. Ever since Neela had begun spending more time with Chris, Min and Frank had become an item again – kind of. Tara knew her friend was hoping for more. Hoping for some kind of acknowledgment. She also knew that the stress of the status quo – late-night booty calls as well as Frank's drinking – was taking its toll. Min was drunk or high more often than not these days, which probably explained why she'd ended up pregnant back in November. At least, Tara hoped it was a mistake, rather than some crude effort to trap her man. At any rate, Min had terminated it, with a few curses but no tears that Tara had seen. Not when she'd accompanied her friend to the clinic. Frank had paid for the procedure, at least. He'd done that much, although it had been Tara who sat with her that night, feeding her Advil and Scotch.

Frank hadn't come around since, though, as Min had admitted late one night the week before. Whether that was due to some latent attack of conscience or because of the requisite month of abstinence following the procedure, Tara didn't want to speculate.

This, though, was something different.

'Hey, Min, want to get some air?' Tara didn't like the look of this boy: raw, crude, and way too young. Didn't like the way he smiled, more of a sneer really, as he pulled her friend closer.

'I don't want *air.*' She nuzzled the boy's neck.

'Come on.' Tara reached for Min's arm, only to have the boy pull her closer.

'Lady's made up her mind,' he said, one hand sinking to cradle her ass. 'She's old enough for sure.'

'Fuck off.' Tara didn't know where that came from. Neither did the boy, apparently. He straightened up and began to laugh.

'Your dyke lover's jealous, baby.' This to Min as he began to unbutton her jeans. To Tara, he was more direct. 'Fuck off, bitch.'

'Fuck yourself.' Min pushed him away. Tara would've liked to think that her friend was coming to her senses or even to her defense. More likely, she knew, Min had simply crossed the line, her easygoing drunk turning mean.

'Crazy bitch.' The pimply youth glared at Tara and back at Min and stalked off.

'Good riddance,' Tara muttered as she watched him go, ready to intervene if Min went after him. Her friend was looking pale, however. Sweating more than even the crowded room merited. 'You OK?' Tara reached for her arm to steady her.

'Fuck you.' Min pulled away and stumbled off. 'I think I'm going to be sick.'

'Let her go.' Phil, from the Whirled Shakers, had come up behind Tara. Put a hand on her shoulder. 'She's been like this since she got here. Maybe she'll puke or pass out finally.'

'I don't know . . .' Tara, unsure whether to follow, watched her friend lurch through the crowd.

'She'll be OK,' Phil interrupted, drawing her back. 'There's too many people here for her to do a Spinal Tap. Besides, we're about to play.'

Tara turned from the muscular singer, but Min had already disappeared – into the crowd or one of the few other rooms that had been carved out of the industrial space. With any luck, she'd have managed to get into the bathroom. Phil was right; Min would be a lot better without the belly full of whatever she had ingested. Besides, Tara told herself, she was here on assignment – if not for the *Dot*, not yet, then for *Underground Sound.* She had to look out for herself.

Grabbing a beer, Tara made her way to the front of the room. Phil and the band had already set up, their makeshift stage a mess of jury-rigged chords.

'Thanks for coming tonight.' Phil spoke into the mike as one of his band mates turned off the music and fiddled with the PA. 'As you know, we've been working on a new recording for a while now, a follow up to our hit single. But before we preview the new song, we're going to give you what you really want to hear. So without futher ado, here it is: "*I love you, baby, and that ain't no crime!*".'

The stage was only a corner of the room. The crowd more friends than fans, and more sloshed than sober. Phil didn't care. He grabbed that mike stand and swung it, nearly decking Joey, who was reaching forward to untangle the wires. It was a rough start, but Joey quickly scrambled back behind his set. Grabbing his sticks, he beat out the time. '*One, two, three, four!*' And they were off.

'*If we had world enough, world enough and time . . .*'

Phil was singing his heart out, but Tara couldn't get into it. Some of that was the sound. The loft wasn't made for music, and the band's makeshift set up didn't have the punch of the Oakie's soundboard or even the Casbah's, with its booming overkill. More than that, though, she couldn't stop thinking about Min. As the crowd around her began to dance, she craned around, concerned, looking for her friend.

'Hey, Gina!' Tara shouted, unsure if she could be heard. 'You see Min?'

'*Ain't no crime! No crime!*' Gina took Tara's hand. Tried to draw her into the dancing.

'Min!' Tara yelled in her ear and got bonked in the nose as the other woman began to pogo.

'*No crime!*' The oblivious woman bounced off. Tara retreated in disgust, pausing briefly to fish an ice cube out of the sink – the remaining cans were bobbing by then – and heading into the hallway. She held it to her nose, but then let it drop, adding to the slop on the floor. If she could find Min, she'd make her leave. Take them both to IHOP, if her friend was up for it. Get some food into her. Or just home to her place, until her friend had slept it off.

The first room was a bust. The small bedroom, partitioned off the hall with unpainted plasterboard, was full. But even though there was a sleepy call for her to close the door, Tara took her time. Stared at the bodies lying on the futon, slumped on the floor. The sticky-sweet hash smoke coiled and slid in the draft from the open door, but Tara knew there was more at work here. Still, no Min. She shut the door behind her and moved on.

The bathroom was no go. 'I have to pee!' A leather-clad woman with spiked hair was banging on the door, one hand grabbing her crotch. 'Open up!'

'You know who's in there?' Tara asked the next woman in line, a chubby girl leaning against the wall.

'One of the guys from the Exiles.' She rolled her eyes. 'Guess he and his girlfriend made up again.'

A gust of cold air made Tara turn. At the end of the hallway, that scrawny bartender from the Rat had opened a window. He leaned on the sash as he pissed into the alley.

'Man, I envy guys sometimes,' the chubby girl said. Tara nodded in agreement, but there was no time to talk. The open window made her nervous. Min had been so dark lately. Frank. The abortion. Hurrying back up the hall, she eyed the front room. The Whirled Shakers had moved onto the new song. The room was packed and throbbing. Hanging by the wall, she worked her way up to the door. The loft was a fire hazard but, right then, she feared worse.

'Min!' She started calling as soon as she got outside. It must have been fifteen degrees out. Colder. The loft was three stories up. 'Min?'

She found her one floor down. Saw her crumpled in the corner of the landing and almost cried with relief. 'Min!' She ran to embrace her friend. Who hadn't jumped. Who hadn't, it seemed, OD'd.

But Min was bleeding. Her pink leather jacket, crumpled in her lap, was slick with blood and as Min fussed with it – reaching for a pocket, for a sleeve – the blood smeared on her hands. Spread to her face.

'Min, what the fuck?' Tara grabbed her friend's hands, tried to make her stand. 'Did that bastard hurt you? What happened?'

As she pulled Min to her, she heard the clatter. The wood-handled knife, the one by the limes, fell to the floor. That was when she saw Min's arms. She'd turned back the cuffs of her shirt to make four cuts across the underside. All were red, one was leaking blood. It dripped on Tara's boots.

'What the fuck?' Tara didn't wait for an answer. Pulled her own jacket off and bunched it against the wound. Looked around for something better. 'I'm going to get you to a hospital.'

'No, no hospital.' Min shook her head, woozy but awake. 'I can't – no hospital.'

'The hell you can't. Hold this.' Pressing her friend's hand onto the balled-up leather, Tara pulled her shirt over her head. It was soft – flannel – and as Min absently dropped the jacket, Tara took her arm and wrapped the shirt around it, binding it tight to stop the bleeding.

'No, really.' Min shook her off. Started to pull back. To reach for her own jacket. 'I – school. I have – shit. Shit on me. I can't.'

Tara got it. 'What are you on, Min?'

'No, I'm fine. I'll be fine. I didn't – didn't have the nerve.' Min licked her lips and looked up at her friend. Her eyes seemed focused, but Tara couldn't be sure. Those cuts.

'Honest,' Min sniffed. 'It was stupid. Really. I didn't – I drank too much is all. Look, the bleeding's probably stopped.' She held up her arm. Tara couldn't see through the makeshift tourniquet. Then again, no blood had seeped through.

'Min.' Tara couldn't find the words.

'Let's get out of here.' Her friend managed a smile. It was weak, but the effort gave Tara hope. 'Look, let's go to my place and I'll show you how to fix me up. Nursing 101. If you think I should go to the ER after that, I'll go.'

It was a plan, and Tara nodded acquiescence. Min wobbled a bit but made it down the last two flights and over to Tara's car without help. Tara kept one eye on her, though, as she drove.

'I'm sorry.' Her friend's voice was little more than breath. 'I didn't mean to – not like that.'

A movement caught Tara's eye and she glanced over to see her friend gathering up her jacket. Fiddling with the door handle.

'No!' she yelled, hitting the brakes hard. The car squealed to a stop as the passenger door swung open, and she reached for her friend, getting a handful of the pink leather Min had wadded in her lap. With surprising strength, Min jerked it free, nearly falling out the open door as she did. And as Tara slammed the car into park, Min's body convulsed and she doubled over, spewing vomit onto the street. Reaching for her friend, Tara held her shoulders as she heaved, until finally nothing was left, and she could draw her friend back into the car.

'Thanks.' Min's voice was barely a whisper. She raised one hand to wipe her mouth. Tara waited, unsure what to do. Reached into the street to retrieve her friend's pink leather.

'I'm OK now.' Min's voice was clear, if soft. She took the jacket, dirty now, and folded it into her lap. 'Just tired.'

'You pass out on me . . .' The threat was clear.

'Just drive, Tara.' She closed her eyes. 'Please, just drive.'

An hour later, Tara was breathing easier. Min did in fact show her how to apply a butterfly bandage, which she used to close the deeper of the cuts. That Min could demonstrate this, as much as her willingness to be bandaged, seemed major.

'If I'd been serious,' said Min, beginning to sound more like herself again, 'I'd have done something else. Something that wouldn't hurt. I'd just float away . . .'

She stopped there. Tara stared at her friend, too alarmed to ask.

Min avoided her gaze. Stared, instead, at the chair, where her jacket – blood drying brown on the pink leather – lay crumpled. As if a silly fashion statement – 'ironic', indeed – held the answer. As if that thin leather armor could protect her from pain. 'Besides, if I'd meant it, I'd have sliced up the arm,' she said at last, looking down. Drawing her finger along the vein to illustrate. 'See?'

'Great.' Tara slumped back on the sofa, exhaustion taking hold. She dozed, she must have. When she opened her eyes, Min was gone. 'Min?' Panic rising in her throat.

'In here.'

The voice, from the bathroom, sounded normal. Sounded like Min. And anger began to replace the fear, the fatigue. Tara turned on her friend, barking at the door. 'What the fuck were you thinking of, anyway?'

'Hang on.' The sound of running water. 'I'm sorry about your shirt, Tara. If I can't get it clean . . .'

Her voice died out, and Tara jumped up. Pushed the door wide to find her friend leaning over the sink. The tap running cold. 'Don't worry about the shirt,' she said, reaching to turn the water off. Min's head was hanging down, but Tara didn't think she saw the flannel, or the water turned red. A drop broke the surface. Min was crying.

'Min, what happened?' Tara's fury dissipated as quickly as that drop. She put an arm around her friend, waiting. She didn't – couldn't – understand.

'Frank.' The one word, sobbed, explained everything. But Min wasn't done. 'He's proposed. He wants Neela to marry him.'

'But . . .' Tara shook her head. 'No,' she said. 'Neela's with Chris now.' It wasn't the answer Min would want. Then again, it was the one she'd been living with – making a life around – for months by then.

'He doesn't . . . he doesn't care.' Min began weeping in earnest, her body heaving for breath. 'I'd do anything for him. Anything.' She broke off, unable to talk. 'He wants . . . he wants to marry her.'

It still wasn't making sense, and as Min's sobs grew more violent, Tara realized there was more to come. 'Min? Honey?' She held her friend as her body shook.

'She's pregnant.' Min heaved out the words. The ones that hurt her most. 'She's pregnant, Tara. And she's going to keep the baby.'

FIFTEEN

She calls Min while she waits. There's no one else, really, who will understand. Not that her old friend is particularly sympathetic.

'You're kidding, right?' Min sounds busy. Tara shouldn't have called. But she can't shake the fear that her call, the pending interview, is what pushed Neela to try to take her own life. 'She'd do herself in because of *City*?'

'Well, it had to dredge up a lot of old stuff.' Tara isn't trying to justify herself – or inflate the importance of the glossy monthly. She feels culpable. 'And I know we'd end up talking about Frank. Frank and Chris both.'

She bites her lip. It was wrong to call the widow so soon. To get her thinking about her relationship with her husband. About how badly she treated him, back when things were still new.

'Oh, come on. She'd have loved it. Those were her glory days.' Silence. Tara can't argue. 'Besides,' Min picks up again, 'it was only a matter of time.' Tara can hear the rasp of smoke in her voice.

'Min.' Tara closes her eyes. Her head has begun to throb.

'I didn't mean it like that.' Min has the grace to sound embarrassed. 'But that girl was always looking for oblivion, one way or the other.'

'She's not . . .' Tara stops herself. Not a girl, she had been going to say. Not the golden dancer, the wild child. Not anymore. 'Not an addict,' she says finally.

'Abstinence is the flip side of addiction.' Min sounds like one of the posters on the waiting room wall. Mika has gone in to be with Neela, leaving Tara out here, alone. Middle of the day on a Sunday, and the ER is quiet. Even the TV, high in its wall mount, is set on mute. Then again, in a suburban hospital like this, maybe it's always quiet.

'Oh, come on.' It's been a stressful morning. Stressful weekend, come to think of it, and Tara is in no mood. 'Her husband was the one in AA.' She speaks without thinking – without considering. *Husband* is one of those words for Min. 'I mean, she was just supporting Frank.'

It won't help. She knows that. Tries another tack. 'And, I mean, we were all a bit wild, back in the day.'

Does Min even remember that night? Could she have been drunk or high enough that she didn't even recall the blood, the way they talked until dawn. The fact that she had had to wear long sleeves to her nursing classes for almost a month? Min nearly got kicked out of the program, Tara recalls, though that might have been more about the drugs than the suicide attempt. Something had gone missing, she remembers. Someone had pointed to Min.

'A lot of fuss over very little,' Min had said at the time – Tara had been worried – and nothing was ever proved. As if that would make it right.

But Min is speaking again. High on the wall, women are drinking wine and laughing.

'We all fooled around, sure.' Min bites down on her words, as if to make them shorter. 'But Neela? She was into it big time. Loved riding the horse, that girl.'

'Min . . .' Tara catches herself. Her friend is mourning, too.

'Hey, you know what happened to Chris.' Min's on a roll.

'Yeah, but . . .' Tara thinks back. Min, Frank, Neela, Chris; it all happened so fast. Changed, almost overnight.

'What do you think they had in common?' Min's voice drips acid. It could have been yesterday, Tara sees, as far as her friend is concerned. Above her head, the women have stopped laughing. The wine is gone. 'Did you think it was love?'

Tara did, actually. Or something close. The rock star and the dancing girl were the scene's golden couple, enveloped in an aura of happiness and success. Or so Tara thought back then – has long thought. After she and Min hang up – 'My advice? Call a cab. You need to hang out there like, well, like I need another man.' – she finds herself reevaluating. Even discounting Min's bitterness, she wonders if those days were exactly as she remembered. Chris and Neela inseparable. In love.

And, she recalls, oblivious to the effect their affair had on others.

Was it the night the suit from Atlantic showed up, pushing his way past kids half his age to claim a space up by the stage? Or was that particular jerk from Warner? Tara can no longer be sure. She can picture the short, fat man, stubble heavy in the lines of his face. He'd flown up from New York, despite a threatened snowstorm. Late December, the holidays looming, and he'd come in person to check out the hot new talent his local A&R scout had reported. Had stayed up half the night to catch the Aught Nines, who were headlining at that point. The Casbah – the biggest place in town, in terms of capacity, though still a hole compared to the theaters and stadiums the real stars played.

This suit was only the latest to come courting. Rumor had it he was the biggest, though, with the power to sign an artist on the spot. Scott had pointed him out, over by stage right, arms crossed as if he were accustomed to standing next to a mosh pit after midnight.

'I hear he's got a signing bonus in his pocket,' Scott had said, yelling into her ear to make himself heard. 'A grand and a gram.'

'That almost rhymes,' she'd shouted back, a little surprised. That local DJs indulged, she had no doubt. When she'd gone up to the local so-called 'alternative' station to interview the Slushies, she'd seen the smear marks on the mirror, everyone sniffing and blinking like she had brought a spotlight in with her. They'd invited her to join, too, offering to lay out the rest of what the music director had provided. She'd declined, softening her words with a laugh. The Slushies were a power trio riding high on the *NME* charts and apparently anything else the industry would provide, and she didn't want them getting the wrong idea. Thinking that she was another tidbit to be shared around. She could joke about that by then.

But New York? Somehow, she thought at that level, dealings would be more professional. Maybe the difference was that the suit provided, but he expected something more openly commercial in return.

He certainly didn't look high, as he stood there, arms crossed and waiting for the headliners. He was patient, she'd give him that. The Aught Nines were dragging it out, pushing the club up against the old Boston blue laws that would shut them down at two, whether the headliners had performed or not. The room was hot, and he had to have been uncomfortable. The storm had never materialized. The thaw was still on, her boots soaked through from the slush. But it was the crowd that raised the temperature: excited and in constant motion.

Except for Chris Crack. She can still see him, lounging by the door to the Casbah's office. From there, he could see the stage. See the fat man in the thousand-dollar suit as he waited, staring at the empty stage. Chris didn't seem to care. He might as well have been at some Allston house party as a sold-out rock club. The way he leaned against the open door frame, his lace-edged tank hiked up to show some skin. His head lolling back against his upraised arm as if his career wasn't on the line. And then Neela had appeared, coming out from the room behind him to drape herself over his lanky form. She could see Chris's lips move, his head bob as he jerked his chin to point out the suit – or maybe the empty stage beyond, the biggest of any club in town. They both laughed. The spectacle must have looked ridiculous to a boy from the suburbs. To a girl who danced on the bar. Tara lost sight of them when they ducked back inside.

When Chris next appeared, a velvet scarf loose around his neck, it was on that stage. Half past one, almost an hour late, he sauntered up to the mike like he owned it. Like he owned time. And when the band kicked in – Jim's guitar growling like a feral cat – he alone resisted the beat, the throb. He alone felt a deeper pull, something slower, strong and tidal. Hanging onto the mike stand, his caterwaul outmanning even Jim's guitar, Chris Crack was in full rock-star mode. Languid and sweating, his bare midriff snake-belly white, he was every woman's dream and every mother's nightmare. Tara knew at least one straight man who confessed to confusion over his desires from that night on, and from stage left she could see the bright, febrile desire in the eyes of the women. Even the suit responded, nodding his head to the beat. At some point – 'Boy in a Bubble?' that other song? – she saw him reach inside that fancy jacket. Was he making sure he had his checkbook? Had the coke? The glint in his eye was cool, the faint smile as welcoming as a shark's. It didn't matter that the club cut them off after five songs. That the house lights went on and the crowd began to boo. Didn't matter if they wrecked the place, Tara remembered thinking. Didn't matter what the suit offered, or whether the band even signed. Chris Crack cemented his status as a rock god that night.

Looking back, Tara tries to remember Neela, where she would have been during that short set. Not on the bar – the Casbah wasn't Oakie's, wasn't the Rat or Jack's. Brian ran a tight ship – Jonah still showed up most nights. The suit, the looks, and the bouncers quick to act. Besides, Neela was royalty then. Backstage more often than in the room. Waiting for Chris. Waiting. And what else?

No, Tara shakes her head. If Neela was doing more than drinking. More than the occasional snort of coke or, yeah, maybe something stronger, she didn't know it. Min is talking out of jealousy. Out of her own store of memories – how the powders changed. How the high evolved. That slouch? That laughter? That could have been anything. Besides, within a month, Neela would be pregnant. Maybe already was, and married soon after. And Chris? As quickly as Chris Crack had appeared on the scene, he was gone.

'Tara!' The voice calls her back to the present. She turns. Sees the young woman with the familiar smile, only darker. Younger. 'I can't believe you're still here.'

'How is she?' Tara sees something in the younger woman's face, but she wants more. 'Your mother?'

'She's fine.' Mika closes her eyes. Breathes. 'She's going to be fine. Turns out, she didn't take that much. She probably would have slept it off. Only . . .' Another deep breath, and her body visibly relaxes.

'I'm so glad.' Tara feels her own rush of relief and blurts, 'And I'm so, so sorry,' she says. 'I mean, maybe if I hadn't called . . .'

'No, no.' Mika raises her hands. She's laughing. 'It wasn't that you called. Honest. It's Dad.' Another sigh, this one sad. 'She misses him, obviously. She's lost it, a little bit. She seems to feel responsible.'

'But she wasn't there when he fell.' Her words cause the younger woman to start back. 'I'm sorry,' she says. 'I have no filter today. I guess – I heard they were doing an autopsy.'

'No, no.' This time, the demurral is quieter, less upbeat. 'That's what she's said. She was out back. The garden or something. And, yeah, the police.' Another chuckle, softer this time. 'The law's a bitch, isn't it? If only she'd said she was in the kitchen, that would be the end of it. She could have told them what happened. At least, they didn't hold up the funeral.'

'Yeah, really.' Tara finds herself wondering. What are they doing? Testing for alcohol? For drugs? 'Your son!'

It's more an exclamation than a question, but Mika gets it. 'He's fine. He's asleep in Mom's room. I only came out to see if you were still here. And to thank you.'

'Please.' Tara means it. All she's done is step in it today. 'If I helped at all, I'm glad.'

'You really did, and I'm grateful.' Mika clearly wants to return to her son. To her mother. 'I'm sorry you didn't get to talk to Mom. She'll call you, I'm sure, as soon as she's – well, as soon as she's gotten her feet under her again.'

'Please.' Tara knows she sounds like a broken record. Repeats herself anyway, trying to get through. 'Please, Mika, tell her not to worry. Tell her I send my best.' She thinks of Min. Of Scott, even Peter and Nick. 'Tell her we all do.'

SIXTEEN

It hadn't been that late when she'd gotten home. The whole
episode had taken less than two hours. It had left her at loose
ends, though. She couldn't call Peter, not till she was ready
to apologize, and that was a pattern she'd promised herself she
wouldn't fall back into. Min was out too, and work – well, work
was work. She'd made a few calls for the story, knowing her
lunch with Scott loomed. Set up a meet with Jim from the Aught
Nines. Left a message for Gina. Didn't even want to listen to
music after that. It all felt so loaded, freighted with memories
she could no longer trust. She'd stayed up too late watching an
old movie, half wishing that someone would call.

She's paying for it today, her head muzzy despite all that
coffee. Despite hitting snooze one too many times. And of all
the days to get such a summons: Rudy, the VP, wants to talk.
She'd gotten the message as soon as she'd settled in, twenty
minutes late despite ditching her usual T ride for a frantic cross-
town drive. At first, she thinks someone has seen her, mug in
hand, tearing into the lot. The interoffice message marked red
for its urgency. She'd closed her eyes, wishing it gone. Wishing
herself back in bed. But when she opens them, it's still there,
blinking, and although she has no desire to read it, she decides
against deleting it. Better not to touch it at all. Better to leave
no prints.

Instead, she reaches for her phone. Calls AV and tells them
she'll be down in five. What was it Peter had said? That the
police were looking into Frank's death? From him, she had
learned a bit about investigations, that it was harder to clean
something up – harder and more likely to implicate the bad
actor. On that theory, she leaves her office. Leaves the blinking
message unread and sorts through photos for an hour. The
general manager wants a new head shot for his website profile,
and he's old school enough to insist on prints. Bill, the photog,
is fun to hang with. He has his own little realm downstairs,

electronica playing softly and big prints of his dogs hanging at odd angles.

He figures out that she's hiding soon enough. 'You OK, Tara?'

'Monday.' She gives him the universal answer, but he has the grace to look worried as she finally takes her leave, five of the best prints in hand. 'I'll make him choose one of these,' she says, attempting to deflect. 'I'll tell him they all make him look beautiful as sin.'

His eyebrows go up at that. She'd been thinking of Chris. It had been Scott who had called him that, but she'd used it. He was good that way.

And so she doesn't cancel lunch. Feels grateful for it, actually, when she sees Rebecca, standing by her door as she returns from Bill's lair. Worry furrows the secretary's brow despite the bun drawn painfully tight.

'Mr Hughes has been trying to reach you,' she says. It's her job, as departmental secretary, to convey such messages. To make sure they are received, and Tara feels bad.

'I'm sorry.' She is. 'I got caught up in the whole photo thing.' She raises the folder, as if presenting evidence, but the other woman doesn't respond. It could have been the hair, freezing her face like that. 'I'll give him a call,' she promises.

Door closed, she finally reads the message. It is ominous. The quarterly report has problems, it says. Mistakes. He wants her to come by at the earliest available. He'd sent it at eight-oh-three. Without giving herself a moment to think she messages back, explaining that she has a lunch appointment. That she'd be by as soon as she returns, and then she heads out.

The devil you know, she tells herself again. At least she cares about this story. About her old friend. Only how well does she know Scott anymore? What kind of devil is he?

'A suicide attempt.' Scott takes a bite of his salad and chews, thoughtfully. Mulling over her news as well as his food. 'Interesting.'

'I guess.' Tara is distracted, her appetite gone. She'd been dreading this lunch with Scott anyway. This morning she considered cancelling, even when she got his voicemail about making lunch special, about reservations at Brasserie Zou. Probably should have. She thinks about the situation at work.

The report. She's not ready for Monday, not even her dull as dishwater job.

'I mean, it kind of makes sense.' Tara talks to fill the space. To distract herself. She can't read Scott's reaction at all. 'Losing Frank and her grandson being sick. It's a lot.'

Scott eats and manages to look pensive at the same time. Careful. A far cry from the man she remembers. The old Scott would close his eyes in ecstasy as he inhaled a pizza. 'I guess the interview is off,' he says at last. 'Can you get anyone from his old band – Last Call?'

'I spoke with Onie.' She feels uneasy. 'But I don't know if we should go that way. I mean, maybe the Aught Nines should be the focus. I'll be talking with Jim tomorrow, and then Gina.'

'Gina!' His face lights up. 'That's right! She was at the funeral. Gina being Gina.'

'Pretty much,' Tara admits with a grin. 'Did you two . . .?'

'No.' His exaggerated expression says it all. 'Did you?'

'Me?' Her voice squeaks. It's embarrassing. 'No. Objectivity, remember? We stayed above the fray.'

'Whatever.' He tilts his head, a twinkle in his eye. 'But I think you've got to keep Frank's death in the story. Otherwise, it's old news. Frank gives it pathos, ties it all together. I mean, he married Chris Crack's old girlfriend. Became a father, then a grandfather, while Chris . . .' He stops talking. Takes another bite of salad. 'I really wish you could talk to her.'

'Maybe I can.' She hates herself a little, but she can't resist. 'Mika – her daughter – said to give her a few days. I'll talk to Jim and to Gina. Get more background.'

'That's my girl.' Scott's beaming now. 'I always knew you had it in you.'

'Whatever "it" is.' She finishes their old refrain. Picks up her burger with renewed appetite. The place may have a French name, but they know their American basics.

'So what's the deal with this Nick?' Scott's question catches her with her mouth full. 'Are you going to be talking to him again?'

She swallows hard. Hopes he doesn't see the tears that spring to her eyes. 'I don't know.' She shrugs and reaches for her water glass. 'Not sure he's that central to anything anyway.'

'He ever work at the Casbah?'

'No.' Her voice is once again under control. 'Why, did Jonah say something?'

Scott shakes his head. 'I don't think he knew him. Except for his own club, Jonah wasn't that into the scene. He remembers Chris, of course. But . . .' Scott's face is unreadable. Bosses. Tara waits until he leans forward, his voice dropped to a conspiratorial pitch.

'Jonah's why I think you need to keep Frank in the picture. He's been leaning on me. Says the focus is tired, that it's stale. That he didn't bring me in to rehash my glory days.' Scott pauses, shakes his head. Suddenly, Tara realizes there's a reason for the fancy lunch. For the reservation.

'This wasn't a treat,' she says, putting it together. 'You didn't want me coming into the office.'

'It's not you,' he says. 'He's the one who's been bringing up objections. I reminded him of our agreement. That if I could get the edit board to agree with me, I could overrule him. And they still love it – as long as it comes up to the present.'

'Hey, I don't want to be responsible for you losing your gig.' They both know publishing by now. They both know publishers.

'I don't want to lose it either.' He's still leaning in. Still talking low, but that hint of a smile is back. 'So you better do a kickass piece for me, Tara. I'm counting on you.'

In a strange way, hearing about the pressure is a relief. Tara still feels uneasy about the story – about the new Scott, as she's come to think of him. Knowing that he's worried about his job, that he's pushing back against the *City* publisher, explains why he's leaning on her. Plus, she's picking up on his anxiety, she figures. On his desire to make his mark. Set his boundaries, without losing his job. Besides, his faith in her is flattering. She leaves the lunch on a high that even her two iced coffees can't explain. She's ready to get back to work.

On the story, that is. She's so preoccupied with it – with Scott and *City* – that she almost forgets her own workplace drama. She's thinking she'll call Jerry. See if she can line up an interview with him for after she talks to Jim, as she walks in. See if Onie can put her in touch with anyone else – maybe someone who

was at the Casbah that night. Maybe Katie . . . Only when she
sees Rebecca standing in front of her office does she remember
Rudy. Rudy and the memo.

'Tara.' The dark-haired secretary clasps her hands. Wants to
wring them, Tara can see. 'Mr Hughes has been calling for you.
He's—' her voice drops to a whisper – 'he's very upset.'

'Thanks, Rebecca.' She takes a breath. Steels herself. Opens
the door.

Her office is empty, and she almost falls in with relief. Relief?
She can't fool herself. Part of her wants to get fired. To get out
of here. She has to recognize that. Own it.

She takes a seat and another deep breath. Tries to remember
her process.

Back when she and Peter were splitting, she'd gone to therapy
briefly. It had been his idea, though she'd been willing enough.
Wanting something to stop the constant ache, the confusion. To
make the world make sense.

The shrink had been OK, a nice lady. Suburban. She'd pointed
out how passive Tara was being. Like a turtle withdrawn into
her shell. She called it dysthymia – a mild, persistent depression.
Tara kind of liked the idea. Why shouldn't she withdraw from
a painful and confusing world? But she'd bought the idea that
her movements should be conscious. Should be her choice. The
therapist had given her breathing exercises designed to help her
be more aware. For a while, Tara had kept at them, though now
she can no longer remember the last time she tried. Clearly, she
has fallen back into her old habits.

So now she takes a moment. Takes a breath. Does she want
this job? She visualizes a chalkboard. Two columns outlined in
white. On one side, she'll list the plusses – the reasons to stay.
The first item that comes to mind is the pay. It's been nice not to
worry about money. Not to have to ask Peter for cash, like in
the old days. Almost immediately, her mind flips to the opposite
side. She'd never really wanted this gig. Hadn't been seeking it,
or anything like it. Might never have even known about Zeron
if Peter hadn't pushed her toward it. Sick of supporting her, she'd
figured at the time. It's not like there are any newspaper jobs out
there, not anymore. Though if she can nail this piece . . .

A deep breath. Cleansing, brings her back in focus. She's not a pinball, pinging around reactively. It's her life, and she decides. She'll do what she can to salvage the situation. It's a good job, if not one she wants. But she will continue to put energy into the article. 'Be open to opportunity.' Had her shrink said that or had Peter, back in the day? Maybe it was a fortune cookie.

She laughs at herself, at the predicament she's gotten herself into. At the silly process – breathing exercise and all – and picks up the phone.

'Rudy, I'm so sorry.' Voicemail, but she sits up straight, remembering that client who talked about phone voice. 'I've been tied up with the brochure photos. Please let me know when I should come by.'

She hangs up and looks at the clock. Checks her cell for the numbers Nick gave her. Greg, the Aught Nine's drummer, should be around. Nick said he'd set up his own shop. Contracting and construction, working in his old neighborhood.

'Condor Consulting.' The same gruff voice, maybe a little deeper.

'Greg?' She smiles. Wants him to hear that in her voice. 'It's Tara, Tara Winton.'

'I was wondering when you'd call.' An exhalation and she pictures him leaning back, his belly as round as a bass drum, most likely.

'Sorry.' She's tickled. This is how it used to be. 'I've been slow getting started on this one, but I've been meaning to call you. Would you have time to talk this week?'

She reaches for a pad. Looks at the week ahead on her desk blotter calendar. If she speaks to Jerry tomorrow . . .

'To talk about the old days? The Aught Nines?' She catches herself. His voice is off. Too high, too tight. 'About Chris Crack?'

'Well, yeah.' Something is wrong. She needs to reel this back. 'But about all of you. All of us. The scene.'

'Let me guess.' There's no denying the sarcasm in his voice. 'You're going to finally figure it out. Solve the case of who killed Chris Crack.'

'No.' She's shaking her head. Forgets he can't see her. 'No, I'm not . . .' She remembers the rumors. There were always rumors. Especially with someone as handsome and talented as Chris. 'That's not the story.'

'Cause I have no desire to live through that bullshit again, Tara.' He spits out her name like he remembers her all too well. Like he remembers an old grudge. 'Chris was a sick guy. Always. He was weak. His girlfriend had just dumped him, in case you don't recall. And, yeah, he had a habit. But he was my friend, OK? I'm not going to help you dig him up, all over again.'

She sits there, holding the phone, even after he cuts her off. At least with cell phones, there's no more angry slam. This used to happen, she remembers, after a bad review. She's gotten soft, she realizes, here in her cozy office. Does she really want to go back to those days? Does she have the energy for the rough and tumble of journalism – for the anger?

Her desktop phone lights up. It's Rudy, most likely. Or, more likely, Sally, the executive secretary, sent to make her do cartwheels in penance even before they talk. She sits up straight once more as she reaches for the phone. Shoulders back, head up, as she readies herself to apologize and more. But even as she fixes a smile on her face, one she knows will be clear in her voice, she can't help but wonder at what Greg has implied. That cold night, way back when – could Chris Crack have committed suicide?

SEVENTEEN

Maybe Greg did her a service. After his spurt of nastiness, Rudy is a teddy bear. Yes, he does make her wait by Sally's desk. And, yes, he does express his extreme dismay – his words – at the monumental errors that have managed to get into the report. Something about last quarter's conclusion, following on this quarter's numbers, Tara knew she'd been playing fast and loose with her files.

'I understand that the quarterly report is important, sir.' She keeps her voice soft, her tone deferential. She doesn't need a therapist to know how to placate an angry boss. 'I will, of course, redo the report immediately. In its entirety.'

Because, ultimately, no harm has been done – no real harm, if she doesn't count the black mark on her reputation. The report hadn't gone to press yet, and that as much as her deference and her apologies are what probably save her job.

'You know, we all knew you were going through a rough time a few years ago.' Her boss stands, pushing himself out of his leather chair – not to see her out, she understood, but because he had better places to be. Because he is done with her. 'We thought you were past that, Tara.'

He scowls at her, his eyebrows bristling. 'I very much hope you are.'

'Yes, sir.' She ducks her head, almost a bow, and resists rolling her eyes even as she leaves, knowing that Sally is looking on, both in concern and in order to gauge her own next interaction with her boss.

Back at her desk, Tara takes a moment. Stupid, really, what she did. Five minutes to re-read the opening paragraphs, she would have caught the errors. Ten minutes checking and she'd have retained her halo as the golden girl of Zeron.

Golden girl? Maybe not, from what Rudy said. Maybe they've noticed her lack of interest – no, her utter disengagement – from the job. It isn't fallout from her divorce that's distracting her. It was her marriage that had brought her to the firm in the first place. Without Peter's urging, she never would have interviewed for the gig. Never would have heard of it, probably, and certainly never would have ventured into the latest incarnation of the waterfront, the old warehouses replaced by gleaming high-rises. The Innovation District, they call it, in the latest rebranding. As she calls it, every time she refers to her employer in print. So much for street cred.

She spends the next two hours rewriting the report. Re-typing, actually, as much penance for being so careless as to make sure she doesn't cut and paste any errors back in. After checking, she goes for coffee. The break room falls silent as she enters, and she knows word has spread.

'Hey, it's not like I killed someone.' Her voice sounds too loud for the small room. Too chipper even for the lemon yellow walls and the bright orange chairs. Margie from Legal ducks her head and turns away.

'All righty, then,' she says as she leaves, more to buoy her own spirits than because she expects any response. This is what happens when you hold yourself aloof. When you still call it a 'day job' after five years. In the silence, she hears Peter's reproofs. Wonders, not for the first time, if maybe he – if maybe that therapist had been right.

She is active. She does have control. At least of some things, and for the rest of the day, she dives in. Scott isn't the only one to praise her writing, and Rudy had been in charge of hiring her. At some point Rebecca sticks her head past the door, knocking gently on the frame.

'You're the last one here,' she says, that neat bun nodding. She seems to approve. 'Should I do the alarm?'

'No.' Tara manages a smile. Team building. 'I'll undoubtedly forget it's on and then set it off. Besides, who's going to break into a building in the Innovation District?'

That comes out snarkier than she intends. 'I mean, I feel safe here. I'll set it when I leave.' Rebecca relaxes at that. Score one for Team Tara. She hears the other woman's heels as she crosses the lobby by the elevator. Hears the whir and hum as the lift whisks her away. And then she gets back to work.

In truth, it takes two more hours. This stretches to three, as she makes herself slow down and check a source. Even with breaks for coffee and the bathroom, it is not an insurmountable task, and she reminds herself again of how foolish she has been. How lazy. If she leaves – when – it will be her choice. And with that in mind, she steels herself for one more read-through of what has become eye-crossingly dull.

But first, a break. Her chair leans back, and she puts her feet up. Considers music, and decides to deny herself a little bit longer. She should put off Jerry, she decides. Eat lunch at her desk for a day or two, just for show. She looks at the clock – not yet eight – and reaches for her phone.

'Jerry?' Voicemail, and now she's having second thoughts. 'Tara here. Would you give me a call?' She leaves her cell number, in case it's not apparent. Leaves the office number too, before she hangs up.

When her phone rings ten minutes later, she grabs it. 'Jerry?'

'No, ah . . .' A chuckle, half embarrassed. 'Nick.'

'Nick.' She can feel the smile forming. 'How are you? I got the horse.'

'The horse? Oh, yeah.' Another laugh. 'Yeah. It told me I didn't appreciate it enough, and so . . .'

The silence is more cordial than awkward, though Tara is grateful he can't see the warmth rising to her cheeks.

'So how was your weekend?' She's the one to break it finally. She is, after all, an adult. 'Your kids?'

'Oh, lord.' She can picture him, leaning back, his eyes closed. 'It was – well, they're getting used to the drama, I guess. And Jack, especially, can be a handful. They're good kids, though. I've got to give them that.'

She likes how he doesn't talk about his ex. Doesn't blame her or the boys.

'Anyway, that's sort of why I called.' He sounds back on track. 'I was wondering if we could make up for that lost dinner? We could grab a burger, or I could even grill.'

Suddenly Tara is hungry. 'Wow, that sounds great. I mean, either, but I'm stuck here tonight. I'm still at work. Zeron.' She allows a note of scorn to slip into her voice. Surely, Nick will understand. 'I kind of screwed up, and so I'm trying to make things right.'

'Good for you.' He sounds serious, just when she kind of wishes he wouldn't.

'Maybe I could play hooky.' She's bad at flirting, always was. 'I could be talked into it.'

'No.' He's not playing along. 'I'm not going to help you hurt yourself.'

Or is he? 'I wasn't . . .' She stops, the edge of an idea tickling her mind. 'Hey, Nick, do you mind if I ask you something?'

It's an odd question. Leading, and she realizes she's stalling. Trying to figure out how to put her thought in words.

'I don't – no, I don't mind.' She's put him off. There's distance in his voice.

She doesn't care. 'Someone said something to me today. About Chris Crack.' She pauses, waiting for him to remember. 'Do you think there's any chance that his overdose was intentional?'

'Do I think . . .?' Caution has tightened his voice.

'I mean, could it have been suicide?' There, the word is out. 'I mean, he did have a song called "Hot Shot", after all.'

'Suicide.' He exhales into the phone. 'Well, I'd never thought about that. I don't know, Tara. Do you really want to get into all of that again?'

'It's kind of relevant to the story.' She hears him withdrawing. Feels it. 'Don't you think?'

'The story.' Another sigh. 'Yeah, maybe. But – I don't know, Tara. I just don't know.'

The call ends soon after, without any further talk of a rain check. It surprises Tara to realize how this disappoints her, and she consoles herself by thinking of the little carving. By thinking that he called.

The invitation has another consequence, one that's less easy to dismiss. She's suddenly famished. It's been hours since that lunch with Scott. All the coffee she's had since has done nothing but sour her belly. The need for food is medicinal, she tells herself. Primal.

But she's so close. She hears Nick's voice in her head – the serious one – as she wakes her computer to review the copy one more time. Only after she prints it out to read and redline a paper copy – underlining every fact to check against her source material – does she finally send it, along with an email apologizing once again. Nine thirty-seven, she notes with satisfaction. If Rudy doesn't notice the time stamp on the file, maybe he'll see it on her email and know she's done her penance.

Gathering up her jacket and bag, she heads toward the door. The building is quiet, the dim whir and hum of machinery the only accompaniment. For a moment, she imagines herself an intruder. A tourist in a world of computers and printers, much like she was once a tourist in the clubs. Was once? Maybe it's Greg. He shook her up. Maybe it was lunch with Scott, remembering how he labeled them both outsiders. Now she's sorry she isn't seeing Nick tonight. Maybe she'll call him when she gets home. Maybe he'll come over.

Distracted, she nearly walks out without setting the alarm, catching herself as she reaches for the door. It wouldn't do to leave Zeron unguarded overnight, would it? She almost laughs. The whole area is dead at night. Quiet as a grave. But she's going to be a model employee, at least for a while. Punching in the code, she has a moment of anxiety. Then the beep-beep-beep starts, and she races to the door. She's out before it reaches the thirty-second warning, but she double checks anyway. The big glass doors lock behind her, the flashing light now a steady red on the panel off to her left.

Talk about paranoid. Tara can barely hear the traffic from the Pike, six blocks away. She's heard the same rumors as everyone else – that the café by the corner is applying for a liquor license. That it's going to open for dinner by the new year. She doesn't believe it. Ever since the developers leveled the last of the old warehouses – the artists' complex with that good pizza place that had been here for years – the area's been dead after five. The company parking lot, a nice perk but not essential with the T only three blocks away, makes the area even more of a wasteland. In fact, if she didn't have to walk by it, she might have forgotten that she drove in today, running late and in a rush. She looks around. Her car is the only one left.

At least it's under a streetlight. One of those unnaturally bright halogens, though something is wrong with the bulb. It's buzzing, for starters, like it's about to pop or blow out in a shower of sparks. And the shadow is wrong. Too dark, too low, as if her car had been flattened to the pavement.

Unless – damn. She stops in her tracks, twenty feet from the Toyota. It's not the light. Her tire is flat. The car is resting on its rims. Two tires, she sees – front and back. She closes her eyes in exasperation. Tries to remember what she's done. What she missed in her mad race in this morning. Surely, there was glass somewhere or a curb she scraped in her frantic rush. Had she been that out of it? Given herself a slow leak that only now has made itself apparent?

Is there . . .? She walks around the car, dreading what she'll find. A dent. The long scrape of exposed metal. Blood.

What she sees is almost worse. The tires on the other side are flat, as well. Completely, their rubber puddling out around the rim like some cartoon. She stoops to examine the one closest – driver's side, front – under the streetlight. Puts her hand up to confirm.

Someone has slashed her tires.

EIGHTEEN

She does what anyone would. She calls AAA.

'Hi,' she says, when a woman on the other end identifies herself. Her voice sounds tight, even to her. Unnaturally high, as she gives her number, the street address of Zeron, and her phone. 'I need a tow – or, no, what do you call it? A flatbed to come pick me up?'

'Would you state the nature of your problem, ma'am?' The voice on the other end doesn't sound any younger than she is. Still, Tara is embarrassed. She's too old to get into this kind of predicament. 'Is it mechanical – engine trouble – or a tire?'

'It's my tires.' She's grateful to have the words.

'Do you have a usable spare?' The woman is reading a script.

'Yeah, but that won't work.' Tara stands. Looks up at the buzzing light. 'It's all four of my tires. They were – I think someone slashed them.'

The silence on the line makes her pause. Did she sound too dramatic? Is that what actually happened? She looks back at the car, at how low it sits without air.

'I'm sending a truck right away.' She can hear the woman typing. 'Are you someplace safe? Is there somewhere you can wait? We'll call you when our truck arrives.'

'No, I'm fine.' The last time she called for a tow it had been midwinter. One of those frigid nights. The air tonight is cool, but not dangerous.

'Look,' the woman starts talking more quickly. She's left the script behind. 'I don't know what your situation is, but if someone slashed my tires at night, the first thing I'd worry about is does someone want me stranded out there alone. The truck is on its way, but do you want me to call the cops for you? You shouldn't—'

'No, no, I'm on it.' Tara stops her, embarrassed by her lack of judgment. 'You're right, of course. I'm calling them right now.'

'Good.' The woman's voice emphatic. 'And, honey? All our tow drivers carry AAA ID. You make sure he shows you his before you get in any truck with anyone, OK?'

The cops, when they show, are less dramatic.

'At what time did you park the car?' The older one, with an accent from south of the city, is going over her report again. 'And you didn't check it, like when you went out for lunch or anything?'

'No.' She shakes her head before stopping to think. 'No, I walked to the T. Took the T to lunch.' It could have been a year ago. 'I was meeting a friend who works downtown.'

'The driver's ready to go,' says the other cop. He's been talking to the tow driver. Tara assumes he's done all the identity checking that's necessary. 'He can take it to police impound, if you want.'

They look at her. 'No, please.' She raises a hand as if to block the idea. 'I mean, it's not like you're going to dust it for fingerprints, right?'

'Not likely.' The older cop breaks into the faintest smile. 'A car in an open lot like this? Left here all day? I bet half your co-workers probably passed by. Maybe your boss, too.'

'Oh, lord, no.' She hides her face in her hand, as if Rudy could see her. Could see this mess. Feels the headache starting. Hunger. The long day. 'Can't I just have it towed to the garage near my house?'

The two cops exchange glances. 'Suit yourself,' says the older. 'We'll have the report on file, if you need it for insurance.'

Insurance. She nods. She'll need new tires. At least she has the money.

'And you can't think of anyone who has a grudge against you?' The younger cop sounds concerned, or maybe he's tired too. 'You haven't made any enemies?'

'I work in corporate communications, writing quarterly reports.' It sounds dull, even to her. 'I'm amicably divorced. My ex and I get along great. I don't . . .' She stops. Considers, and then rejects the sliver of an idea. 'No, no enemies.'

'Maybe it was kids, then.' The older cop is looking at her like he sees something. She stays silent. 'Or they got the wrong car. If you think of anything, you let us know.'

'I will.' She nods. It's an effort to talk at all. 'Thank you.'

Another glance between the two policemen. 'That's all then.'
The older one smacks the flatbed's hood twice. 'Hoist her up!'

She calls Peter, almost by reflex, the moment she gets in the door.

'Wait, what?' He interrupts before she can finish. Before she
can explain why she was working late, why she drove at all.
'You walked from Iggy's?'

She closes her eyes. Breathes. The whole point of having her
car towed to the local garage is that it is local – three blocks
from her apartment. They know her there. Know her car. 'Of
course.' She's trying to hold her voice steady. Hears the tremor,
the slight breathlessness. She ran, after all, more spooked than
she cares to admit. 'I mean, I'm home now.'

'Tara, someone slashed your tires. Someone targeted you.'

'It may have been random.' She tries to remember what the
older cop said. 'Besides, that was over by the waterfront. Not
here.'

'I'm coming over.' She can hear him moving about. Imagines
him grabbing a jacket. Looking for his keys. 'Lock the door,
will you?'

'It's locked, Peter.' She hears the peevishness that has crept
into her voice. Can't believe she called him; can't believe she
was afraid. But since she did . . . 'Hey, one thing?'

He grunts. She can tell that mentally he's already out the door.

'Would you stop by Emma's? I'm starving and it's too late to
have them deliver.'

She's on her second slice before he can start with the questions.
The first one, she inhales, only vaguely aware of him talking.
Ranting, really, about corporate responsibility. About Zeron's
culpability for what he is calling 'the attack'. He's been frightened. She knows that. Knows he doesn't like feeling helpless.
Doesn't like that he wasn't there, and so she lets him vent,
knowing he'll settle down faster if she doesn't interrupt. Besides,
by the time he shows up, the adrenaline has worn off, leaving
her shaky and weak. She's starving, and the smell of the pizza
hits her like a drug.

'It's this stupid article.' He's eating, despite his anger. He could always eat. 'Not that I expect the cops to get anything. Who'd you speak with? I used to know a few guys at that precinct. Timilty, or no—'

He's reaching for his jacket. For his phone, when Tara realizes she has to speak up.

'I didn't.' Her mouth is full. She pauses. Chews. Swallows, all the while the horrified comprehension dawns on Peter. 'I mean, I did talk to the cops.' She pauses to take a drink. At least she had beer in the fridge. Wipes her mouth. 'I just didn't tell them about the article. They asked if I had any enemies, and it didn't seem relevant.'

She shrugs and goes back to her pizza, which seems to upset Peter more.

'Tara, what the fuck?' He's got a focus for his anger now. 'I told you they were investigating Frank Turcotte's death.'

'Yeah, but that's not what I'm writing about.' Years ago, his tone would have riled her up. Would have her oscillating between anxiety and rage. Kind of like he is now, she realizes. 'I'm writing about the past. About the scene.'

He ignores her. 'Who have you interviewed for this piece? Who did you speak to last?'

She finishes the slice, chewing slowly to give herself time to think.

'Come on, Tara. Someone wanted to scare you, at the very least.'

Peter is like a dog with a bone, she knows that. Plus, he did come over when she called. Min would call it capitulation. Min was never married.

'I've spoken with a few people. Most of them really quite happy to talk.'

Peter snorts in disbelief.

'No, really. It was nice to reconnect with Katie and with Onie.' Tara is warmed by the recollection, but Peter knows her too. He can see when her smile falters.

'What?' He questions her almost before she realizes what has changed. Fear – the idea of scaring her. Fear made her call him, after all.

Could *Peter* have done it? No, he wouldn't. Not after Saturday night.

'Well, Greg Burdick was kind of a jerk.' She gives him that, to buy herself time. 'But he just didn't want to talk.'

'Who else?' That doggedness. His years as a reporter. She knows he hasn't moved on, simply noted one name and is waiting for the others. 'Come on, Tara,' he says, when she doesn't respond immediately. 'Maybe it was random, but maybe not. Maybe someone wanted to scare you – or maybe someone wanted you stranded out there. Alone. Who else did you talk to?'

He's grilling her like a husband. She thinks of Nick.

'Tara?'

'Nick Linbert.' She turns away. Doesn't want him to read her face.

'Nick who?' He sees something.

'You don't know him.' She shakes it off. 'He was a bar back. Someone I knew.'

'A bar back where?' He's leaning in. 'What club?'

'Peter, about Saturday . . .' She's not a kid anymore. She needs to talk this out.

'Look, I get it.' He bites down on the words. 'That was a stupid idea, but I'm not talking about us anymore. I'm talking about you – about your safety. About what you might have blundered into.'

He's jealous, and he doesn't even realize it. She feels – sympathy. Annoyance, and, above all, fatigue. This has been an exhausting day.

'Peter, look.' Suddenly she can barely keep her eyes open. 'I appreciate what you're doing. Really. And coming over with the pizza—'

'Tara!' He's practically shouting. 'Will you listen to me? This is serious. This isn't some punk kid getting pissed off because you ragged on his band. I don't know who you got to or what nerve you touched, but you've got to stop it. You can't just blunder blithely into two open investigations for some feature story.'

'Wait.' She puts a hand up. A confused crossing guard desperate to counter the oncoming traffic. 'Two?' He knows about Nick, she thinks. He has no rights over her, and so he's projecting. Confused. 'You mean one. Frank Turcotte's the—'

'I mean two.' He's almost spitting. 'That rocker. The skinny guy – what was his stupid name? Chris Crank?'

'Chris Crack?' She's lost. Awake but lost. 'You didn't – you barely knew about him. Don't tell me you're one of the people who thinks he killed himself?'

'Suicide?' He stares at her, mouth agape. 'No, I mean he was murdered.'

'Don't you remember?' He's looking at her as if she were a child or, no, a disappointment. An ex-wife who has forgotten the past. 'That was my story. My lede. That's how we got together.'

'Yeah, that's right.' She nods. The story had been insignificant, at least in terms of everything else that had been going down.

It was late February. Must have been. She remembers shrinking into herself from the cold. That her first big splurge was those warm boots.

'Nice boots.' Scott had noticed them right away. Had he known what they meant?

'Thanks.' She'd looked down, discomfited by his words. Not praise – not exactly. The boots weren't pretty. Big and thick, years before Uggs would become a fashion statement, they were waterproof and lined. And for the first time that winter, her feet had been neither damp nor cold. Even if they did look gigantic.

It wasn't his implied criticism of her stylistic choices that made her flinch, though. And after several minutes of working quietly, side by side, he finally broke.

'So you got it.' He wasn't looking at her boots. Wasn't looking at her, at all. 'The job.'

'Yeah.' Tara reached over. Took the straightedge and lined up the photo. When she reached for the X-Acto knife, he barked out a short, choked laugh.

'What, you think I'm going to hurt myself?' He'd turned as if to take her in, all five-eight of her in her leather jacket and fancy new boots.

'You know Raspberry is a stickler.' She didn't look at him, either. She was focused on the flat before her, giving the record store ad more attention than it needed, finicky customer or no.

'Yeah.' He sighed. 'I don't know how I'm going to get this rag out without you, Tara.'

She paused to look at him, realized she was blinking back tears. 'I could still help out.'

'And steal all our scoops?' He turned away, back to the flat, his own voice suspiciously hoarse. 'Besides, the *Dot* is a sweatshop. They'll be running you ragged.'

She already had an assignment – an assignment and an impossible deadline. She hadn't wanted to tell him. Hadn't wanted to not show up, to help paste up one last issue. Instead, she finished the ad. Collected herself.

'I wanted to thank you,' she said, as soon as she could trust herself to speak. 'If you hadn't pushed me – made me write. Made me apply . . .'

'Bullshit.' He sounded like himself again. 'You were always a writer. I was just smart enough to get you to work for free before you figured it out.'

The next day, she started work. Not paste up – not anymore – but as a staff writer, with a desk and everything. The everything including, apparently, Peter.

'May I help you?' She came back from orientation – forty minutes of form-filling with HR – to find him at her cubicle, head bent over – yes – her review.

'Tara Winton, right?' He looked up with a grin. Tall and surprisingly boyish looking, he dressed so square she had trouble seeing him as a colleague. Khakis and button-down shirts were the province of an older generation, or so she had thought. But he was her age, or maybe only a little older. And he knew her name.

'Yeah?' She thought back to those forms. Had HR said someone from management would be speaking to her? He was cute, in a straight way. 'I mean, may I help you?'

'I hope so.' He brushed back those bangs in a move that would soon become familiar. 'I'm hoping you can take me out. Introduce me around the rock clubs.' Her surprise must have registered on her face. 'I'm Peter.' He held out a hand. 'Peter Corwin. News. I'm working on a piece about drugs in the clubs, and I'm told you're our new girl on the music beat. That you can hook me up.'

NINETEEN

Things were moving so swiftly, it all jumbles together in retrospect. Some things she knows for sure. She took Peter out that night. The Exiles were playing and she wanted to go anyway. To celebrate her first day on the job. She'd told him to meet her at ten. That she'd be at the upstairs bar. She hadn't said anything about his clothes. She didn't know him well enough. And besides, surely he'd figure it out.

She remembers Min laughing. Pulling her aside. 'Your date's here,' she'd said, the words slurring.

'He's not—' Her protests only made it worse. Peter had changed the khakis for jeans, the button down for a worn-out sweatshirt, the logo faded to indecipherability against a blue-grey background. Still, he looked too preppy – too clean – for the scene. 'Look, he's a reporter. He's on a story.'

'That's what he's calling it?' Min's voice had an edge, an archness that made Tara squirm. The night of the knife had been a week before, maybe two. They didn't speak of it, not since then, but Tara could feel the change in her friend. A new hardness. As cold as the winter. 'My, these creative types sure are . . . creative.'

The drugs, the booze. Tara didn't want to argue.

'He wants to meet some regulars. You know, musicians. The folks on the scene.' She remembers Min's eyes, unnaturally bright. Piercing. 'You want to talk to him?'

She offered her new colleague up like a sacrifice.

'Me? No way.' Min laughed, the demon appeased. 'He's all yours, my friend. He's just your type.'

It wasn't just the drugs. That laugh. 'You seeing Frank again?' Tara worked to keep her voice light. Min hadn't mentioned Neela since that night. Hadn't mentioned Frank or a pregnancy either.

Min's smile, her shrug confirmed it – confirmed something, anyway. 'We're talking about you, Tara. Hey, your future husband is waiting.'

She remembers that. The way he peered over the heads of everyone at the bar. Looking for her. It made her feel connected. Important, maybe. Responsible, at least.

'Don't book,' she'd said to Min. 'I want to introduce you. You and Frank.'

'Right.' She'd laughed. 'Anyway, Frank's working. The Cash Bar's giving him some shifts.'

It might have been that night. It's hard to remember now. She'd taken Peter out a few times that week, a few the next. She had a beat now, an editor who expected a story a week. Min had ducked out that first night, she was pretty sure. But before long, she had introduced Peter around, and he'd managed to get some of the regulars to talk. Brian, who'd left Oakie's by that point for the Casbah but who still came around on his nights off. Katie, who'd been hanging with Phil.

It was Katie who first made her realize that Min was right. That she at least wanted this clean-cut reporter to notice her.

'Your friend knows a lot about the clubs.' They'd been at the Rat, at the upstairs bar. Peter just back from going off with Katie to talk, the blonde taking him downstairs to someplace quieter for a good half hour. Not that Tara was timing them.

'Katie? Yeah.' She watched as the blonde climbed the rickety stairs, rejoining Phil, who now stared over at Peter. 'She's been with Phil for ages.'

'She has some ideas about what's going on.' Tara kept her eyes on the other couple. Didn't want Peter to see her face. 'About the drugs.'

'What?' At that she turned. 'What drugs?'

He looked at her as if she were a child. 'The heroin. Don't tell me you didn't know.'

'Don't be silly.' She raised her hand in protest. Shook her head. Suddenly, it seemed important that he not view her as naïve. 'I know – there's a lot of smack floating around. More than there used to be.'

'Damn right.' Peter leaned in. 'No one knows who's bringing it in. Or no one who will speak to me anyway, and I've got my connections.' His voice dropped lower, and he leaned in so close that Tara could feel the warmth of his breath. 'There's some scuttlebutt that someone's going to talk. Going to give up the connect, but I don't want to wait. I want the story before the bust.'

'There's going to be a bust?' Tara swallowed. Min only used at parties. If someone was holding. Someone always was these days.

'So I hear.' Peter's eyes glittered. His breath yeasty from beer. 'Somebody didn't get paid or had a beef. That's usually what happens,' he said. 'Someone on the scene. That's why I wanted to go out with you.' He stopped, as if hearing his own words. 'I mean, one of the reasons. The initial reason, Tara. I mean, besides spending time with you.'

Was that a week after Min's breakdown at the party? A month? Yes, it had to be. February dragging on, and Min acting foul, secretive and unhappy. But maybe she'd sensed something going on. Seen how Tara was changing, even before Tara herself knew it. That night, Tara invited Peter up to her apartment, after he'd driven her home. What he'd said – the way she'd felt when she'd seen him with Katie – outweighing any scruples she had about a workplace romance.

'Fuck it,' she'd said, when she'd called Min at home the next day. 'It's not like it means anything.'

'Yeah, right.' Her friend knew better. Sounded better, too. 'Meanwhile, I've got some news of my own.'

'Oh?' Tara looked around. Thursday morning, and the arts department was empty. She'd only gotten up this early because Peter had. 'Frank?'

'I'm not hearing wedding bells yet,' she said. 'No lullabies, either, if you get my drift.'

'Neela's not pregnant? I thought she wanted to keep it.' Tara knew better than to pry, but her own disclosure seemed to prompt sharing.

'Who the hell knows?' Or maybe it didn't. Min certainly didn't sound like she cared. 'All I can tell you is she's spending time with Chris again. Maybe she got rid of it. Maybe it's his. Maybe there never was a baby in the first place.'

'Well.' Tara heard voices over by News. 'That would make life a lot simpler.'

'No shit, sister.' Min was getting up. 'Hey, I've got to run.

You going to the Casbah on Saturday? The Aught Nines are doing a surprise gig. A makeup for that shit show before the holidays. Last show before New York, they're saying. Frank will be on the door.'

'Maybe,' she said, already wondering if Peter would want to go. If Peter would want to be with her again. The way things turned out, it hardly mattered. That was the show that never happened.

'You never did get that story, did you?' It's after midnight. The pizza's gone, and Tara is lying back on the sofa, half asleep.

'There was no bust.' It was a non answer. He was sensitive about that. 'The snitch bailed. Or disappeared.'

'That's right.' She'd been so busy back then, Peter's concerns had faded into the background. What with everything that happened, the editor had wanted a special issue – her first cover – on the rise and fall of Chris Crack. By the time it ran, she and Peter were seeing each other regularly. 'I should have remembered.'

'No reason.' He sounds sad. He's remembering too, she thinks. 'But there were no busts, and now here you are, asking questions.'

'For a feature.' Her eyes are closed. 'On the clubs. The music.' She can't keep having this conversation.

'You've got to tell the police about what you're working on.' He's repeating himself. He hasn't moved. 'You've got to tell them that it wasn't random. Wasn't some kids.'

'We don't know that.' The long day, the fright, the hunger . . . all she wants is her bed. She could ask him to stay. It might be easier.

'Well, you shouldn't go in tomorrow.' He knows her. Stands and reaches for his jacket. 'It's not safe.'

'I have to.' Tara rouses. Rubs her face with her hand as she gets up to see him out. She hasn't told Peter about the screw up. Doesn't need the lecture. 'We're . . . I'm on a deadline for the quarterly report.'

He nods. She's saying the right things. Sounding corporate. 'Yeah, well, keep in mind that someone knows where you work. And these people you're asking questions of – they're not the cream of the crop.'

'G'night, Peter.' She's leaning on the door.

He pauses, and when she looks up, she can see that he's worried. That the worry lines are permanent now.

'Peter?' She's too tired. Not thinking. Doesn't want to think. He turns, his face so sad it could break her heart, and she reaches for him. For his hand, and she pulls him back.

It's comforting to have him there. Companionable. But even though she wakes enough to want him, to want the release, she finds she can't sleep afterward. His presence, after Saturday, is too confusing. Either that or the pizza is keeping her awake. She's not twenty anymore. Not even forty. And as her ex-husband lies there, snoring softly, she finds herself revisiting the early days of their courtship. Thinking of Peter, and Min and Frank. Of Chris Crack and the scene, and how it all fell apart.

They heard the news like they always did back then. Someone talking in a club. In the shadows of the ceiling, Tara pictures Oakie's, the way it used to be.

'Did you hear about Chris?' Gina, always wanting to be part of the story. Then again, she'd been hanging around with the Aught Nines.

Tara remembers looking over at her. Seeing . . . more of a mess than usual. 'He's signed with Epic?' It was what everyone assumed would happen. She'd told her editor to expect an announcement at the show on Saturday.

'No.' Gina's voice dropped away, breathless. 'He's gone.'

'Gone?' She thought of the gig. The time spent in New York, LA. 'Where?'

'No.' Gina shook her head. '*Gone.*'

It hadn't made sense. Tara didn't believe it. Chris Crack was on his way. Headlining the Casbah that weekend. Signing, everyone said, and then on the road.

Only he wasn't. He was dead at twenty-eight. Killed by the heroin he loved so much. A hot shot, people were calling it. Just like the song. There'd been an autopsy, Tara remembers. But the verdict had been what most expected. Chris Crack had died from the drugs, alone in his apartment. The needle still in his arm. Not that the heroin was pure. The street drug had been cut – 'stepped on', the word had been – with something stronger. Something to give a user his money's worth. Odds were, it wasn't anything he hadn't had before. But maybe after his stint in rehab, it had been too strong for his emaciated frame to handle. Maybe after some time away, his resistance had gone down. However it happened, it had been too much.

She'd written the story – part appreciation, part reporting – and it cemented her status at the paper. And with her star on the rise and Peter's momentarily dimmed, they'd found an equilibrium too. They'd kept seeing each other. Moved in to his place, over by the Fenway. Gotten married. As the clubs started closing, it had seemed like the way forward.

The morning is easy. They have a routine. The smell of coffee wakes her. Groggy still, she makes her way into the kitchen.

'Here.' He hands her a mug, done up with milk and that fake sweetener she likes.

'Thanks.' She takes it. 'Peter, I was thinking . . .'

He tenses. Even with his back to her, she can see how his shoulders rise, waiting for the blow. She rushes to fill the gap. Pity, but also curiosity.

'About your story, you know, back in the day.' The coffee is good. Stronger than she makes these days. 'You never found out who the snitch was, did you?'

'No.' He draws the syllable out, waiting.

'But you think it was Chris Crack? Or, that's what you thought, right?'

'I couldn't prove anything.' He leans back against the sink, relaxed. 'And none of my sources would go on the record. All I know is it was someone in the rock world.'

She drinks more of the coffee. Tries to make what she remembers fit. 'But why would he? Why risk it?' The question isn't really for Peter, although he answers.

'Maybe he made a deal. Maybe it was part of getting clean. Maybe he was ready to start a new life. Ready to move on.'

She thinks about Neela. About Frank and Min. 'Maybe,' is all she says.

TWENTY

Thanks to Peter, Tara is in early. He gives her a searching look as he drops her off. 'Tara.' She sees him holding back. 'Think about it.'

'I will,' she says, although she's uncertain whether he's talking about his own suit or calling the police. She has no thoughts to spare for either, though she's grateful for the ride. She's at her desk when Rebecca comes in, that line of worry still creasing her brows.

'It's Mr Hughes.' She looks like she's ready to apologize. Like she wants to say something. 'Calling *himself*,' she whispers, like it's a scandal. 'On line four.'

'Thanks, Rebecca.' She reaches for the phone, gives the poor woman a smile, and turns away. 'Good morning.'

'Tara!' The VP shouts in her ear. 'Glad to see you're up and at 'em. Got the revision you sent last night, too.'

'I'm sorry it was necessary, sir.' Rebecca has retreated, but Tara resists the urge to roll her eyes. She needs to sound serious. 'I hope to make it up to you.'

'It's not me you need to make it up to.' The VP is still yelling. He's on his cell, Tara realizes. Outdoors. 'I'm off as soon as this is published. I'm forwarding it to graphics now. But when I'm back, we need to have a heart to heart, Tara. And you need to do some thinking about where you see yourself in five years. About whether Zeron is really the place for you.'

Tara makes the right noises, but she still feels bruised by the time she hangs up. *No*, she wants to shout. This isn't where I want to be. But she's not a kid anymore. She can't just pinball around.

She's about to call Peter when her phone rings. This time, the call is direct – Rebecca doesn't announce it – and she picks up, grateful for the distraction.

'Tara Winton.' She's closed her eyes. She could use a nap, if Rudy really is out of the office.

'Tara, it's Greg.' At that she sits up, alert for the threat, the danger. 'I wanted to apologize for going off yesterday. I guess I'm still sore – and with Frank gone . . .' She doesn't respond. Barely relaxes. 'I'd like to talk – you know, set the record straight. I mean, if you still want to interview me for your story.'

'Yeah, sure.' She reaches for a pad, a pen. 'Are you still free for lunch?'

'Yeah, I can be in the Seaport area around one, if that works for you.' She picks the café at the corner. He knows it. Of course he does, she thinks. He's a contractor, and this whole area is a work site. Not to mention that the waterfront was part of Southie – South Boston – long before it became the Seaport or, God help us, the Innovation District. Greg's Boston Irish. If he didn't grow up here, he probably knows tons of folks who did. And he knows full well where she works, too.

It's not an easy morning, and the lack of sleep doesn't help. When she talks to the garage, she balks at the price. She needs brake work, and the tires aren't salvageable, Ed, the owner, tells her. They've been punctured – stabbed rather than slashed – all the way through. It's not that she can't pay it – all that money in the bank. Only when did tires get so expensive? She and Ed reach a compromise, finally, but neither ends up happy.

'You can pick it up before we close,' he says, and hangs up.

With Rudy out, she expects some of the pressure to be off. Only word has gotten out that she's on probation of a sort. That she's being watched. She can almost feel the eyes on her as she walks to the break room. She retreats to her office and, in a break with decorum, closes her door. Only then does she see that she's missed a call: Nick. His voice is warm.

'Hey Tara. Hope you made your deadline,' he says. It's enough. She closes her eyes, leans back. Nick. Peter. Min is right. She can't keep fucking her ex-husband. Not even when he rescues her from a jam. Not if she wants to move on.

She calls him back, gauging her fatigue, and is almost relieved when she gets his voicemail. 'Hey, Nick,' she pauses. Wonders how much to tell him. 'Thanks. I made it, but it's been crazy.' She stops herself before she can say 'call me'. He's a grown man. She's an adult, too. She feels better when she hangs up.

Not so much better that she wants to work on Zeron copy today. It's not the company's fault that she needs four new tires, but she resents the place anyway. Resents the scare Rudy put in her. Besides, she tells herself, if she's going to meet with Greg, she might as well work up some questions. Her interviews thus far have been way too casual. More reminiscing than digging up facts.

She spends the next hour reading. She starts with her old stories, the ones she archived on her website when she heard the *Dot* was folding, before she realized she'd stay so long at Zeron. They were good, she decides, with a faint flush of surprise. Sure, she had some unfortunate tendencies. Too many quotes, for starters. And the buzzwords of the day – from post-punk to psychedelicized – recurred way too often. How does a guitar 'chime', anyway? And did she really use 'thrash' as a noun, adjective, and verb in that profile? But these are the sins of youth. The foibles of deadline writing in what was essentially a hothouse environment, where everybody shared the same fifteen descriptors like cold germs.

She pauses before opening that final Chris Crack piece. In retrospect, it doesn't read that much different from her *Underground Sound* work. Maybe the *Dot's* punctuation is cleaner. Maybe that's the typeface. By comparison, the 'zine pages she scanned in look pockmarked and cheap. What comes through, though, is the emotion. Not only hers – Scott had taught her to scoff at the idea of journalistic distance, of fake objectivity – but those of everyone she interviewed. People had loved Chris, loved the Aught Nines. She reads that now and she remembers how fresh it all was. How young they were.

She flips back to the *Underground Sound* pages and her first write-up of the band. Yes, it was all there, between the lines. She'd described how skinny he was. How pale, and she'd referred to the controversy about authenticity. At the time, it had seemed so important. Now she reads about a group of club kids looking for a savior, and a sickly suburbanite who happened to catch their eye.

No wonder Frank couldn't compete. None of them could, and Neela was probably lucky that her old flame stuck around, waiting. And with that, Tara gets it – the tickle of an idea. She switches over to the present day, to her interview notes, as skimpy as they are. To the questions she'd typed up, sitting by Peter on the couch. The memories she'd recalled. She's looking for the theme – the through-line – that will tie the article together. The motion from here to there.

What she finds isn't enough for a piece, not yet, but maybe it's enough to start with. To build on. There was a community, she finds, and she had documented it. A ragtag coming together. And while it existed before and after in a shaggy, adolescent form, there was a year, maybe two, when it coalesced into something magical both in terms of the artistry and the fellow feeling.

Reading back now, she can see. The elements that created it also tore it apart – the eccentricities. The pushback against convention, and the drugs. But maybe that's part of the story, the underlying tragedy. In this narrative, Chris Crack and Frank Turcotte epitomize opposite ends of the spectrum. Chris was the outsider, the wild genius who burned bright and flamed out. Frank was the neighborhood boy, along for the ride. The one who survived – until he didn't.

Tara starts jotting – lines and arrows, linking one idea to the other. Noting the gaps. The holes she needs to fill. When she's done, she sits back. Taps her pen on the pad and thinks about what she's just read. It's a story, sure, but is it enough for Scott? There's no edge here. No spark. Should she work in the rumors? That Chris Crack had killed himself or been killed by some darker force than addiction? If it weren't for Peter, she'd dismiss the idea. Nobody likes an accident, especially when the victim is young and popular. Only Peter wasn't some conspiracy theorist. He was a journalist back then, a good one, and he'd been on a story. He'd had it from good sources that someone was going to talk.

She laughs and pushes back from the desk. Wouldn't it be something, she thinks, if after all these years, she's the one to finally finish her ex's investigation?

'Hey, Peter.' She gets his voicemail too. Tuesdays are his meeting days. The corporate quadrille, he calls it. 'Do you still have your contacts from the clubland story? I know it's been years, but . . .' Her voice trails off. There is no exception – no counterintuitive reason. She wants to figure out what happened, that's all.

*　　*　　*

Greg is seated when Tara enters. He's leaning back, holding a hot cup on his belly, and looking out the window. His face is grim, though it's possible age has set it that way, and Tara finds she has to buck herself up a bit to approach him with a smile.

'Hi, Greg.' She walks up. Reaches out her hand. 'Thanks for meeting me.'

'No problem.' He puts the cup down. Pushes himself up using the table for leverage, and Tara lets her hand drop to her side. 'Before we start. I want to make some things clear.'

'Of course.' She puts down her bag, takes her recorder out. Clearly, this isn't going to be a companionable lunch.

'First, I don't know why you're digging this shit up again.' He glowers, then looks down at his coffee. 'I mean, the man's got family. Think of them.'

'Chris Crack?' She remembers his parents, or at least some mention of them. 'His folks are still alive?'

'Don't you even . . .?' Greg's voice sinks to a growl. 'Two sons, they lost. And you, like a vulture or a leech or something. Fucking clueless. Look, I said I'd talk to you, because I know you're going to write this anyway. And I care about a lot of it. The music. What we did. But you can't act like Chris was supposed to be something other than a normal guy.'

'He was a big deal.' She won't be intimidated. 'I mean, he wanted to be a star.'

'What Chris wanted . . .' Greg pushes back from the table. Looks away. 'Look, he had something, all right? Something everyone wanted a part of – and that crazy girl. She didn't help.'

'Neela?' Tara thinks back on the timing. 'You mean, because she chose to get back with Frank?'

'Chose. Shit.' He shakes his head and Tara waits, unsure what the big man before her means, when a thought hits her. So obvious.

'You mean, she married Frank because Chris wouldn't marry her?' The timeline fits. 'Was Chris the father?'

He shrugs. 'Maybe, who knows? Though there was talk that Frank knocked her up on purpose. Make her settle down.'

'He must have known. Suspected, at least . . .' Tara does the calculations. The repercussions.

Greg has no time for that. 'Look, Chris didn't want a baby.

Who did, back then? But he'd have come around. Made a good dad, even. She was the one who didn't care.'

'So, she didn't want the baby?' Tara can't help it. She thinks of Min.

'Didn't act like it.' He scowls. Anyone else, Tara would ask – he must have children of his own. 'God, she was a terror.'

'I didn't know.' Her mind reels. If Neela didn't want to have a child, she could have had an abortion. It was easy enough. There weren't even protesters back then, before the backlash. The clinic shootings.

Greg laughs. It's a joyless laugh. 'You were always clueless. About Chris, about Neela. Shit, that bartender – the one who was so sweet on you? He could've clued you in.'

'Wait, Nick?' She doesn't remember. He has to be wrong.

'You should've asked him about Chris and Neela. He could've told you some stories. Look, this was a mistake.' He pushes his chair back. It grates on the tile. 'Chris, shit.' He's shaking his head as she stands. As he turns away. 'The kid didn't have a chance.'

Tara doesn't feel much like eating, but everyone is watching. The other patrons turn away as Greg lurches out, and Tara's cheeks are hot as she approaches the counter.

'Turkey club. To go.' The counter man nods and turns away.

'Are you all right, dear?' A voice beside her. An older woman, her face pale and drawn despite her rose-red lipstick.

'Yeah, thanks.' She summons a smile for reassurance. 'I'm . . . researching an article. I'm a journalist.'

The woman shakes her head. 'That's no job for a nice girl,' she says. 'Not with hooligans like that around.'

Tara's smile widens. Greg is a businessman. One of the successful ones. 'You're right,' is all she says.

TWENTY-ONE

I t's funny how they never talked about family. As if the only way to be was to have created oneself anew, out of whole cloth, in the world. Her own parents never understood why she did what she did – staying in Boston. Becoming a journalist. They weren't crazy about Peter, either – he'd made the mistake of talking politics with her father. But at least, once he'd married her, they'd stopped nagging her to move back.

Now that so many of them were parents, those strictures had loosened. Or maybe it had only been her family that turned inward, afraid of the world their daughter sought to join. Onie had spoken fondly of his mother, of how she'd supported him in his band days. And Chris Crack?

Back in the office, Tara does another search – this time for Chris/Christopher Kantrowitz, instead of Crack. This time she gets a hit. Chris hadn't been famous, not yet, not in the wider world by the time he died. But drug casualties had already begun to pile up. The *Herald* took that angle – 'Dead Too Young', the headline reads – and Tara clicks through. But there's no story. Only a photo and a caption. His name, a street address in the Fenway, and a date in March, twenty years before. The basics of a crime scene report, nothing more.

The grainy black and white shot doesn't show her much. An empty apartment, a mess. Whatever money Chris had earned – been promised – he certainly wasn't spending it on furnishings. The couch in the background is shredded, the stuffing poking through. The table before it is littered with styrofoam cups, one spilling out ashes. Cigarettes smoked down to the butt. There are no drugs to be seen. Any substances, or his works, must have been taken for evidence, before the journalists were allowed – snuck? – in. Some of the clutter, Tara realizes, might have been made by the EMTs. By the police who responded. Maybe by Neela, who was reported to have found him. Who was taken away, hysterical. Crying.

Still, the photo is moving in a way that a write-up might not
have been. The room it depicts is sad. Poor. A pair of jeans lies
bundled in the corner, with a crusty towel or maybe two. Band
T-shirts that looked the worse for wear, and some of the lacey
cast-offs he wore on stage, ripped and frayed. A few records,
too, scattered on the floor. Vinyl, because Chris would have
been a purist. The flash picks out the covers, glossy still, despite
the general grime. Reflects off a jacket, as well. Leather, studded
with hardware, and its mate, lighter in the black and white shot,
crumpled behind a chair. Tara sets the photo aside. Even without
a body, the shot makes it all too real. Someone lived here.
Someone died.

Tara bookmarks the site. Scott wanted art, and this was
certainly lurid enough. Without knowing the names of his parents
or his siblings – a sister? that brother? – she is pessimistic about
finding anything more. Anything that can help her search. Finally,
in a suburban weekly, she finds a lead.

'Christopher "Chris" Kantrowitz,' the piece begins, 'had a
promising artistic career cut short on Friday.' The *Haverhill
Examiner*. Tara vaguely recalls going up there for a job interview
when she first graduated from college. An office in a strip mall
that smelled of gas. 'A talented trumpet player, the Hamilton
native had performed in All-County and All-State bands before
leaving school to pursue a singing career . . .'

No wonder Chris had left. Had re-invented himself. She reads
on. 'He leaves behind his grieving parents, Sarah and Ronald,
and a sister, Madeleine. His older brother, Daniel, pre-deceased
him as an infant.'

In the back of her head, she hears the lyrics: *'Boy in a bubble
. . . Coddled, fondled, packaged, bundled. I barely survived,
barely got out alive.'* Funny, she'd always thought he was talking
about himself. Maybe he was. The Hamilton she's been reading
about certainly sounds isolating. Out of touch.

'Tara?' The sound of her name breaks into her thoughts.
Rebecca, looking more worried than usual. 'Are you joining us?'

'Of course.' Tara clicks into work mode. 'I guess I lost
track of the time.'

The two thirty meeting should be easy. She doesn't have to
present, only take notes on what the other departments will be

doing. She gets copied on all their memos, so there are rarely surprises. Only today, she's aware of a difference. Partly, it's that she's late – the last one to the conference room, where the seven other department heads are waiting. All eyes rise as she walks in, and it hits her once again that her screw-up is common knowledge. That Rudy's words were not an empty threat. She needs to reclaim some ground.

'Sorry, I'm late, everyone.' She takes her accustomed seat, halfway to the window. 'As you've probably heard, I had to rework part of the quarterly. I guess I got bogged down in my notes.'

'Tara, would you like to chat?' Martha heads up HR, so it's not an empty question. 'I've been hoping to talk with you.'

'I'm fine, Martha.' Tara takes care to enunciate carefully. 'I simply confused some files. Believe me, I've undertaken a thorough reevaluation of my labeling and storage procedures.' After five years here, she can talk the talk as well as any of them.

'It's not the report I'm worried about.' Hugh and Donnie nod, Tara sees, as the HR boss keeps talking. 'I'm sorry. I was hoping to discuss this in private, but I'm afraid it's now general knowledge, at least at this level.' She looks at the assembled faces. Licks her lips and continues. 'We've had reports – disturbing ones – that you've been involved in extracurricular activities that have put you in touch with some unsavory characters. And while your private life is, of course, your own, Zeron has to act when you bring the threat to our doorstep.'

The car. They're talking about the car, as if an intervention were in order.

'Excuse me?' She's not faking her outrage. Maybe misdirecting it a bit. 'I did not "bring a threat".'

'Your extracurricular—'

'My car was vandalized.' She's gaining steam. 'On Zeron property, which brings up the very real question of culpability.' She scans the table, as another question comes to mind. 'Of course, I would hate to think that a member of the Zeron family was responsible.'

Nobody gasps. Not audibly. But she sees a few heads jerk back, ever so slightly.

'You're clearly upset.' Hugh is trying for comforting but

even with his deep voice, he only sounds patronizing. 'Which is understandable.'

'What isn't understandable—' Tara is not going to let this pass – 'is vandalizing my car.' She scans the table. Nobody blinks. 'And blaming me, rather than coming forward to offer support.' She stands to leave. 'I have work to do.'

'Tara, please.' Martha rises. Follows her into the hallway. Stops as Tara turns to glare at her. 'I didn't mean – not like that.'

'Really?' Tara lets the acid drip. She's tougher than these corporate types. They wouldn't last a night. 'Then why don't you tell me what you did mean, Martha?'

'I got a call.' She's stammering. 'About you being here late. Hanging out after the building was closed.'

'A call? From who? When?' Her mind reels – works backward. Peter. The police. Greg? 'What did it say?'

'It – he – just sounded concerned.' Martha is in full retrenchment mode. She is even wringing her hands. 'That one of our employees seemed to be loitering – to be spending time with unsavory characters, and weren't we concerned about the safety of our other employees.'

'Loitering?' Tara had left the building and gone directly to her car. True, she had had to wait around for the auto service and the police. But besides that . . .

'And also,' Martha's voice dropped to a whisper, 'he said you'd been overheard asking about drugs.'

She goes back to work. She has to, really. No matter what she thinks, she's not twenty anymore. Not that she'd been the type to walk off a job even then. But as she extricates herself from Martha, she realizes how grateful she is that she hasn't given in to Peter's urgings. That she doesn't have a mortgage, not yet.

But she does have rent and a car that she now owes twelve hundred on. And so she begs off as gracefully as she can. Tells Martha that there must be some mistake. That she has been meeting with some old friends, but nobody disreputable. Only when she mentions Frank – his funeral – does Martha relent.

'I'm so sorry,' she says, and Tara dips her head in gratitude, accepting the misplaced sympathy. By that point, she'd have brought up Frank's twelve-step program, if it would have gotten her back to her office. Away from that meeting, and off the hook.

'Thanks.' She knows she ought to leave it at that, but she can't resist. 'I don't know why anyone would make a call like that,' she says. 'I mean, if someone saw me in the parking lot, waiting for AAA, why not come wait with me? Or offer me a ride?'

Martha doesn't have an answer to that one. Not one she's willing to voice, though the tight-mouthed smile implies something other – something that goes beyond one call, one night. One messed-up report.

Back at her desk, Tara calls Scott. He's got to know about this – know that someone wants her off the story. It's the only reasonable explanation. Peter may be paranoid, but the anonymous tip has convinced her. But reaching her old friend isn't as easy as it once was, and by the time she gets through the receptionist and Scott's personal assistant, she's feeling better. Defiant.

'Whoever it is,' she says, when she finally gets him on the phone. When she finishes laying it all out. Rock and roll, she thinks. Scott will understand. 'He's overplayed his hand.'

'That's great, Tara!' Yeah, she's feeling tough. But still, this shocks her. In the silence that follows, she can hear him rising from his desk. Walking with the phone. She imagines his office as big and airy as his apartment, though minus the waterfront view, and feels her anger – for it is anger that has caught in her throat – turn inward. This isn't her old friend. Not anymore. 'This means you're onto something,' he says. He's walked away from his desk for a reason, she realizes. His voice has dropped to confidential. 'You've touched a nerve.'

'I'm not getting paid enough.' She grouses. It's reflex. Their old joke, from back when neither got paid at all. Back when what excited Scott was the music. The writing. Not whether the writer had been threatened.

'I'll see if I can squeeze more out of the budget.' He doesn't remember. Thinks she's serious. 'This is worth it.'

'You don't—' She stops herself. More money might be useful, especially if her job is on the line. But there's something else going on – something she can't quite identify. The lowered tone, the distance from his desk. From the office door? 'Scott, how badly do you need this story?'

The pause is telling. 'Scott, are you OK? I mean, at *City*?'

'Yeah, I'm fine.' The old Scott. Dismissive. Almost jovial enough. 'Jonah's being a hard ass is all.'

'In general, or about this piece?' She thinks about their lunch, but there's something else. A thread she can't quite grab. An off note. 'Is it your job?'

'No.' His chuckle sounds forced, but she's out of options. 'It's been – well, maybe I pushed for this story a bit too hard. But it's worth it. I know how good you are, and once I bring you in . . .'

She bites her lip. That had been her dream, too. She thinks of the photo. Knows Scott – this new Scott – will see it as sensational, rather than sad. 'I may have some art for you.' It feels dirty even to offer.

'I knew I could count on you.' Hale and hearty again, as if someone had entered his office. 'Look, I should go. Back-to-back meetings today. Keep at it, kid. We'll talk, OK?'

She's too paranoid to work on the story for the rest of the day. Feels like someone's watching her. Watching what she does on the office computer anyway, and the afternoon ticks by as slow as molasses. She waits until after five to leave, making sure Rebecca knows she's still at her desk. She's on her way to pick up her car when her phone rings, and she jumps. The T is crowded. Rush hour and the Sox, and there's no room for excess movement.

'Tara, it's Nick.' He sounds so calm – so happy – she's a bit taken aback. 'Congrats on making your work deadline.'

'Thanks.' She puts her hand to her forehead, as if to contain all the thoughts. To block out the stare from the woman she's bumped into. 'God, that feels like a year ago.'

'Rough day?' His voice is warm. He's in a good mood.

'Kind of.' Her stop is approaching. She begins to maneuver toward the exit. 'At least it's over.'

'Well, that's good,' he says. 'I was wondering about that dinner. We can make it a celebration, if that's in order.'

'Hang on.' She pushes between two backpacks. Makes it to the door. 'I'm in transit here.'

'Sure, sorry.' She walks to the stairs, trying to gauge her mood. Yesterday, she was looking forward to seeing him. The day has been a bear. Is it that they're not aligned – he's not reading her mood, her mind? Is this because she let Peter spend the night?

'I'd love to have dinner.' The words burst out of her. Min was right. 'Just don't make me talk about my day.'

Two hours later, she's glad of her decision. Mellow with wine and with a surprisingly good spaghetti puttanesca, she leans back on Nick's sofa and closes her eyes.

'That bad, huh?' The cushions move as he settles down beside her, his own glass in hand. 'Wait, you don't have to tell me.'

'No, I'm good now.' She looks at him. Those blue eyes are warm. She made the right choice. 'It's – well, I was going to say it's this article. The one on the scene. But it's more than that.' She closes her eyes again, this time to gather her thoughts.

'I don't like my job.' It feels good to say it out loud. 'It pays well, but I'm bored to tears. I mean, that's why I screwed up, the report I had to re-do in a hurry.'

She peeks at him, but his face is still, somber. Concerned, she thinks, but not judgmental.

'I miss doing journalism. Writing stories like this one.' She stares at the ceiling. 'I don't even know if I could make a living anymore doing this kind of thing. I mean, it's not just that I'm used to earning more, it's that the outlets don't exist any more. The papers.'

'The *Dot*,' he says, nodding.

'Yeah, or any of them. *The Weekly,* the *Real Paper.*' A moment of silence as they remember. 'And this story. I'm finding more questions than answers, which is cool, but . . .'

'Questions about Frank?' His curiosity is piqued.

'About the scene. About Chris Crack. I mean, do you think he killed himself?' She pulls herself up on the sofa and turns toward him. He's the one staring into space, distracted.

'I don't know, Tara. He was into some stuff.'

'That's just it.' She's waking up. 'I've even heard that maybe he was murdered somehow. That he was going to snitch.'

He shakes his head and looks at her, confused.

'You know there was an investigation going on, right? That one year, when smack was everywhere? Well, I have it on good authority that somebody knew who was bringing it in. That somebody was going to talk.' She's so excited that she chooses not to see how his brow furrows. How his mouth opens to protest. 'Then Chris dies, and the lead disappears.'

'Tara, no.' He reaches for her hand. For her glass of wine, which he places on the table, 'You can't – this isn't the music story you told me about. You know what was going on then.'

'Well, that's just it.' She draws a knee up, as if to prop herself up. As if to stand. 'I don't know. Just that there were no drugs – nothing serious – and then suddenly there were. I mean, what if Chris was the police informant? What if he was murdered to keep him quiet?'

'And what if those people are still around now, Tara?' His face is serious. Sad, even. 'You said you're having problems at work, right? But they're normal problems. Safe problems. Please, Tara, let this go.'

She pauses, and it hits her. She hasn't told him about her car. About the call to her office. Only that she screwed up at work. At her safe, dull corporate job. Who else knew she was working on this story? That she was working late last night at Zeron? Suddenly, she feels nauseous. Dizzy from the wine.

'I've got to go.' She pulls herself to her feet. What was it Greg had said? *That bartender – the one who was so sweet on you?* 'I – I'm sorry. I didn't sleep, and the wine . . .'

'Of course.' He's beside her. Takes her hand. 'Do you want me to give you a ride home?'

'No, no, I'll be fine.' She grabs her coat. Takes the car keys in her hand. 'I'm just tired, not drunk.' She manages a smile and hopes it looks less fake than it feels. 'Thanks for dinner, Nick.'

'Anytime.' He looks a little dazed as he walks her to the door, and she almost relents. Then she remembers what Peter has said. Min. And she turns and nearly runs.

TWENTY-TWO

S he could be twenty-five again. Only not in a good way. She's pulled the afghan over her as she lies on the sofa, calling Min for solace.

'I should have known better.' She sniffs, a little weepy. The wine she's poured herself might not have been the best idea. 'He seemed so nice.'

'A divorced bartender?' Min is arch, as always. 'What a prize. So what'd he do?'

Tara hesitates. She's shaken. That's real. But here at home, under the afghan, glass in hand, her fears seem groundless. Any way she tries to phrase them will come off as silly.

'Oh, it's stupid.' If Min were here, she'd have a harder time evading her. Min has a way of staring, one brow raised. Of waiting. 'I just – I don't know what I expected.'

'Ah, nostalgia.' There's relish in the word, and Tara seizes on it.

'Yeah, maybe.' She sits up. Remembers. 'Min, when Frank called to ask you about his grandson, what did you say the diagnosis was?'

'Fabry's.' Min's voice is flat. She's not giving anything away.

'And that's genetic?' She's remembering what Mika said. What Nick said, too.

'Yeah.' Min draws it out, waiting for her to connect the dots. 'X-linked.'

'Does Mika's husband have a history?'

'Tara, this is private, OK? I can't be talking about someone's medical history.'

'Mika's not a patient.' Tara isn't put off. She's too busy trying to work through the implications. 'Neither is her son. Min, did Frank know?'

'He wasn't a fool.' Min spits out the word. Still bitter or – no – still mourning. 'I mean, even at the time, there were rumors. He didn't care.'

'You don't think . . .' It was so long ago, why would anyone care? 'He wouldn't have done anything – to Chris I mean?'

'She'd already agreed to marry Frank when Chris died.' Min's voice is clipped. Curt. 'She was already pregnant.' As if Tara could forget that night, the party. 'I mean, yeah, some people said that's why Chris OD'd. Cause he'd fucked up with her. But, you know, if he'd snapped his fingers, Neela would've gone back to him. With or without the baby.'

'But what if it wasn't an accident? What if Frank was worried about Neela going back to him? You don't think Frank would've . . . done something?'

'You've been reading too many murder mysteries.' Min's laugh has little of humor in it. 'Besides, Frank had no beef with Chris. Not anymore. He got what he wanted. He knew having a baby would settle Neela down. That was it for him, the reason to clean up and fly right. All he ever wanted.'

If she listens, she'll hear the edge. The brittle bite to Min's words. But Tara can't let it go. Not yet.

'You think Chris was going to snitch?'

'What?' Min laughs in surprise. 'Where'd you get that one from?'

'There was an investigation.' Tara knows better than to bring up Peter. 'The cops were looking into the drugs, all the heroin that showed up that winter. I heard they had a lead. Someone was going to talk.'

'Sounds like a *City* story to me.' The sound of a match being struck. An inhale. 'Is this what your old pal has you working on?'

'Kind of.' Tara doesn't want to go into it. 'His boss is less than enthused.'

'Jonah Wells, right?' Another laugh. Softer this time. 'Yeah, he's put all that rock and roll mayhem behind him. Kind of surprised he hired Scott, actually.'

'Scott's a good editor.' She doesn't want to defend her old friend. Not tonight. 'But isn't it possible? Chris Crack was going to testify. Turn state's evidence and then – boom.'

'He was a junkie, Tara.'

'He was cleaning up. He'd cleaned up.' He was on the brink of fame, she wants to add. So close to having it all.

But Min is still talking.

'He was a junkie.' She says it again. 'A junkie who'd detoxed. Whose family made him clean up, because they cared. Because they still had hope. And then as soon as he was free, he went right back to the shit. Shooting anything he could get his hands on. Only he couldn't handle it, not after a few days' clean, and it killed him. We see it all the time in the ER, Tara. All the time.'

She sleeps badly, her dreams a jumble of shadowy figures. She wakes to the knowledge that she has to go into work. That someone is trying to sabotage her in the present day. In the daylight world.

On her way in, she calls Scott. 'It's Tara,' she says, in case the voicemail won't identify her. 'I'm having serious second thoughts about this story.' There, it's out.

When her phone rings – an unknown Boston number – she picks up right away. 'Scott?'

'Sorry.' A familiar voice, a warm burr. Phil from the Whirled Shakers. 'Is this Tara Winton?'

'Yeah.' She stops on the sidewalk. Confused.

'I got your number from Katie,' says the singer. 'She said you're doing a story on the scene?'

'Yeah,' she says. It's useless. She's a lifer. 'Yeah, I am.'

She can't play hooky. Not after the last few days. But she gets precious little done while waiting for her lunchtime interview with Phil. One press release, straight from the boilerplate. A draft of an update that will announce the ill-starred report, which she sends to Hugh, asking for feedback that she really doesn't want. It's more than she'd do most days, and it's not even eleven. Time, she decides, for a break.

Days like this, she's glad to be in Boston. Crisp, not cold, and clear, the sky an otherworldly blue. On an impulse, she begins to walk toward the harbor. It's not far, but she's never done it. Never walked farther than the T. She thinks of Scott's place, with its fantastic view. Breathes in deeply and imagines a hint of salt. It makes Zeron more attractive, in theory, at least until she runs into a construction site bordered by mud and gravel. The chain link stretches for at least a block around the 'Future Home of the Hub's Best Views'.

The Hub. Back in the day, that was one of those words – a tell that someone wasn't local. Wasn't authentic. Scott, joking around one day, had laid out a headline: 'Hub Heartbeats'. Tara couldn't even remember what band he was spoofing. She'd changed it to 'Heartthrobs', and they'd both laughed so hard, she'd nearly pissed herself. Of course, the beer hadn't helped either.

What happened to Scott? She turns and begins to walk along the fence. There's no sidewalk here. Some earth mover has chomped up the pavement. The slabs that remain are tilted at crazy angles, and she steps into the street, where it's easier.

Her memory sparks. She used to walk in the street on her way to the Casbah. The sidewalks weren't broken then, not that she can remember, but they were empty, and the shadows cast by the silent warehouses were dark. She looks around and it's as if the daylight recedes. The club wasn't far from here, she realizes, though it could have been another world. She checks her watch. She's not due to meet Phil for a good twenty minutes yet, and if she recalls correctly Summer Street should be only a block over. Two blocks, maybe, the construction as disorienting as the bright sunlight.

She finds the street by its sign, eventually, three blocks down and another over from where she started. That lane, she thinks, wasn't there. Was, if anything, an alley as threatening as those shadows. She'd seen a rat run out of there once, as big as her old cat. What it was running from, she didn't dare guess. Though she'd heard the laughter at her own gasp. Voices back in that alley. The slurred invitation to come join in. Maybe the drugs had always been a part of the scene. But, no – Peter wasn't an insider. Wasn't smitten or infatuated or whatever word he'd used for her. He saw something new. Only to him, it was a story to be written, and not a personal tragedy.

Not until she steps up onto the old stone curb does she get her bearings. She remembers that curb, a little too high and slick when it froze. The building behind it, a restaurant, is new, though it too is stone – some hipster concoction of granite and glass. This street: if she closes her eyes, she can see it. Paving stones covered with a thin coat of asphalt. The ancient heart of a working city. Still working, in its own way. She opens her eyes and continues on. Zeron is only about five blocks behind her, but she's passed into another world. Sees them shift and change. Southie. The Seaport, and now the Innovation District.

Progress is on its way. Past the chic bistro, she sees sunlight and catches her breath. The Casbah stood here, until it didn't. The long, low building must have been a warehouse of some sort originally. A loading dock. Storage. She can picture it, set back behind the large lot that served as the last obstacle course for a pedestrian. She remembers running through it, past parked cars – a few left there for good. Anxious not to be late. Eager for the evening to start. For a moment, she thinks she can even see Frank, those last few months when he was working the door. Jonah, lurking, in those stupid suits. Chris and Neela laughing. Falling into the wall.

She'd go there now. Trace the footprint of the cavernous club. Only there's nothing there, not even the lot. A giant pit in its place, and the entire lot – it must be an acre – surrounded by chain link eight-feet high. The site is quiet, work stalled by her memories, or maybe it's the economy. There are rumors. Maybe the innovation hasn't reached this far yet, but that's OK. She leans into the fence, hooking her fingers through it. She remembers that night, the last night. The music. The scene.

'Sure looks different, doesn't it?' The voice, with its warm rumble. Tara turns, as if in a dream. Phil is standing beside her, hands up on the chain-link fence as if he, too, would vault it. Back in time.

'No shit!' She huffs a little laugh, startled. The sun is brighter than she'd remembered.

'I saw you.' He's apologetic. 'I mean, I was walking this way to meet you. Figured it's such a nice day, and then I saw you here. Amazing, huh?'

'Yeah.' She turns back toward the pit, peering through the wire of the fence. 'It looks bigger than I remember. Though I guess some of that was the parking lot.'

'Looks the same.' She turns to see if he's joking. 'I mean, they never repaved it.'

'That's right.' She nods. 'The potholes that could break your axle. I'm surprised Jonah never got sued.'

'Jonah?' Phil's looking at her, the lines between his brows, bracketing his mouth have deepened.

'Jonah Wells. Wasn't he the owner?'

A shrug. 'Those days? Who knows. I mean, he ran the place.'

'Well, he did well for himself.' She thinks of *City* and of Scott.

'That place was a gold mine.' Phil is staring ahead, as if he can still see the club.

'Well, the land, sure.' Tara looks at where the club stood, its logo – a caricature oasis, complete with palms – painted on the wall. 'But back then?'

'Hey, it was the Wild West back then.' He turns from the site and shrugs, a faint smile playing on his lips. 'But what do I know? The Whirled Shakers weren't exactly a Casbah band.'

'You should've been.' As if by agreement, they both begin to walk away, over the broken pavement and back toward where the corporate world has already staked its claim.

'So what else can I tell you?' Phil leans back, smiling at the memories he has shared. The stuffy practice rooms, the lousy gigs. The night the toilet at the Rat overflowed and flooded the room. 'What else do you want to know?'

'Anything else you care to share.' Tara leaves it open. Loose. The café is nearly empty this early and talking with the singer is easy. Easier than she'd expected. Or maybe it's just the memory of her last interview here – with Greg – that has her looking for shadows on this sunny day. 'What was it like, back then? You must have felt like a king.'

He laughs, but there's warmth in it. 'A duke, maybe.' He shakes the compliment off. Bends over his latté. The smell of the coffee is as rich as his voice, but as he leans forward to sip from the big cup, she sees the grey in his hair. The way it's receding at the temples. 'We were never a part of the inner circle.'

Tara leans her seat back. 'Oh, come on!'

'No, really, Tara. You were one of the only ones who thought we were stars. Well, you and Gina.'

He looks up, licks the foam from his lip. An image comes unbidden. Gina, her head bobbing, backstage. She turns away so he won't see her blush. Picks up her own oversize mug to account for the color in her cheeks.

'I like to think . . .' She stops herself. Phil and Gina were close once, at least as far as she knew.

'Gina's a bit of a mess.' He gets it. 'But she's a good egg. And, hey, she had an all-access pass to everything that was going on back then. She *was* the all-access pass.'

He's staring out the window as well. The cars in the lot glitter in the sun. Tara can only guess at the memories. 'Hey, I thought you wanted to talk about Frank?'

Suddenly, the bright glare from the window is too much. She leans forward. Turns away.

'What is it?' Phil sits forward. 'You OK? Did I say something – is it because of Frank?'

'Sort of.' She manages a grin. 'I'm just . . . I interviewed Greg here, and he got upset.'

'Greg's a bit of an asshole.' Phil doesn't sound surprised. 'He's still pissed that his brother did time.'

'He did?' She catches herself. Remembers hearing something. 'Drugs?'

Phil nods. 'Smack. Fool. He's lucky he didn't get busted for intent to distribute.'

'Was he dealing?' Tara tries to remember if she knew him. If she saw him with Chris. Then it hits her. 'Would he have turned informant?'

'Gary? No.' A wave of sadness passes over the singer's face. 'He's not together enough. He just had a habit. Like a lot of folks back then.'

'But not Frank.' Tara feels like she's looking at a puzzle. Like if she could just twist the pieces around.

'No way.' His eyes widen. 'He drank, sure. But smack? No. Not even . . . you knew about Brian, right?'

She nods. He'd been managing the Casbah bar by then. A success. The needle was still in his arm when they found him. She thinks of Min, of what she said.

'Hey.' She lowers her voice. 'Do you think Chris Crack committed suicide?'

He exhales noisily. They're so close that she feels his breath. His warmth. 'Junkies,' he says at last. 'That shit is slow suicide anyway.'

'Did you ever?' She wants to ask. Remembers Min in the

bathroom. Remembers too much. But he's put his mug down. Pushing his chair back.

'No, that wasn't my scene ever.' One last smile. A flash of the star. 'The music was always the buzz for me. Like you – and like Gina.' He stands. Pulls his jacket off the chair. 'You should talk to her. She likes you.'

She follows him out. The breeze has picked up, bringing with it the salt of the harbor. The warm tar smell of construction, and suddenly she's back.

'Kind of hard to believe the waterfront has changed so much,' she says as they step outside. 'Gotten so . . . clean.' That's the wrong word. Modern. Sterile.

'Yeah, times have changed.' He's looking around, and she wonders what he sees. The old buildings, now replaced or refaced with chrome and glass. The dank nights banished by the bright day. 'Some people made some money when they cashed out.'

'That they did.' She thinks of Scott's apartment, with that view. Of Jonah Wells. 'I guess it was all about timing. The new boom.'

He leans in, and for a moment she thinks he's going to kiss her. 'More like getting out before the old bust,' he says, his mouth right near her ear. 'Anyway, this has been good. You should come out next month – the fourteenth.'

'Another reunion show?' Her voice is too loud. Too hearty. 'You're making this a regular thing?'

'The boys have football practice on Thursdays.' That smile is back, but it's for another life. 'Joanie says I need to get out of the house more, too.'

He walks off leaving her oddly bereft. Maybe, she thinks, she understands Gina a little more. Phil was wrong about one thing. He was always a star.

TWENTY-THREE

No matter what Phil says, she wasn't the only one. And it wasn't only women – Katie, Gina, OK, Tara adds herself to the list – who fell prey to the singer's charisma. It was Scott, after all, who had wanted her to write about the band. Who had sent her off to interview them, back when they were just beginning to get the headline slots.

'Check it out,' he'd said. They were laying out the listings. Or she was. He was more what he'd call multitasking – looking over her shoulder for bands to feature in the next month's issue, fussing with a photo as he did. 'The Whirled Shakers are headlining a Thursday at Oakie's.'

'Oakie's?' She straightened the type. Let her tone speak for itself. The club was a bit of a backwater. The action centered on Kenmore Square back then – Kenmore or the waterfront.

'Yeah, Oakie's.' She'd been a bit aimless still, unsure of who was worth writing about and who, for some then inexplicable reason, would be considered beyond the pale. Scott knew it. She was his project, as much as *Underground Sound.* 'You should go to the show. Talk to them after. They'll love you.'

'What do you mean?' She didn't know that then, the evening Scott sent her off on assignment. 'They'll love me?' She hadn't seen Gina, then, down on her knees. But she wasn't a fool, either.

'You're press!' Scott's emphasis sprayed her with his beer. 'That's what I mean, silly!'

'Oh.' She'd adjusted the X-Acto knife in her hand. Trimmed a strip of copy. 'So why aren't you going?'

'They're sick of me.' He reached across her, brushed a whisker of paper away. For all his personal slovenliness, Scott was finicky about layout. 'And you need to become a regular. You need to learn.'

He was right, of course. Hearing them again – that combo of hooks and rhythm, the whiplash guitar and Phil's command of the stage – helped hone her sensibilities. Not so much her critical abilities – she always knew what she liked, right from the start – but what worked. What would connect with the leather and denim crowd she was so eager to join. By comparing the Whirled Shakers with the Exiles, she learned about the range of the rock world. Its capabilities, so that by the time she heard the Aught Nines – the new Aught Nines, with Chris Crack – she could speak with authority.

She thinks of that, on her way back to Zeron. Remembers the thrill. Being lightheaded from forgetting to breathe.

'They're something, huh?' Gina, slimmer then. Her lipstick wet and bright.

'Really.' It was all the response she could conjure but it was enough. Gina had taken her hand and dragged her out, the floor already filling up.

Maybe Phil was right, she thinks now, as she enters the antiseptic office building. As she returns to her current job. The day job. Maybe she should call Gina. But he's wrong that they were his only fans. Scott knew. He always knew the band was great. He was the one who had sent her there to cover them.

Her cell begins ringing as she gets off the elevator, but she reaches into her bag to silence it. She's been out for nearly two hours, and she doesn't like the looks.

'Dentist.' She mouths the word as she walks by Rebecca's desk. Only after does she realize that anyone walking by would have seen her, sitting by that big window. Fuck it, she tries to buck herself up. Wasn't it Rebecca who was pushing her to join that lunch dates club? Wasn't she wondering if she was sick of this job anyway?

As she walks to her office, she hears that phone begin to ring. For an awful moment she fears the worst. Her parents, back in Ohio. Peter. Min. She races the last few steps and grabs it, breathless from the fear.

'Hello?'

'Ah, you're answering now.' Peter, so annoyed he could be the one vibrating. Not an emergency then.

'Did you just try my cell?' She fishes it out of her bag. No, it's another number – no ID. Local.

'Please.' Peter's voice drips acid. 'You're in enough trouble there. What the fuck, Tara? That's a good gig you've got.'

'Excuse me?' She keeps her voice down as she walks to the door. Closes it as much as she dares, then returns to her desk, turning her chair to face the wall. 'May I ask what you're talking about?' She's not whispering, but her voice is low. Inaudible, she hopes, from the hall, and chilly. She knows Peter, and she can do cool, too.

'Your job.' He's practically hissing. 'I'm not going to call you on your cell on work time unless I know you're out of the office. You're already doing freelance on company time and—'

'Hang on.' She cuts him off. 'What are you talking about?' She rummages through her memories. Monday, she was distraught. Overwhelmed, when he came over. What did she tell him?

'Look,' says Peter, 'I know Rudy, OK? He called me to see if I could talk some sense to you.' She sits down hard. Unable to respond. 'He likes you. He likes that you come from a newspaper background. He knows that makes you . . . different from the corporate clones. Only—'

'Wait.' She puts up a hand, as if she could stop him. 'You know Rudy? My boss?'

'Slightly. From when I was in the business section. He was a source.'

'So, my job . . .' She closes her eyes against the dizziness.

'You knew I recommended you. And I knew you'd be good for the job.' He pauses. She's supposed to respond. To thank him. Only she feels sick.

'Did you tell him I was working on a story – on the piece for *City*?'

'What? No.' He scoffs. 'I'm not going to sabotage you. I'm trying to help you here, Tara. This is a good gig.' His voice drops to a whisper. Urgent, almost pleading. 'Tit jobs like this aren't easy to find anymore.'

'Why'd you leave journalism, Peter?' He starts to speak, but she keeps talking. 'I know the *Dot* was failing. I'm not a fool. But why didn't you go someplace else? Someplace bigger? New York or—'

'Tara, please.' Calmer again, but contemptuous. 'We were married. We were building a life.'

'I would've moved.' She's never thought of it before. That

doesn't mean it isn't true. 'Was it the money? Or were you afraid?' Silence. She knows some things about this man. 'You were afraid you weren't good enough.'

'That's preposterous.' Scorn, but sadness too. 'I broke some great stories.'

'Yeah, but your biggest – the heroin connection – never panned out. Hell, your best source was an ex-cop. Oh, and your girlfriend.'

'Tara.' He's not arguing, and she spins her chair around. Pulls a pad from her desk drawer.

'Tell me what your connection said. Timilty, his name was? I have no doubt you remember everything.' She grabs a pen. 'Clubland', she writes. 'And while you're at it, what did you find out about Frank Turcotte's death?'

He doesn't give her much, but it's likely all he has. This many years in, she knows his voice. His tells, his pride.

There aren't many details in the tale he spins her. He claims he can't remember, but the gist is there. That heroin was flooding the clubs wasn't news to her. She'd been there, she reminds him. She'd seen the transformation. What she hadn't known was that it was spreading. A bus boy from a local burger joint was found unconscious by the dumpster. A cabbie. Then some college kid, whose panicked friends dropped him off at the ER when he started turning blue.

'That's when the heat came down,' said Peter. He couldn't see as Tara rolled her eyes.

It was Timilty who called him first, he confessed. Remembered him from his days on the police beat. The eager pup who came out to every call. Timilty had been old school. An Irish beat cop who'd worked his way up. Who'd wanted to get the word out, he'd told Peter. Spread the news. 'The shit you're snorting? It's not fun anymore,' the grizzled detective had said. 'It never was.'

He'd not been able to give him names. The bus boy had been busted. The cabbie, too, and the college kid had disappeared back to some suburban rehab joint. The one connector was the club scene, Timilty had told him, but she knew that. He wanted an in. She'd known that from that first night he'd asked her out.

He needed her. Even more so once Timilty had stopped talking to him. Stopped feeding him news of the investigation. The leak about the snitch had been stupid, and the veteran cop had taken flack for it. A brag, said Peter, though Tara saw it more as incentive – a way to keep the bored young reporter going. When that fell through, so did the tips. Reprimanded, moved, or maybe disenchanted, the cop had clammed up and retired soon after, beaten by the scourge. It was only after Frank Turcotte's funeral that Peter had reached out to him again.

'So you called him?' Tara wanted to be clear.

'I was curious. Seeing all those people again. Your old friends.' The malice gone, he sounded tired. 'I wanted to know if they'd ever figured it out. You know, found the source.'

'You're bored too.' A simple fact.

'I don't know,' he said. 'I do know I'm not going to fuck up a good job for some freelance story.'

'Oh, Peter.' She couldn't hide her sadness. 'It's not that good a job.'

Now, looking over her notes, she sees the pattern. Peter, wanting to investigate, saw it too. The clubs were the perfect conduit – young people looking to get high and a business model based on cash. Bands, bartenders – anyone could have been dealing. She could've helped Peter more, she realized. Could have asked Min where she scored. Asked any of a dozen scenesters. But it wasn't her story. And she had wanted to belong.

She opens the desk drawer to put away the pad. It's time for her to focus. To salvage the Zeron job and then, maybe, figure out what to tell Scott. The piece is going nowhere. She's enough of a reporter to know that. A bunch of memories is all. An interlude before real life. She clicks the pen closed. Reaches for the mouse.

And then she retrieves the pad again. The investigation on Frank Turcotte's death hasn't been closed. 'Inconclusive,' she has written, quoting Peter who was quoting someone – Timilty? – about a clock running out. Only that's not the question in Tara's mind as she stares at the sheet of paper. As she grabs her phone and punches in the number for Peter's cell.

'Tara?' He sounds beaten. Tired. But at least he doesn't reprimand her for the call.

'Peter, why did you call Timilty?'

'You asked, Tara, and I thought – after Saturday—'

'No, I mean, after the funeral.' She knew he was bored. That these weren't his people. 'You said you saw the old crowd and you thought of the case, I know, but . . .' She's not sure what she's going for. 'But, why?'

'It's silly.' She waits. Lets the silence do its job. 'I just remember talking to Frank one night when we were out. You'd gone to talk to some band guy or other, and I asked him, you know, about the drugs and shit. I figured he knew what was going on. I thought he might even be the snitch. Only of course he wasn't, right? And, anyway, now he's dead.'

'Everything OK?' Rebecca is at the door. Has been standing there a while, if that furrow of concern between her brows is any sign. Waiting while Tara digested that last call, silent at her desk. The secretary has a paper in her hand, which she holds out as an offering.

'Yeah.' Tara sits up. Wakes up, more like it, from her stupor and reaches for the sheet. Vacation policies have changed. Or, no, the policy for requesting them, she reads. 'Yes, I'm fine. Thanks.'

She isn't, though. And while she wants to follow up, she's not sure how. So Peter and Rudy are friends? Or, no, contacts? She sighs heavily, all the disappointment flooding out, and then looks up quickly. Yes, Rebecca has retreated. Wouldn't do to tarnish her reputation further.

Twenty years, more or less, she's been with Peter. On and off, sure, but . . . She's not sure what surprises her more. She knew he was a hustler. That he worried about her, that he tried to fix her – fix her up. His ongoing crusade to get her to purchase a condo is only the latest manifestation.

What she didn't expect was his insecurity. His fear. It's as if he doesn't believe he was ever a good reporter, when she knows how dogged he was at getting at the truth. At putting the facts together.

Or was he? She thinks about his last admission – the one that left her speechless and led to his stumbling apology. That led to him ending their brief second call. He'd reached out to his old contact on the force because of Frank. Because he'd thought of *Frank* as the potential informer. Not Chris.

Tara can't take that in. If Frank was the informer, then why did he back out? And did that mean that Chris Crack's death was either the conscious or inevitable result of the slow suicide of addiction?

There's another question, though. One that's more to the point, and that dawns on her as she reads and re-reads her notes. Why did Peter think Frank might be the informant? She should have asked. And although she knows she's being a nudge, she can't resist. She reaches once more for the phone.

Which rings in her hand. Not Peter, she sees – that other number, from before. *City.*

'Scott?' She remembers that she called him. It feels like years before. 'I'm sorry. I know I was trying to reach you before.' She pauses. How to say that she's distracted. 'Now's not a great time.' The advantage of a job.

'Yeah.' One syllable, but as flat as she can imagine.

'Scott, you OK?' She pushes the pad aside. 'What's wrong?'

'Did I say . . .?' He stops himself, halting his disclaimer half formed. 'I'm sorry. Today isn't turning out well here, either.'

'I'm sorry I bothered you then. I mean, earlier. It wasn't important.'

'No.' His voice is thoughtful. 'It is. And we should talk.'

'That doesn't sound good.' She knows this man. She can say things like that.

'It's not that bad. Why don't you come over for dinner?' He's not convincing. She knows him too well.

'Sure,' she responds. Knows him well enough to not press – not now. 'I'll bring wine. Lots of it.'

It's the kind of thing they used to say – though she's switched in 'wine' for 'beer'. The kind of thing that used to get a smart retort. Only Scott doesn't, and she remembers. 'Sorry, I mean, I'll bring soda.'

A soft laugh. 'Thanks, Tara. But you can bring a bottle. You might want some,' he says, and she realizes that he's serious. 'See you tonight.'

There's no working after that. Her concentration is shot. Even calling Peter back is out of the question – the urgency is gone. The question on the tip of her tongue confused now. What exactly did she want to know? Besides, she's done nothing related to her job since the morning. She might as well not be here.

The sheet. The new instructions. It's all on-line, the page explains. Requests going into a central calendar that tallies up available days, 'keeping supervisors informed', she reads. A few clicks and she's in. There's Rudy – marked in red – out until Monday, the third.

An urge takes her and she starts to type. She's got more vacation time than she can use. Loses days each year, but not this time. A few keystrokes and it's done. She's requested the next week off. There's no form to fill in about why; no curious glances from HR. She simply wants to. She can work on the piece, at her leisure. And she can avoid talking to Rudy for one more week.

The job is more pleasant knowing she's got only two days left. She files some old releases, the ones that have already been distributed. She even manages a jaunty email, alerting her colleagues of her impending time off.

'Please send along any time-sensitive material by Thursday EOD,' she writes, and resists the urge to tack on an apology.

Before she knows it, the day is gone. Quarter to five, she realizes, when she hears Rebecca washing out the coffee pot in the break room. Fifteen minutes later, she steps out, in time to see the secretary donning her coat.

'Have a good one,' she calls.

The secretary looks up, a little startled, although it could be that tight bun that makes her eyes so wide.

'I'm just going to finish up some work,' adds Tara, a tilt of her head back to her office. 'Don't worry. I don't think I'll be the last one out tonight.'

In truth, she waits only until the dark-haired secretary has gone before she prepares to leave. The computer, a company desktop, she powers down. The pad she starts to pack, folding it to fit into her bag. It's too big – a yellow, legal pad leftover from some earlier era – and finally she rips out the sheets she's written on. They fold neatly and she slips them into her pants pocket. Better she shouldn't be seen removing company property. A joke she can't share, bitter with rue. But then she's out. The sun's still up, and she's got plans to keep.

TWENTY-FOUR

'I brought two bottles. Red and white.' She holds them up as evidence when Scott opens the door. 'I didn't know what you were cooking.'

'Thanks.' He doesn't look at them, and as she follows him into the kitchen she sees why. He's got another open, a full glass on the counter. 'I've already started,' he says.

'OK then.' She watches him. His hands are steady as he pours her one, as he puts her white into the fridge. Something is wrong. That's clear. She's later than she'd said she'd be, and she wonders if he's bothered. She'd made a detour for the wine – gotten it downtown and then turned herself around in her attempts to walk from Zeron over here. Not turned around, she corrects herself – she admits, but spooked as she walked past another construction site. The crew had cleared out by then. The shadows were just long enough. And once she'd passed the T, all the other office drones were gone, drained into the station like so much runoff.

If it were earlier, she'd have kept walking. Fewer shadows, or maybe the scare of the week before. As it was, she'd spun around. Hurried as if she were running late and caught the T inbound several stops before realizing that Scott's place was actually one stop the other way. She'd felt funny about the wine, what with Scott not drinking and all. Funnier still, now that she's shown up and he's already poured himself a glass. Her old friend is avoiding her gaze, and she decides to be honest. With herself, for a start.

'Scott, what's going on?' He's chopping vegetables. Onions and now celery. A pan on the stove glistening with oil. In the pause, she pours herself a glass from the open bottle on the counter. The wine was cold and warming both. Better, probably, than the bottles she has brought. She drinks some more. 'It will be easier if you just say it.'

'It's the piece,' he says, brushing the vegetables into the pan

with the blade of the knife. 'I mean, I know you've been ambiva-
lent about it, and I've been wrong to push.'

'The story?' She wants to ask him about the wine. About his
drinking. He's deflecting. She knows he wants to kill the piece.
Maybe he has to, but his reaction is too strong. 'Yeah – I mean,
maybe you've pushed me. But, Scott, this isn't like you.'

Even as she says it, she knows that's wrong. The old Scott,
the one who sat up drinking with her, would pick apart a story
just for fun. Hers, anyone's. Even pieces in the *Dot* – no, especially pieces in the *Dot*. 'Pretentious claptrap,' he'd snort. Then,
wiping the beer from his beard, he'd point out the flaws in the
argument. The hyperbole and the cliché. The old Scott didn't
care about her feelings. He cared about her copy – and respect.
But this new guy? Even the way he drinks is different, and she's
no longer sure what he was about.

It isn't dinner. He's put the knife down. His back is toward
her, and he stares at the pan as if the sizzle speaks to him. She
sees his shoulders rise and fall. This new Scott wears form-
fitting clothes, the kind of long-sleeve T she suspects cost more
than that wine.

'Talk to me,' she says. She takes a step, reaches up. His
shoulder is warm – the oven, that shirt – and she remembers
the frisson of desire she felt when they'd first met again. He's
a good-looking man now. Trim and fit, but he's also her old
friend. The one who felt more like a brother than, well, than a
mate.

'You've got to understand.' He's talking to the pan, but he's
talking, and that's something. 'When I first met Jonah, back in
the day. I hated him. I mean, he was everything I despised. The
power and . . .' A pause. He swallows. 'The way he used it.'

She waits, remembering. The rumors about the bands. The boys.

Scott keeps talking. 'He approached me, way back then. Not,
you know, coming onto me. But as a friend.'

She's glad he can't see her recoil in surprise.

'He said he knew. That it was hard, but that I'd be happier.'
Scott picks up a wooden spatula. Pokes at the vegetables in the
pan and adjusts the heat. 'I hated him even more for that, of
course. I mean, the man was a fucking predator. I didn't want
. . . I mean, I'm not . . .'

She wants to touch him. To let him see she is his friend, but she waits. The onions are collapsing in the pan. The air is growing fragrant.

'Anyway.' Another sigh, as if to punctuate the thought. 'I came out, and he was right. Life got better. And so when the Portland job ended, I got in touch.'

It could be the onions. Tara is famished by the time they eat, the smell of the dish – some stir-fry – driving her mad.

'It's nothing special,' says Scott. 'But, you know, it's a weeknight.'

'It's great.' Tara barely pauses to chew, let alone drink the wine. They've finished the open bottle, and by then it doesn't matter that the one she brought isn't as good. She's relaxed. They're both relaxed, and for the first time in a long time, Tara feels she's got her old friend back. 'Where'd you learn to cook like this?'

That's not what she wants to ask. It doesn't matter. Everything makes sense now. Everything about him, anyway.

'Cookbooks. Newspapers.' He tops off her glass. He's put his own away. 'My first boyfriend – first real boyfriend – was a fitness nut. That helped.'

She nods, her mouth full. The brown rice is nutty and picks up the sweetness of those onions. She's tempted to follow up. To hear more about the transformation. How the happy, slim Scott – the one who doesn't drink, or barely – came to be. But really she wants to talk music. Music and writing, like the old days. Now that maybe they can again.

Business, however, comes first.

'So, Scott.' She wipes her mouth. He has cloth napkins. 'My piece. What's up? I thought you had free rein?'

'I did, too, kiddo.' He pushes a green pepper around his plate, then leaves it be. 'That was my agreement with Jonah when I came on.'

She waits. He's talked a bit about Jonah, about how the older man mentored him. How Jonah was different with him. She knows he considers the former club manager to be more than a boss.

'But . . .' Time to prime the pump.

'I gather someone up the food chain doesn't like it.'

'Someone up the food chain?' She puts her wine down. She wants her head clear. 'You mean, like an advertiser?' She shouldn't be surprised, not really. She knows how these big glossies work. She's seen the four-color sell sheets, advertising their content months in advance, long before any mere scribe puts a word on paper. But, no, Scott is shaking his head.

'No. He didn't say – and he would've.' Those eyes. A glance laden with meaning. 'I'm thinking it's one of the big investors. Or one of the owners.'

'Owners?' Maybe she's drunk too much wine. 'I thought *City* was an independent.'

He reaches for the rice. 'Nobody's an independent anymore,' he says as he spoons out a mouthful. As he studies it on his plate. 'We're not talking a 'zine here.'

'Scott?' His plate is not that fascinating. She reaches across the table. Puts her hand on his. 'What's going on?'

'Nothing.' He doesn't pull away. Doesn't look at her either. Instead, he turns back toward the kitchen, although she knows for a fact that he turned off the stove before they sat down. She wonders about the wine. The glass in the sink, but then he's back, a tumbler of sparkling water in his hand. 'It's just business. And maybe I hear more about it, because Jonah and I . . .'

'You're not *with* Jonah.' She hears the judgment in her voice. Regrets it just as quickly as it's out. 'Are you?' The question comes out in a squeak.

'Me? No.' He laughs. He even looks at her. 'I'm not his type. But he does talk to me. We have history – I mean, the scene – in common, among other things.'

The silence that follows isn't uncomfortable. Isn't happy, either.

'Look,' he says, after a moment has passed, 'you really think you have something, right?'

She nods. Against all her better instincts. 'I don't know what yet. But there's something . . .'

He holds up a hand to stop her. 'Let me see what I can do. I mean, I know it's going to be a great story, and I think once he sees it, Jonah will know that too. And he can talk any investor around. I mean, shit, this is the man who sold ice cream as a February cover story. And speaking of, dessert?'

TWENTY-FIVE

Tara sleeps better than she has in ages. Wakes feeling almost hopeful about the future. The article. Scott. Two more days at Zeron and then she can hunker down. See about putting some kind of a story together.

There's another message from Nick by the time she exits the T, and she's glad she missed it. As she climbs Zeron's front steps, her phone rings again and she looks at it with annoyance. But, no, it's Mika. Tara stops halfway to the front door to answer. The young woman puts Tara's fears to rest: Neela is fine. In fact, she continues, her mother is home and ready to talk.

'I told her how great you were, with Henry and everything.' The young woman sounds relaxed. 'And I never really got a chance to thank you.'

'It was nothing.' It's a reflex response. It doesn't mean anything, although as Tara says it she feels a pang. Despite what Mika said, she still wonders if her reappearance in Neela's life drove the widow too far. The more she learns – the more she remembers – about those years, the more difficult they sound. She looks up at the building behind her. 'And, I mean, she doesn't have to talk to me, if it's too painful, or something . . .'

'No, I think she should.' Her daughter cuts through her mumbling. 'I think it will be good for her to talk about the past. About my dad, and everything.'

Tara opens her mouth. Remembers what Min has told her. What Nick has said. And then simply thanks the younger woman, as she waits for her to put her mother on the line.

'Tara?' The widow sounds shaky. Her voice thin and weak.

'Hey, Neela.' Tara isn't going to push. 'How're you doing?'

An exhalation, half laugh, half sob. They were never close, back in the day. But Tara feels they've shared something, even if it's simply history. They've got a bond at least as deep as Scott and Jonah Wells do, don't they? She waits.

Only the sound of breathing lets her know the other woman is still on the line. Tara is close to breaking in. To excusing the other woman and letting her go back to her mourning, undisturbed. Only it really would make the piece if she could get her to talk, and Tara wants that, she realizes. More than she thought.

Finally, Neela breaks the silence. 'Mika says you still want to talk to me.'

It's a statement, and it seems to cost her.

'I do, if you're up for it.' Tara bites her lip. Waits.

'Yeah.' Another pause, and then she comes back, her voice stronger than before. 'Yeah, I think it would be good for me,' she says. 'I think it would be healing.'

'Great.' Now it's Tara's voice that quavers. She clears her throat. 'How about Saturday afternoon?'

'Sunday would be better, if you don't mind coming over in the morning again.' There's a note in her voice that Tara can't identify. Resignation? Sadness? A touch of dark humor? Whatever, it fades as she drops her voice to the barely audible. 'My daughter will be at church, and I could use the company.'

That's a lie. It hits Tara. An excuse. She doesn't know what it means. Maybe Mika won't go off to church unless she knows someone's with her mother. Maybe Neela wants to talk about her wild days. Tell the truth about her daughter's paternity. It doesn't matter any more. Mika is a grown woman, with a child of her own. Still, Tara is excited. This is what she needs – Neela's input. An unexpurgated account of her history, her take on the music world. She thinks of Neela as she was – the golden girl, dancing on the bar – and agrees. Besides, she thinks as she waits for the elevator, she's got all of next week to work on the piece. It will be good to get this final interview done so she can get her notes in order.

Knowing that she's only got two days till she's out of there makes the morning sail by. Sara's input on the press release? Done – and she doesn't even pause to remark that what the purchasing manager calls 'grammar' is really just her personal preference. The monthly newsletter? Drafted, with copies sent to everyone who contributed – and who will doubtless want to revise and enlarge their short items. The department heads get competitive about these.

With each item checked off her list, she emails Rudy. She's still not sure what to say to him – if she says anything at all. Whatever it is, she wants it to be on her terms. To her surprise, she finds she wants him to think highly of her. To value her apart from his friendship with her ex.

It is with some annoyance, then, that she sees a text from Peter pop up, just as she's formatting a notice. *Did u call*, it reads.

No, she types back and remembers: she had wanted to follow up with her ex. To ask why he'd settled on Frank as the snitch. He hadn't told her, but she has her suspicions. If he'd gotten a lead from his cop contact, she wants to know – to hear it all. She no longer believes Peter ever had an innate sense for news. The idea that he was some kind of super reporter was just part of his image, a persona that she has finally debunked. She should have seen it years ago, of course.

The police?

The new text follows her own thoughts so closely it startles her. Then she realizes what's happened. Peter was interrupted. He's only now finished his query. The car, the tires – but he's only now remembered? With a glance at the door – slightly ajar, but closed enough – she hits Peter's number on her phone.

'Tara, I was just texting you.'

'I know, Peter.' She keeps her voice low. 'And, no, I didn't call the police. What am I going to say? I'm talking to people about their lives more than twenty years ago, and so someone might have targeted me?'

'Maybe.' He sounds like himself. Which is to say cocky. Confident. 'I mean, you've clearly pissed off somebody.'

'Me?' She can't help it. She's angry. 'You're the one who's been manipulating my life for years. Since day one . . .'

'Hey!'

She catches herself. There was a time. 'I'm sorry, Peter. It's been tense.'

'I gather.' Sullen. 'I'm sorry too.'

'Hey, Peter?' She looks at the door. There doesn't seem to be anyone in the hallway, not that she can see.

'Yeah?' His voice is soft. Warm even.

'Why did you think that Frank was the informer? Potential informer, I mean.'

A burst of laughter, as if it has been punched out of him. 'That's what you want to ask me? Shit, Tara, you're even colder than I am.'

She doesn't respond. What's to say?

'OK, I'm sorry.' He gives it up. 'I'm just . . . surprised. Let me think about that. I'm not even sure that I remember. Only a lot of the drugs seemed to be coming out of the music clubs, as you'll recall. And he was working at that bar – the one down by the water—'

'Wait, the Casbah?'

'Yeah, that was it. It was the biggest place in town, at the time. And, well, it was in Southie. So you know . . .'

'Southie?' The word conjures up the townie neighborhoods. Mobbed up. Tough. 'The Casbah was on the waterfront.'

'Same thing, Tara.'

There had to be more. 'And why Frank?' There's something she's not seeing. 'A lot of people worked there.' She sees them in her memory. Brian. Jonah.

'Yeah, but there was something. He wasn't happy. He seemed to have a beef.'

'Well, yeah.' She doesn't know what Peter remembers. What he knows. 'His girlfriend – fiancée – was probably cheating on him. Plus, he was an alcoholic. I mean, he had a lot of reasons to be unhappy.'

She's on the defensive, and she's not even sure why. 'There had to have been more to it, Peter.' Silence. 'Please, tell me.'

'I'm sorry.' His voice is flat now. Final. 'I really . . . it was just that when I spoke to him, he sounded like a man who had been pushed too far. I thought I could get something from him. I mean, he was about to break.'

'Yeah, he was.' Tara goes back in her mind over what was happening. Neela. Chris. 'But he wasn't the one who cracked.'

It's unsatisfying, but there isn't any more. Peter's much vaunted reporting boiled down to one police contact and his girlfriend – her – who showed him around the scene.

'Maybe you should have been the one investigating,' he says. Not humble, exactly. Conciliatory.

'It wasn't my story.' She responds slowly. It's dawning on her:

Min is right. He wants her back. The condo, the job. Maybe he never let go. And now, he's ceding his turf to her. His investigation. After all these years, he still doesn't understand. 'All I ever wanted to do was write about the music, Peter. That's what I cared about.'

Or maybe he does. 'Yeah,' he says. His voice is softer now. Sad. 'Yeah, I know.'

She tries to shake it off. Calls Min once they hang up.

'Hey, girl.' Her tone sounds fake, even to herself, as she leaves the message. 'I'm taking next week off. Want to do something?'

When she hears the soft knock on her door, she's tempted to ignore it. Her colleagues have finally gotten around to reading her memo, and the requests have begun pouring in. Suddenly it seems like everyone has an idea for a marketing outreach. Clients who need to be soothed and coddled while she's away. Two more days, she tells herself.

'Come in,' she calls. More like one and a half.

'Steve asked me to give this to you.' Rebecca enters. 'He thought you could make something up.'

Tara takes the file and opens it. In the first photo, white men in dark suits are smiling and shaking hands. Her colleagues – Steve Hellman, vice president of corporate development. Rudy. Hugh. The fourth man is shorter, although his suit fits better. Familiar. 'Thanks,' she says, as she turns the print over. Jonah Wells, she reads, fourth on the list. 'The Boston Vitality Summit?'

'Some charity function,' Rebecca says. 'Steve likes the other photo better. The one I marked.'

Sure enough, one has a Post-it stuck to its border. Steve and the mayor, also shaking hands, flanked by the other Zeron execs.

'Great, thanks.' Tara closes the file to dismiss the secretary. 'I'm sure I can do something with this.'

She's looking at the photo – the one with Jonah in it – when the phone rings again. She picks up without thinking, and immediately regrets it. Nick, and she's not prepared.

'Hey, Nick.' She closes her eyes. Tries to remember what spooked her. What she felt before. 'I'm sorry, I've been—'

'Please.' He cuts her off. 'We're not kids, Tara. But I did want to touch base with you. To see if there was something I said or did . . .'

She takes a breath. The idea that this man would have punctured her tires, would have threatened her seems crazy now. She's spent time with him. Been intimate with him. And, yet, someone did. It's all too much to explain. 'It's complicated, Nick.'

A sigh, or maybe it's a soft laugh. 'Look, can we try again? Dinner? Someplace neutral?'

It's a joke. She knows that, but she's grateful anyway. 'Sure.' The word is out before she can stop herself.

'Tonight?' His voice may be soft, but he's pushing. 'You say where.'

She names the pizza place and instantly regrets it. 'Look, how about lunch? Saturday?'

'I've got the boys.' His trump card. 'But, if you really want, I mean, they're old enough.'

'No, it will be fine.' They pick a time, and he rings off. Before she can change her mind, she realizes. Too late, she realizes that she should have changed the venue. If this goes badly, she won't be able to go back there for at least a month.

Min gets back to her later that day. She's almost forgotten she'd called her friend. Hopes she doesn't ask about Saturday – about Nick – about Peter. Instead, Min takes her by surprise.

'I got your message.' She sounds – lighter. That's the word. 'Want to go hear some music?'

'What?' She doesn't even try to hide her surprise.

'Yeah, yeah.' The old Min, but still with that note of cheer. 'I know. But some of the old crowd is getting together to honor Frank. Do a set of Last Call tunes. Katie called me.'

'Katie?' She sounds like a parrot.

'Don't worry.' Now its Min's turn to mock. 'It'll be early.'

'Tonight?' She chokes out the word. Doesn't want to have to explain her plans with Nick.

'No, silly. Next week. I just got the call and had to let you know.'

'Ah.' That was better. 'Yeah, sure. But, Min?' She's not even sure how to ask.

'Hmm?' The sound of a lighter. A drag.

'You never want to go out anymore.' It's easier to phrase it as a statement. 'I thought you didn't like it.'

'This is different.' She hears the exhalation. Pictures the smoke. 'This is for Frank. And Greg and the others specifically asked me to be there.'

TWENTY-SIX

Mystery solved. The night won't be about music so much as it will be about Frank – about Min, really. The acknowledgment that she never received. Well, Tara is happy enough to sign on. It's not like her own marriage lasted any longer – or forged any more passionate a bond.

She thinks about Peter. About the friendship she thought they'd settled into. Something easy, lower key. At least Min and Frank were talking at the end, she thinks. What the hell. At least they'll go hear some music.

Thinking of the evening ahead, she clears her desk up early – earlier than she'd intended at least. Waits for Rebecca to leave, of course. And the rest of the department, but she's out by six. September. The light has already begun to fade, the shadows lengthen. It's that, she tells herself, that's making her sad. Autumn means the end of things. Death, even.

It's not cold, but she's shivering by the time she reaches her apartment, which feels more empty than before. Maybe she should get a cat again. It's not like she travels. Not like she spends that much time at work. In her mind, she can hear what Min would say, and her answer surprises her.

'No.' She finds herself talking out loud as she pulls on a sweater. Pours herself a glass of wine. A generic Chardonnay, bought on sale. 'I'm not waiting for someone. Some man.'

She catches herself and makes a silent correction. It's Peter's censure she anticipates as much as Min's. Not that she wants to get back with him. Only, he's been there – been the constant – for so many years.

The wine tastes sour, after what she had at Scott's. She makes a face as she carries it into the bedroom. As she thinks about what to wear. Part of her wants to consider this a date. A quick shower and shave. The nice panties. She's still got her figure, even if her skin tone is off, and the lace boy-cut briefs make her ass look good.

She stops. Puts the glass down. The last time she saw this man, she was frightened. She really needs to think. And so turning from her closet, she returns to the living room, where there is no cat. But a small carving of a horse stands at attention, tail like a flag, as if ready to run.

What does she know about Nick? What does she want? She washes her face and puts on some lipstick, ready to find out.

When she hears the knock, she ignores it at first, hoping whoever it is will go away. When it repeats – a simple *tap, tap, tap* – she fears the worst. Greg, come to call her out. Threaten her – or expose her. The words come to her as she rises from the couch. *Expose her*? As what, she wonders.

A fake. A tourist. Her worst fears answer for her. *An outsider, always, merely looking in.* Facing off with him can't be worse. She goes to open the door.

'Gina?'

The name pops out. The woman, already walking away, can't be anyone else. The jet-black bob. The pleather mini that cuts into her thighs. But at the sound of her name she turns and fixes Tara with a grin.

'This is your place. Awesome.' She nearly bowls her surprised host over, as she pushes the door further open. As she strolls into Tara's home. 'I wasn't sure you still lived here. It's been years.'

'Yeah.' Tara struggles to remember when Gina had ever been here. Back when she first got the apartment, she'd had a party. Peter had always been uncomfortable with her friends. Her gang, he called them. His, too, if he wanted. Which he didn't. So she'd thrown a shindig to celebrate her independence. Her freedom. She still remembers cleaning up the mess. 'Yeah, I do.'

She follows the other woman into her own living room. Watches her collapse on the sofa and eye her glass of wine. 'That looks good,' she says.

'Hang on.' Old habits die hard. Tara heads to the kitchen. Takes down another glass. The Chardonnay is nearly gone, so she pours out what remains. Considers opening another. Considers the situation. 'So what brings you to my place?'

The question should be normal, but it sounds rude, and so she fetches another bottle from the metal rack on the counter.

One of Peter's purchases, but she likes it, and he seemed pleased that she wanted it. Gina's voice reaches her as she wrestles with the cork.

'I ran into Phil.' A low chuckle. Not an accident, then. 'He told me you were talking to people for a story? About the scene? Chris Crack and the Aught Nines?'

'Yeah, I am.' Tara fills the second glass and puts the bottle in the fridge. 'It's not cold,' she starts to say, as she returns to the living room. She stops short. Gina is holding the figurine – Nick's carving. Turning it over in her hands. Tara puts the glass down carefully, aware of a sudden urge to grab the piece from the dark-haired rocker.

'That's OK.' Gina puts the figurine down and reaches for the glass. She means the wine, but for a moment Tara wonders if the other woman has read her mind. 'Anyway, I'm here.' Gina grins up at her, and the illusion dissipates. 'So who else are you talking to?'

That's it. Tara nods. Gina always wanted to be included. To be part of the action. 'Well, Phil,' she says, since Gina knows that anyway. 'Onie from Last Call.' She skips over Katie. Over Greg, too, for different reasons. 'And Nick,' she says. She has to work to keep her voice level. 'Used to be a bartender?'

'Yeah, Nickie.' She nods so hard her body shakes. Tara watches the wine slosh around the glass. 'He had the sexiest eyes.'

'He gave me the horse.' The words come from nowhere. As if she were claiming him as hers.

'The horse?'

Tara reaches for the little creature. Almost misses how Gina's eyebrows disappear beneath her bangs.

'I knew he wasn't squeaky clean, but I didn't think – oh.' Tara looks up. Gina is grinning. She picks up her glass and takes a deep drink. 'Sorry,' she says and nods toward the figurine. 'That. That's cute.'

'What did you think I meant?' The germ of an idea is tickling her brain. One she can't quite shape. Gina looks down. Her glass is empty.

'Hold on.' Tara gets up before the other woman can start talking. Can leave. Gets the bottle.

'Thanks.' Gina takes a swig. 'I'm sorry. I shoulda . . . I mean,

I knew he worked at the Casbah. But, like, he was one of the good ones.'

Tara freezes, still holding the bottle. She makes the effort to put it down. To speak.

'One of the good ones.' She repeats the words. 'At the Casbah?'

'He put me in a cab a few times when some other guys wouldn't have, if you know what I mean. And he wasn't one of the Casbah cash cows. He wasn't even there that night.'

'That night?' Gina can't be saying this. Can't be talking about Chris Crack, not after saying that about Nick – about him working there. But she is.

'I thought I had a chance with him – with Chris, I mean.' She's picked up something. Seen how Tara is looking at her. How she looked at the carving. 'I mean, it wasn't like he and Neela were going to get married. But I don't know if he could even get it up anymore, and Neela wasn't letting go. She just wanted to be with him, no matter what.'

She shrugs. Disappointment. Regret. It's hard to tell.

'They were getting high together?' Tara whispers. Her mouth is so dry. 'Neela was shooting up when she knew she was pregnant?'

Another shrug. 'She didn't even care about the baby. Isn't that funny? Frank was furious when he found out. I thought he was going to kill her.'

'How'd he . . .?' She has to pause to swallow. 'How'd Frank find out?'

'Don't know.' Gina's almost done with her second glass. Tara slides the bottle over. 'Somebody had been talking to him. Asking questions about the club. Really riled Frank up.'

'Riled him up?' She can barely form the words.

'Yeah, for real.' Gina's nodding, lost in her memory. 'Telling him he should care, what with his girlfriend using and all. Really pushing him about all the shit that was coming in.'

She's talking about Peter. It hits Tara like a flash, only – nothing adds up.

'This was at the Casbah?' It's the first question she can muster.

'Think so.' Gina shrugs. 'I can't say for sure. I only snorted a little. You know, to be with Chris. But they didn't call that place the Cash Bar for nothing. Someone made some money there.'

'Yeah, someone did.' Tara is glued to her seat. The question she asked, and the question that was answered. Gina has emptied the bottle into her glass.

'So, you wanna talk about the music? About the old days?' The plump woman blinks. Her eyes are filling with tears.

'Gina.' Tara sits up, another question forming. 'Why did you come to me? Why are you telling me all this?'

Surely the woman must know what she's saying. What she's revealing, after all these years. But her guest merely shrugs. Spills a little wine on her skirt. Rubs at it, to make it go away.

'Because you get it.' She says it like it's obvious. 'I mean, you were always a bit of a tight ass, but you love the music. The bands. You saw how it might have been. That the Whirled Shakers should've been huge.'

TWENTY-SEVEN

It's an effort to get Gina to leave after that. The dark-haired rocker is drunk. Probably was before she arrived, and she wants to reminisce. But Tara is driven. Frantic, almost, and the empty bottle helps her trundle Gina out the door. Next week they'll talk. At the tribute. The one to Frank. She has plans, she tells the pudgy rocker. She doesn't say with whom.

'Hey.' Nick rises as she walks toward the table. Leans forward as if to kiss her, only the table is in the way, and so they sit. 'Thanks for coming.'

'Thanks for calling.' She hears herself: too hearty. False. 'I mean, for keeping after me. It's . . . things have been weird.'

He nods, waiting. He's not a fool.

'Hi, I'm Monique, and how are we this evening?' The waitress speaks as if they're children or unspeakably old, a forced smile on her round face. 'Would you like to start with a cocktail?'

Tara would, most definitely. But her head is already spinning.

'I think we need a minute.' Nick sends her on her way. 'Please?'

It's unclear if he's addressing the waitress or Tara. The girl has already retreated, taking temptation with her, and while Tara watches her go, the green apron string cutting into her waist, Nick begins to talk.

'I should start by telling you that I know I move too fast.' She turns back to him, but he's looking down at the table. 'Maybe it's because we knew each other, long ago. Or maybe I've just been too lonely, but I think I rushed things. I think I may have scared you off.'

'Nick.' She wants to stop him. To get to the point.

'Going over to your place after.' He chuckles, but it's a humorless sound. 'Leaving a kid's toy.'

'No, that was sweet.' Min had called it creepy. What was it Greg had said about 'that bartender'? 'It was, but – Nick?'

She has too many suspicions. She has to know. She takes his

hand. She wants him looking at her, not at the plastic breadbasket
that neither of them has touched.

'Back in the day . . .' She pauses, then dives in. 'You knew
drugs were moving through the clubs, right?'

She has his attention now.

'Yeah.' He draws out the syllable. Quizzical. Cautious. 'Yeah,
of course, I did.'

'Did you ever . . .?' This is the tricky bit. The question she
doesn't know how to ask. 'Were you aware of any drug trafficking
in or around any particular club?'

'What are you asking?' He sits up now, pulling his hand back
in the process. 'Are you asking if I was a dealer? I was a bartender,
Tara. That's all. My first real bartending job after years of humping
cases and glassware.'

Suddenly, she cannot breathe. 'Your first . . .?' She makes
herself inhale. She's trembling. 'So you did work at the Casbah?'

He nods. He's cast his gaze down at the table again, but she
can see how his mouth has set in angry lines.

'But you said . . .' She can't go on. Shakes her head.

'I know.' He raises his hands as if to plead for sufferance.
'Look, Tara, I lied about never working at the Casbah. I lied and
I'm sorry. It wasn't . . .' He sighs and the tension leaches out of
him. 'I didn't plan it. I just – you asked and I spoke without
thinking. It's a period of my life that I'm not particularly proud
of. A place I'd rather forget, even if it did get me actually tending
bar.'

'And you knew.' She's still kind of stunned. 'You knew about
the drugs.'

'I knew a lot of things, and nothing at all.' He's looking at
her now, his eyes sad and tired. 'I knew the bouncers beat up on
kids. Sometimes just for fun. I knew the booze was watered – not
by me, but I knew it. And I knew that there was a lot of shit
around. I mean, maybe it was everywhere by then. But . . . yeah,
I knew.' He shakes his head, as if there's just too much to carry.

'But you didn't think to tell me?' She takes a breath and
tries again. 'I'm not . . . Look, you know my ex, Peter, was a
reporter, right? And that I'm working on this story now. About
the scene?'

'Your article?' He's acting like he doesn't know about it. Like he didn't agree to be interviewed. 'Is that what this is about? I thought you were writing about the music. About the community. I thought—'

'I am.' She keeps her voice low. Monique is hovering. 'I mean, that's how it started. But then Peter started telling me about the story he was working on, back in the day. About all the drugs. The cheap smack. I mean, you worked with Brian . . .'

It's the wrong tack.

'And you think I had some part – that I sold him the shit that killed him?' He pulls the napkin off his lap and throws it on the table. 'Shit, Tara.'

'No, I don't think that you . . .' She stops. She can't deny that she wondered. That she wants to ask him. 'But maybe, you knew something? Or . . .'

'Shit.' His hands are flat on the table. 'I'm sorry, Tara. I guess I was too lonely. Or maybe I was just a fool. I'm sorry I lied. I thought it wouldn't mean anything. I mean, we're talking twenty years ago. I thought you wanted something – something other than a story.'

'Nick, please.' She reaches for him as he starts to rise. He pauses, searching her face.

'You know Brian was crazy about you, right?' His voice is soft. Sad. He shakes his head. 'He had such a crush on you. I thought about that that first night. I actually felt like maybe he'd want us to be together. He was my friend, Tara. Shit.'

And then he pushes back his chair, and he leaves.

It's not like she can sleep. Between Nick and Gina, her brain is racing. She wants to call – someone. To talk it over. She thinks of Peter, of Min, and stops herself. It's late by then, and she's drunk too much, too. At least for one more day, she has work in the morning.

Somehow she gets through the night. Wine doesn't make her sleep anymore, and she wakes sweating, the sheets a tangle. Coffee helps, and she makes it into the office before nine.

'Ready for vacation?' Marie's grin is so wide Tara knows it's fake. 'You look ready.'

Tara smiles back. Crocodile teeth. 'Fuck you,' she mutters, under her breath, as she turns into her office. It's not like she can concentrate, and the inevitable last-minute requests – for a memo, a statement, an ever-so-minuscule revision on a website profile – take too long, trying her nerves, and as soon as she gets a chance, she calls Peter.

'Where are you?' She's whispering, but so frantic it comes out a hiss. 'We need to talk. Now!'

'Peter?' She tries his office line next. It's Friday, a work day. He should be answering. 'What did you say to Frank? What did you ask him?' It's not enough, she's well aware. Her query is too vague, and the incident too long ago. But surely he must remember something. If he said what she suspects . . . If he outed Chris as the would-be informant.

She waits. The clock on her desk does not tick. She almost misses the sound. The audible passage of time. After two digits have turned over, she tries again. Leaves similar messages. Considers cabbing over to his condo after work. Or, no, his office. Now.

Only she's got her own life to clean up. She takes a breath and exhales slowly. Then she calls Nick.

'Hey.' She modulates her tone. It's easy. Her sorrow is real. 'I want to apologize for what I said. Can we talk?' It's unsatisfying. Another voice mail, but she makes herself hang up at that point. She's learned that much since she and Peter split.

When her phone rings a minute later, she grabs it all breathless anticipation.

'Hey, girl!' Min is laughing. 'That hot to talk to me?'

'Hey, Min.' No response is the best tactic.

'I finally listened to my voice mails. Psyched you're taking some time. Wish I could. Though I am thinking about the day after the tribute. I mean, that's going to be intense. But, this weekend? Might you be up for some antiquing Saturday? We'll go out early, then get some brunch?'

Tara could cry. She hardly sees Min these days. Certainly not in the daylight, outdoors. And yet . . .

'I don't know, Min. I've got an interview early Sunday.' Silence. 'For this piece.'

'Oh, yeah.' The liveliness is gone. The spark. 'Your story.'

'I'm definitely going to the tribute show next Thursday.' It's too little, too late. 'That'll be something.'

'Yeah,' says Min. 'It will.'

Her office is quiet after that. The late requests continue to trickle in, and she eats lunch at her desk to get through them. It's after four when her desktop pings. A message, she sees. Rudy.

About our talk, it says. She closes her eyes. Mulls over a response. *I know you're on vacation next week.* That, at least, is a mercy. The on-line calendar keeping everyone in the loop. *Monday you're back.* A statement, not a request.

Sure, she finally responds. *Tanned, rested, and ready.* She hits delete, erasing all but the first word, and watches him blink off. Too late, she realizes she doesn't know if the system shows her words as she types them. If he'll get the reference. If he's the sort to be amused.

'Damn it, Peter.' She gets his voicemail again. He's the one who got her into Zeron. The least he could do is return her calls. She has so many questions.

While she refills her coffee, someone has touched base. Her office line is blinking, and she spills in her hurry to find out who has called.

'Tara? It's Scott.' She slumps in her chair, disappointed. 'Call me?'

She needs to speak to Scott for sure. About this article. The magazine. His publisher. But she wants to get things clear in her own head first, and so she hits erase and watches the message disappear. Dabs at her blotter, the paper already puckered and brown, and then it's time to leave.

Any other night, she'd pick up a pizza. Have a glass of wine to celebrate the week's end. Any other night, she'd find a movie to watch. Wouldn't worry about her work. But the dinner last night has spoiled pizza for a while, and Gina has finished her wine. She swings by the deli for a rotisserie chicken and a six-pack and settles in at her kitchen table, notepad and pen in hand.

An hour later, the chicken is cold. But she's still on her first beer as she wipes her hands clean and pulls up yet another search engine, tries yet another search. Peter's right. There's precious little on the scene. The cops never did make any major busts, although the cheap heroin seemed to fade away as quickly as it appeared. She can list the casualties, most of them anyway. Brian. That college kid. Chris Crack. Count as well the clubs that closed, not only the Casbah but Flash's and the Dive.

Between the deaths and the closures, the all-ages scene disappeared as well. The hardcore bands lost their places to play, and the unofficial venues couldn't last, not once parents had ammunition to keep their kids away. Yeah, Oakie's hung in. Cover bands and suburbanites helping to fill the void. She has her own archive up on another window and she switches over. How could she not have seen what was happening? How could they all have missed it?

She doesn't need Peter to spell it out. She didn't care. It wasn't her story. Just like Gina said, all that mattered was the music.

She closes her eyes. It's late, and she's tired. She thinks about turning on the radio. About playing some of her records. The old ones. Vinyl. The compilation or, no, the Whirled Shakers single. Only she can hear it in her head already, and so she cleans up. Throws the rest of the chicken in the fridge, and falls into a deep and dreamless sleep.

Saturday passes in a daze. She writes – poring over her notes to find connections. Highlights the research she needs to do. The questions she still has to ask.

When Peter calls, she has her list ready. Who he talked to. What he said.

Scott she puts off. 'Don't worry,' she promises. 'I know you were speaking in confidence. And I appreciate what you've done for me.' They make plans to talk again on Sunday. He offers to cook again, but she suggests they play it by ear.

Sunday morning, she wakes early. Makes herself wait, drinking coffee, until ten. As the time clicks by, she realizes she's been holding her breath. Expecting Neela to cancel. For Mika to intervene. But the phone does not ring, and she turns it off as she sets out for Mika's place. For one final interview.

She finds the street easily this time, driving once more through the newer subdivision to Mika's neighborhood. The SUV is gone, the driveway empty, but Tara parks on the curb, under the shelter of an old maple. The house looks quiet. Deserted, and she checks her phone one more time. Scott has called, but there are no messages. She turns the device off once more and heads toward the house.

She hadn't noticed the doorbell before. How loud it is, audible from the stoop, where Tara stands, waiting. It must echo throughout the entire house. Must wake the baby when it rings. Unless the volume is in some way a reflection of the house. Of its emptiness. Yes, she thinks. That's it. Neela has changed her mind and left. Or the other woman has simply forgotten. Has joined her daughter at whatever church the family attends.

The thought is almost a relief. She has followed this story far enough. But just as she turns to leave, she hears the click of a latch. The door opens, and Neela greets her. She looks older – old, suddenly – a frail shadow of her former self. She walks slowly as she leads Tara inside, into the split level's sunny front room. Toys have been stacked in a plastic bin, beside an overstuffed sofa that shows signs of wear, but the house is quiet. Clearly, Neela is alone. Henry has joined his parents at church or some other arrangement – a babysitter other than the unsteady grandmother – has been found.

Neela gestures toward the sofa. The sun has faded its floral print, but it looks comfy. Lived in, and Tara sits down. She pulls both her pad and a recorder from her bag. Neela still has not spoken, and the silence has grown oppressive.

'If you don't mind,' Tara says, more to break the silence than to ask permission. Neela seems to understand, because she doesn't answer, except to take the wingback chair opposite. It is large and upholstered, its arms – the encompassing wings of the high back – both isolating and supporting her in her weakness and her grief. Only then, when she has settled in – sunk in, really – does she take a deep breath and begin to speak.

'I don't know what to tell you,' she says. She looks away, embarrassed. As if she had broken a vase, rather than tried to end her life.

'I think you do.' Tara speaks softly. 'I think you want to confess.'

TWENTY-EIGHT

She calls Scott back as soon as she's home. The drive has given her time to think, a little distance. She wants to tell Scott first. To give him a chance.

'We need to talk,' she says. He doesn't question it. Simply reiterates his invitation for dinner. She doesn't ask about wine.

She spends the rest of the afternoon at her computer. All these years later, writing something out helps her understand. Only, this time, it's not how a series of changes tugs at the heart. How a dash of dissonance sets off that pure pop chorus, turning its sentiment into something conflicted and rare.

Or maybe it is. She pauses, halfway through, to laugh. The scene she loved. This tribe. Maybe they knew they were doomed. Fated to die or fade away. Maybe its ephemeral nature is what made the music so powerful. One brief chance, one stab at fame or something greater. Immortality, wrapped in transience. Because all the while, time lurked. The dulling of age, the vulnerability of youth. Loss, whether gradual or abrupt.

As the afternoon light dims, she thinks about putting on a record again. Vinyl, old school. But it's almost time to go, and she needs to get this drafted – get it clear – before she meets with her old editor, the one who got her started.

It's Sunday night, and so she drives. Passes one of the new places – a seafood restaurant that plays up the waterfront theme – a stylized fish outlined in neon and steel. Two young men lean against the wall. They stand as she slows. Valets, but she's not some suburbanite, and they're not what she thought, in that moment, when she first spied them, huddled, heads together.

Past the restaurant, the street is dark. The area still hasn't come into its own, and she finds a spot beneath a streetlight. A chuckle surprises her as she locks up. She didn't have a car this nice in the old days. Min did, but that's when she learned about parking down here, especially toward the end when things got bad. About looking for a light. Maybe this is better now – the construction, everything new. Maybe these things come in cycles, like the tides.

She's thinking of the tides as she walks to Scott's apartment, that beautiful space with its view of the harbor. A flicker of movement catches her eye, even as she approaches the condo, its foyer lit and bright. She stops and turns, but it's gone. Paper, maybe, only there is no wind tonight. A rat, then. This is still a waterfront, no matter what else may have changed.

And Boston is still a port city, a place for trade and commerce. That can't all have gone now, even with the condos. The restaurants. No, the trade must have shifted. Moved underground, like that rat.

She holds her bag tight against her side up the walk to that well-lit door. Is it that different, then, the way she hurries, slightly breathless from anticipation? Back then, her only fear was missing the set. Missing the show. The band. The story. God, she was fearless then.

And now? She presses the button for Scott's apartment, and the door buzzes open in response. He's expecting her. He has bigger worries than a break-in, she realizes, as the elevator takes her up.

'Hey.' He greets her with a quick half hug and ducks away. 'Be right with you.'

'No rush,' she says, grateful for the time. Alone in that beautiful room, she crosses to the window. The autumn sky is clear. Night now, dusk long gone, but the sky is far from dark. The ambient glow of the city silhouettes the buildings across the way. Running lights on a motorboat late to dock pass silently below.

She takes a moment to enjoy it all. The view, the quiet. When Scott comes up behind her, she takes the glass he offers silently. Drinks without speaking. Red this time and good.

'It's Jonah,' she says at last. 'Isn't it? He's killing the story.'

'I'm sorry.' Scott comes up to stand beside her. He's back to seltzer. The bubbles fizz and burst. 'I should have known.'

'You couldn't have.' She turns to look at her friend. So handsome and so miserable. 'Not all of it.'

They sit and she spells it out – speculation, for the most part. Only it all makes sense. The money, the drugs. The unknown backers who ran the city in its bad old days. Who run the city now, only their hands are clean. Cleaner, she corrects herself. By the time she's done, her glass is empty.

He goes to the kitchen for a break. Probably to turn off the stove, too.

'How did you know?' He's brought the bottle and refills her glass. He's topped his own off, and added a slice of lime.

'It was the story of Chris – of Frank and Neela.' She pulls the printout from her bag. Watches as he reads.

He nods when she covers the territory he remembers. About how Chris Crack appeared from nowhere, as ethereal as a sprite. As skinny as one too, following his own sickly childhood, the source for 'Bubble Boy'.

'I thought it was a metaphor.' His voice clues her in.

'Yeah,' she agrees. 'We all did.'

Maybe it was that childhood – overprotected, his parents so scared of losing him – that drove him to the scene. To the drugs on offer. Maybe it was his looming fame. His fear of being called out. A fake, a tourist.

Maybe it was something built into his DNA, along with an early childhood condition – the inability to process certain proteins. Whatever the key to his own addiction, Chris was the perfect proselytizer. Heroin chic, before that phrase ever hit this dirty town. He got Neela using, even if she never shared his addiction. Even when she was carrying his child.

'I wasn't, you know, shooting up,' she had told Tara that morning. 'I snorted it and, yeah, I skin-popped but . . .' She hadn't been able to look Tara in the eye. Instead, she had stared out the window. Maybe she was hoping for her daughter to come home early. Her daughter and the grandson who had inherited Chris's condition. 'I wasn't a junkie.' Her voice was soft. 'No matter what Frank thought.'

Tara had waited, then. Confident that the rest would come. Sunday morning. It was time.

'He didn't know about the drugs – that I was using – when he proposed,' Neela had told her. 'He found me there, in the back room, right after I'd told Chris.' She'd sucked her lips in, the memory still bitter. 'I'd told him I was pregnant. I didn't . . .

I don't know what I thought. He'd just come back from rehab, and I didn't really think he'd marry me, only . . .

'Only he didn't care. Not about anything but the smack. About scoring again and getting high. And then Frank came in and found me crying. He figured it out. Said he'd marry me right then. Said he didn't give a shit whose it was. That he didn't want to know.'

She shifted to face Tara. 'I wanted to hurt Chris then, like he'd hurt me. So I said yes. I never thought . . .'

She swallowed. Looked away again.

'You never meant to go through with it. Did you?' That much, at least, was clear.

Neela shook her head. That radiant hair grown thin now, drawn back in a tight bun.

'And then it was too late.' Tara kept her own voice soft, knowing there was more to come.

'I loved him so.' Neela stared. Seeing a slender golden boy, incandescent and now gone. 'I knew it was over, but I couldn't stay away. And if that meant getting high . . .'

She stopped then, and Tara filled in the rest. That a reporter – Peter – was researching the drug connection. Was in the clubs, observing. Waiting to find out who was going to talk. To snitch to the police. Peter might not have been the ace reporter that Tara had thought him to be, but he had an edge. A girlfriend on the scene who introduced him around. Who introduced him to her friend, a woman with her own agenda.

Even knowing Min's history, Peter bit. He thought he was smarter. Always did, and he would have seen Frank as the obvious candidate to tell him everything. To tell the cops. Not the rising star, a user with no real interest in getting out. No, an angry man with a grudge against the club owners, against the men who had fired him and ruined his life. Peter must have worked on Frank, prompting him to spill all. Only in the course of his prodding, Peter had revealed too much. Min had shared too much, and he'd let Frank know that Neela was still seeing Chris. Worse, that she was getting high with him. Shooting up.

It must have unspooled from there: Neela was pregnant, and Frank was out of time. Getting Chris busted wouldn't help, not if Neela was caught up in it too. Instead, he changed his plans.

He had the shit he'd taken off a kid, and he'd spiked it with something. Something to make it just a little stronger. He got it to Chris, maybe through Brian. Maybe just by leaving it in the Casbah office – everyone rifled through the lost and found. Through the bags and the pockets of the coats left behind. Maybe in some other way that Tara would never know. And then Chris was gone.

'How did you find out?' She wanted to be gentle with Neela. The woman had been through so much.

'It was when Henry was first having trouble. Frank had a friend who helped us. She steered us toward testing. Toward the right doctors at Children's. And that was when I realized that Mika was Chris's, and that Frank had known all along.'

'You must have known.' This part made no sense.

Neela shook her off, biting her lip. 'No, not really. I wasn't ever sure, and I didn't think he could be, either. Because, if he was, how could he be sure that I'd . . . well, that I'd come around?'

'Ah.' It hit Tara, a moment before Neela could say it.

'Yeah.' The word a barest breath. 'With Henry's diagnosis, it all came out. Frank knew. He always knew. But it didn't matter. Cause he also knew I'd stay with him. I'd marry him, because he knew Chris wouldn't be there. That he'd be gone.'

'You confronted him?'

'We had a fight. I pushed him. I think the cops suspect.' She said it quickly, glad to have it out. 'I'd kept my end up. I'd been a good wife. A good mother. But Chris . . .' She covered her mouth with her hand, but still the words leaked out. 'I loved him so,' she said.

Sitting with Scott, waiting as he reads her pages, she feels at peace. The fairy tale ending was never going to be, but now she understands. About Peter, maybe, and his desperate drive. About Scott, her friend, who took so long to find his way. And maybe now she has a clue about her own. This is what she's meant to do, even if the article in her editor's hands never runs.

'It's quite a story.' He looks up at last, the ghost of a grin on his handsome face. 'No wonder Frank went quiet. He'd gotten Neela out, and he wouldn't want to raise any questions about his own involvement. And now that Neela's talking to the cops, I'm almost tempted . . .' He stops, looks down at the pages again. 'You wouldn't consider rewriting the drug connection out of it, would you?'

'It wouldn't make sense without the Casbah.' Neither of them mentions Jonah's name. Besides, they both know Jonah was only a front man. Maybe still is. Tara thinks of her car, sitting low on its rims. The timing fits. 'Scott, my tires. You think . . .?'

He shakes his head, as if willing her not to finish her question. 'I don't know, Tara, and I can't ask. I'm sorry.

'Let's eat.' Hands on his knees, Scott pushes himself to his feet. He leads the way into the kitchen. 'If this roast hasn't completely dried out.'

An hour later, it's gone. They've both eaten heartily and have now pushed their chairs back in the relaxed manner of old friends.

'That was great.' Tara feels her eyes closing. It has been a day.

'Thanks.' Scott is staring at that window. If he can see more than his reflection now, she can't tell. 'I enjoy it. Cooking, I mean.'

She follows his gaze. The night outside is full, but the indoor lighting is well done. Indirect. She can still make out the distant shore. Or maybe that's a ship at anchor. It's hard to tell.

'One thing, though.' Scott isn't talking about the boats. Maybe he isn't seeing them. He's lived here long enough. 'One question that's still bothering me,' he says. 'What did Frank spike the heroin with? I mean, where would he get something that could do that?'

TWENTY-NINE

The next morning, Tara wakes with a start. Only after she remembers that she is, in fact, on vacation does she lie back and relax. Settling on her pillow, she thinks about the dinner with Scott. It was nice. Easy, as if with all the unspoken that lay between them finally voiced, they could go back to being friends again. Maybe better friends, Tara realizes. For while Scott has no intention of confronting his boss, he has promised to make some inquiries about her story – see if he can help her place it elsewhere. He has always been supportive of her, of her work.

Did she reciprocate? Staring at the shadows on the ceiling, she wonders. Tries to remember if she was a good friend or simply an acolyte. For all the time they spent together, she can't remember ever talking about anything but music. Still, how could she not have known that Scott was gay?

Bewildered – amused, almost – by her own cluelessness, she rises to begin her day. There's no sense fretting over the past. It had always been about writing with them, anyway. Writing and the music, of course. Both of them outsiders, looking in.

Which doesn't excuse everything. Far from it, although she's thinking of more than mere amends as she calls Nick.

'Hello?' He sounds sleepy and she kicks herself. The man manages a bar. Has two teen boys. She should have waited.

'Hey, Nick.' She makes her voice soft. 'I'm sorry to have called so early. Only, I wanted to talk to you.'

He doesn't reply, and she hesitates too. She knows she's been – not unfair. Uneven, maybe. That she's run hot and cold.

'I want to apologize,' she says. 'For what I said. Implied, anyway. I was caught up in something. Not that that's any excuse.'

'Thank you.' His voice is hoarse. 'I appreciate that.'

In the silence that follows, Tara finds herself waiting. Hoping, to be honest. She has reached out. She wants this man to do the same.

'Do you think we could have a re-do?' Her voice is smaller now. It is with some difficulty that she swallows. Tries again. 'I mean, I'm not much of a cook, but if you wanted to come over, really anytime this week. I'm taking the week off, you see.'

She's talking too much. Filling in the space, and so she stops herself there. If he picks Thursday, the night of the tribute, she'll figure something out. Just let him name a date. She's on edge, she notices with some amazement. Nervous. It's just excitement, she tells herself. It's been a while.

'Oh, Tara.' He's awake now; she can hear the deliberation in his words. Feels her heart sink, even as she hears the deep inhalation that presages his next words. 'Part of me wants to. Really, I do.'

She bites back the juvenile joke. Bites her lip as she waits.

'I know we wouldn't have met again, if it weren't for your article.' His words roll out with something like inevitability. That long-held breath finally released. 'We've led different lives, you and I, but still . . .'

Another sigh. She can't resist.

'Nick, I've been an ass.' She has. She knows it now. 'I get a little tunnel vision. A little caught up in the past. Min, Peter – my ex – they both tell me constantly, and I'm sorry. But you and I? That wasn't nostalgia . . .'

She catches herself: *wasn't?*

'It doesn't have to be. Look, I fucked up, but I'm human. And I'm sorry. I don't meet a lot of people I feel any connection with. What you said about loners? That's me. That's always been me, and you were always kind to me. And this now? Us? It's been special, Nick. Hasn't it?'

She's run out of words. Out of breath, too. Finds herself remembering. How could she have been so cavalier?

'I feel a connection, too, Tara.' He could be a million miles away. 'But it's not enough.'

'I'm sorry I didn't trust you.' Too little, too late. She knows that. Has to try anyway.

'It's not that – not just that.' Another sigh. She can picture how his brow furrows. How he's probably running a hand across his eyes. 'I used to admire you. You know? You were fearless, in a clueless sort of way. You'd talk to anybody. It was like you wanted to understand it all.

'But now I see the other side of that. When you're writing. It's like – I don't know – blood in the water. You're so single-minded, like the story is the only thing that matters.'

She knows those words. She's said them herself to Peter, to her ex. She has no answer now.

'Let's give it a break,' he says, when the silence has gone on too long. 'I mean, I don't know. I'll call you, Tara. And, hey, good luck with the article. I mean that.'

'Thanks.' She can barely whisper, and he hangs up.

He's wrong about one thing. She's not completely consumed by the need to get the story out there. The need to get it right. Not completely like Peter, like Peter as she thought he was. In fact, she finds herself dodging her ex's calls as the days go by. Weighing what she will tell him when, ultimately, she can no longer evade his questions.

It's not like she's sitting around. Although she's tempted to return to bed after the call with Nick, she makes herself get up and dressed. Makes herself read through the story – the version she'd shown Scott – and finds herself working on it. Tightening the prose. Filling in the blanks with what he'd confirmed, even tacitly.

That's enough for a day, and she leaves it at that, treating herself to a takeout feast and movie binge that keeps her up way too late.

Tuesday and Wednesday follow the same path, although this time her reworking of the article leaves out the speculation about the Casbah. About Jonah and the heavy men who once ruled South Boston, ruled the waterfront. Fashions a version she might be able to defend. More important, to sell. 'A rock and roll tragedy,' she calls it, though a song title from those days kept on playing through her mind.

By Thursday, her Zeron work habits might have never been. She sleeps till noon. Drinks coffee until two, and spends the next hour wondering what she'll wear that night. Her guard must be down, though, because that's when Peter grabs her. Shows up at her door, with an unlikely bouquet and confusion on his face.

'Peter.' She blinks at him, this remnant of another life. Placeholder. Token. Prototype. 'Want some coffee?'

'Sure.' He follows her in, still holding the flowers. Watches as she fixes him a mug without asking: black, sugar. 'I wanted to make sure you were OK,' he says as he takes it. He puts the bouquet on the counter, and she looks at it as if it were an alien thing.

'Yeah, just taking some time off.' She turns to fetch the vase from the high shelf. Hears him come up behind to help her. Reaches it before he can.

'Use it or lose it.' He attempts a smile.

'Something like that.' She clips the stems. Fills the vase. How like Peter, she muses as she arranges the flowers, to see things in such a binary manner. White or black. Right or wrong.

'I needed time to think.' She places the vase on the table and turns toward him, this dear, simple man. 'Time to figure out what I'm doing.'

He looks like he might cry. 'I shouldn't have said anything.'

'No.' He winces, and she catches herself. He's talking about Zeron – the job – not an investigation twenty years before. 'I mean, no, don't sweat it. I don't know if I was ever a good fit with Zeron. I don't care about it at all.'

To his credit, he doesn't speak. Doesn't try to argue with her about adult responsibilities or the dwindling options out there. She hears the catch in his breath, right before he closes his mouth. But she's heard all that before, from him. He knows this, too. He nods.

'You finished the piece?' He blinks. And in that moment, she sees how hard this is for him. He's worried about her, sure. But he also envies her, at least a little.

'Yeah, I think so.' She weighs showing it to him – the expurgated version. Decides against it, at least for now. 'But *City* killed it.'

An explosive sigh. 'So, why?' he asks. *What are your options?* She knows that's what he means. *Why are you doing this?*

She shakes her head. In answer. To stop his further questions. 'I'm working on it, Peter. I'm working on it.'

Min calls at seven. 'You're picking me up, right?' They have nothing arranged, but that always used to be the rule – back when Tara was writing and didn't want to get too drunk.

'Of course,' she says now. Habit, mostly. Nostalgia. That sad, fond feeling for something that's past.

Better to focus on the night ahead. But where once she would obsess about her hair, about the fit of her jeans – that beloved black leather jacket, long gone now – tonight she's thinking of who will be there. And more important, who won't. Frank and Brian. Chris is the obvious name – the biggest. Only in retrospect, Tara isn't sure how much a part of their world the young star actually was. How quickly he burned out, and how much he took with him.

That photo – the one she never showed Scott – comes to mind. She'd pulled it up again for inspiration as she rewrote the piece. How sad it was. The bad couch, the clothing in disarray. Jeans, some shirts. Two leather jackets, one dark, one light. She thinks of the others who survived but have moved on. Greg, with his grudges. Neela. And Nick? No, he's not likely to show either. Not if he's not working.

Min is flying when Tara gets there. Bouncing off the walls. Also, not ready. Some things never change.

'Help yourself,' she calls from the bathroom, after a quick peck hello. 'I got that tequila you like.'

'Thanks.' Tara hasn't drunk tequila in years. Still, it's going to be a night. She pours a shot and throws it back. Damn, that shit is strong.

When she opens her eyes, Min is in front of her, dressed to the nines. Tara didn't know her old friend could still glam up like this. Sees the tint of henna in her hair. 'Wow,' is all she says.

'For Frank.' Min shrugs, but Tara knows better. Tonight is about the two of them. The acknowledgment she never received, despite all the time, all the tears. Everything she did for that man.

The music has started by the time they arrive. The Craters, rocking a blues-based tune that sounds familiar.

'I'll get us a round,' says Min, as Tara stands there staring at the band.

'Tara!' Gina bounds up to her. 'You made it.'

'Wouldn't miss it.' Tara looks around. Thirty people, maybe forty. A good turnout, though half of them are musicians, she realizes. Tom and one of the other Exiles stand over by the wall.

Onie's come out as well. She sees him at a table with a woman she guesses to be his wife. Most of this crew is married by now, or married again. Phil and Joanie stand by the back. Katie and her new husband are at the bar.

Min, meanwhile, is talking to the bartender, a young man with a shaved head who Tara doesn't recognize. Those tattoos would be memorable, she's sure. Still, this club is more his territory than it is hers, she thinks. Nearing fifty. Single. For the first time in a while, she starts to wonder what happened. Where it all went wrong.

'Hey, I know this one.' Gina snaps her out of it. 'You do, too!' Grabs her hand, to pull her to the dance floor. Tara lets herself be led, but she feels too self-conscious, all knees and elbows. After the chorus ends, she retreats to the bar.

'I was watching you.' Min hands her a bottle.

'Thanks.' She rolls her eyes. 'Gina.'

'Yeah, she was always a true believer, that one.' They drink and watch as Gina gyrates and bounces around, not caring that she dances alone. Her enthusiasm, at least, is attractive. Katie drags her husband up front and they begin to move, somewhat more decorously, to the Craters' beat. As they watch, Tara thinks about Katie. Katie telling her about the old days. About Frank taking care of Neela. Insisting she go to the clinic, all the way up in New Hampshire. Saved by a road trip, but how . . .

She shakes it off.

'How was antiquing?' Tara yells, as the song winds up.

'I didn't go.' Min shakes it off. Drinks more beer. 'The weather.'

Tara tries to remember what was wrong with the weather. Saturday, she stayed in all day writing. Stayed in her own apartment, with its own disarray. Sorting through the wreckage.

'Did you get your piece done?' Min might be a mind reader. Except, of course, Tara had told her.

'Kind of.' It's the best she can do. 'I think it's dead, though.' She doesn't say that Scott is shopping it around. Offering it to his former editor in Portland. To someone he knows in New York. There will be time enough for that, if and when.

'Good thing you didn't quit your day job.'

Tara turns. Min's voice has gotten sharp, but she can't see anything in her friend's face. Min is staring at the stage – really just the front of the room. The Craters are finishing up. The drummer rushing a bit as he always did as their big number winds up to a close.

'You do still have the day job, don't you?' Min's face is unreadable.

'For now.' Tara turns toward the bar. All her friend does is work. Dedicated to her career after that one, brief suspension. 'I'm thinking of quitting, though. Ready for another?'

She returns from the bar with two bottles and two shots. The room is filling up, after a fashion. It's darker now, the volume – even between bands – rising with excitement. Min's in her element. Ralph and Tony D have passed by. Even Onie waves, from his table. His wife looks up. Two more shots appear beside them. 'For Frank,' says the tattooed bartender. 'From the band.'

'Everyone's paired off, aren't they?' The room is loud enough, Tara feels like she's talking to herself.

'You seeing that bar guy? Nick?' Min leans over slightly. Keeps her eyes on the bandstand.

'No,' Tara responds, the sadness settling heavy on her. 'I think that's over.'

'Just as well.' Tara starts. Maybe she didn't hear right. The guitarist is tuning. There's feedback. 'Scene guys. They're hard to love.'

Tara turns toward her friend. There's so much she wants to ask. About that night in the loft and a pink leather jacket, cradled as if it were a child. About a hot shot and how much Min was willing to do for the man she adored. Only just then, the room goes quiet. Everyone has turned. It's Phil. He's still got it – that star quality. He's taken the stage, and he grabs the mike.

'*One, two, three, four!*' The guitar kicks in, with a familiar chord. The drums, the bass. The scene.

'Hey, Min.' Tara can't help herself. She yells in her friend's ear. 'Whatever happened to that jacket of yours? The pink one?'

'Seriously?' Min is laughing. On her feet. 'That was so long ago. Come on!'

She grabs Tara's hand and pulls her onto the floor, and Tara lets her. They're part of the crowd. Dancing. Alive. It's that song, the one she loves. The one that should have been a hit, all those years before.

ACKNOWLEDGMENTS

Huge shout-outs to my first readers and former denizens of clubland: Brett Milano, Karen Schlosberg, and Lisa Susser. In addition to the usual plot and character issues, you all caught the references and corrected the anachronisms. Shout-outs as well to all at Severn House Publishers; to Erin Mitchell, publicist and cheerleader extraordinaire; to my agent, Colleen Mohyde of the Doe Coover Agency, who is not a night person and provided a reality check; to John McDonough, for all the answers; and to Kristophe Diaz, who lent his genetics expertise (and patience, during repeated explanations). Jon S. Garelick, as always, doubles as in-house editor and cheerleader, with this book maybe more than usual. I dedicate this book, as always, to you, but I'd also like to tip my hat to the late Rich Cromonic, of Sweet Potato, who got me started. Thank you, all. Rock on.